He's haunted by the past.
She'll bring him back to life.

Wolf's
FALL

AN ALPHA PACK NOVEL

J. D. TYLER

AUTHOR OF COLE'S REDEMPTION

"Readers will fall head over heels."
—*New York Times* Bestselling Author Angela Knight

SIGNET ECLIPSE

$7.99 U.S.
$9.99 CAN.

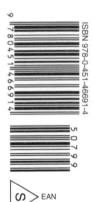

ISBN 978-0-451-46691-4

S > EAN

PRAISE FOR THE
ALPHA PACK NOVELS

Cole's Redemption

"Tyler delivers once again with the fun fifth install-
ment of her Alpha Pack series featuring sexy psychic Navy SEALs turned wolf shifters. Fast-paced
and passionate adventure is a hallmark of Tyler's
writing, and Cole's story is no exception."
—*RT Book Reviews*

Hunter's Heart

"In the rapid-fire fourth Alpha Pack novel from
Tyler (after *Black Moon*), a psychic wolf shifter meets
a wildlife biologist who captures his heart. As the
Alpha Pack—a group of former Navy SEALs turned
shifters—race against time to catch the killer, Daria
and Ryon's romance turns red-hot, even though
they're fighting to stay alive. An unexpected con-
cluding twist provides a little edge and neatly sets
up the next entry in the series."
—*Publishers Weekly*

"Fast-paced with a great sense of adventure, as
only sexy psychic Navy SEALs turned wolf shifters can provide. The characters have a complexity
that brings depth to the story, but the passion between Ryon and Daria makes for a particularly
hot read." —*RT Book Reviews*

continued . . .

"Amazing characters, wonderful drama . . . hot and to die for. Make sure you have a cool drink close at hand because Ryon and Daria together are a romance reader's joy and delight. Final word on this book: Get It Right Now!"   —Dark Faerie Tales

Black Moon

"I loved every single minute of [*Black Moon*], every event, and every twist. This book was action-packed and smexy-packed. You will fall in love with Kalen if you weren't already."
—Under the Covers

"Tyler brings more intense romance and danger to this third entry in the Alpha Pack series. Werewolves and Marines are a heady combination, making the men of the Alpha Pack exciting and passionate. The women in this series are strong enough to stand up to the men without losing their feminine edge, and Mackenzie definitely lives up to the standard."   —*RT Book Reviews*

Savage Awakening

"In a genre with werewolves aplenty, *Savage Awakening* leads the herd with its strong character development and intensity. . . . It's hard not to fall in love with the Alpha Pack."   —*RT Book Reviews*

Primal Law

"With *Primal Law*, J. D. Tyler has created a whole squad of yummy shifter heroes whom readers will fall head over heels for. . . . I can't wait for Tyler's next Alpha Pack adventure!"
—*New York Times* bestselling author
Angela Knight

"Tyler has set up an intriguing premise for her series, which promises plenty of action, treachery, and scorchingly hot sex." —*RT Book Reviews*

"Sizzling and interesting, *Primal Law* pays homage to Lora Leigh's Breed series while forging its own paths. The characters are likable, and the work speeds along." —Fresh Fiction

"In a genre where the paranormal is intense, J. D. Tyler may just be a force to be reckoned with. The book kept me riveted from start to finish."
—Night Owl Reviews

Also by J. D. Tyler

Withdrawn
Wolf's
FALL

AN ALPHA PACK NOVEL

J. D. TYLER

A SIGNET ECLIPSE BOOK

SIGNET ECLIPSE
Published by the Penguin Group
Penguin Group (USA) LLC, 375 Hudson Street,
New York, New York 10014

USA | Canada | UK | Ireland | Australia | New Zealand | India | South Africa | China
penguin.com
A Penguin Random House Company

First published by Signet Eclipse, an imprint of New American Library,
a division of Penguin Group (USA) LLC

First Printing, December 2014

ISBN 978-0-451-46691-4

Printed in the United States of America
10 9 8 7 6 5 4 3 2 1

To my dear friend Tracy Garrett. One of the best days of my life was the day you walked up to me and introduced yourself, taking this shy, new budding author under your wing. Your friendship is a true gift, and I'm so glad we're making this journey together.

Nick's story is for you. I love you, my friend.

ACKNOWLEDGMENTS

Special thanks to:

My family, for supporting and encouraging me during every step of my journey.

My agent, Roberta Brown, and my editor, Tracy Bernstein. I'm so grateful for your support and guidance, as always.

My readers. You make my job telling stories worthwhile, and such a joy.

"It's impossible," said Pride.
"It's risky," said Experience.
"It's pointless," said Reason.
"Give it a try," whispered the Heart.

—Author Unknown

One

Alpha Pack commander Nick Westfall strode from his office and down the main corridor of the compound, his heavy black boots muffled on the carpet.

His hand went to his side, fingers touching briefly on the butt of the firearm tucked into the waistband of his jeans. He pulled his T-shirt down to cover it and kept walking.

I should feel something, *shouldn't I? Fear? Self-loathing? Regret?*

Yes, all of those things shredded his guts like razor blades, but not because of what he might be about to do. He *wanted* to hold on. It wasn't in his nature to give up, ever. But the storm within battered him from all sides, tidal waves washing over his head again and again until it seemed there was nothing left to do but just let go. Drown.

Every time he closed his eyes, he saw Carter Darrow's sinister smile splitting his cold face. Day and night, the phantom press of the dead vampire's body, fangs piercing his skin, unwillingly aroused him all over again.

Worse, he'd begged for it. The nightmare of his time with Darrow never left him. The vampire had broken him down, mind and body, to the lowest common denominator of flesh, blood, and desire. He was nothing but what the creature wanted him to be: enslaved.

Choking off a bitter laugh, he turned a corner and almost mowed down Hammer—aka former Special Agent John Ryder. His best friend and right hand, the one man who'd been with him for years. Endured all sorts of shit with him since their days in the FBI, passing a few years as humans. The one man who would see through Nick's mask in a heartbeat if Nick wasn't careful.

"Where you goin' in such a hurry?" The big wolf shifter was half teasing, but the easygoing smile met a quick death as he studied Nick's face. "What's up?"

"Nothing," he said casually. "Just going out to the hangar to check on the repairs of that Huey, and then I'm heading over to Sanctuary to see how things are going with the new residents."

All of that was the truth. He'd just left out his next, possibly final, destination. Still, the huge bald man narrowed his eyes, shifted his stance, clearly communicating that his bullshit detector was fully functioning. They'd been friends too long to miss when something was off with the other.

"I'll go with you."

A test. One he'd fail if he refused his friend's company, and the guy knew it. Shrugging, he said, "Sure."

Nick could fool most people, but not the former undercover agent whose life had depended on his ability to read the subtle nuances of tone, body language, and facial expression. And he probably knew Nick better than anyone else ever had, even Nick's own brother.

As they headed for the hangar, a buzz vibrated against Nick's thigh. Fishing in his front pocket, he pulled out his cell phone and let out a frustrated breath as he saw his brother's name on the screen. Hell, the guys of the Pack were more his brothers than Damien had ever been.

He should have known. Just when he wanted nothing more than to be left alone, especially by *that* asshole, he had a couple of minders breathing down his neck. "Fuck off," he muttered, pushing the button to decline the call. Then he shoved the device back into his pocket.

"You not gonna answer that?"

"Nope. Thought the 'fuck off' made it pretty obvious."

Hammer was unperturbed, sliding on his sunglasses as they stepped outside. "You know he'll just keep calling back."

"Yeah, he's a dick like that."

"He cares."

Nick shot him a glare. They had been friends for years, since long before the Pack. The others might suspect that Hammer had known the sad story of Nick's past all along, but nobody knew for sure and no one had asked in the days since everything had come out.

Hammer *had* known, almost from the start of their friendship. And he had never told a soul. He was the most loyal, steadfast friend a man could ask for.

Few people knew better what Nick had been through twenty years ago, after making a horrible mistake. He'd used his abilities as a PreCog to change the future, saving his daughter's life. But his actions had cost his mate her life instead—at Carter Darrow's hands. Damien had banished Nick from their clan and forced him to leave a then-eleven-year-old Selene behind. He'd lost his daughter, mate, brother, and clan, in one fell swoop. It was that bastard Darrow's fault—but Damien could have handled things differently. The heartless prick could have supported Nick instead of casting him out.

Which was why Hammer's pushing Nick to reconcile with his brother completely baffled him.

Coming back to the present, he realized he'd stopped to stare at his friend.

"You really want to go there with me?" he asked in a warning tone.

"Just sayin'." Thankfully, his friend lapsed back into quiet mode until they reached the cavernous hangar, and didn't bring up the subject of Damien again.

In the driveway outside the building, some of the guys were waxing the SUVs. Correction: *most* were waxing and two others were goofing off. Jaxon Law, Ryon Hunter, Zander Cole, and Micah Chase were polishing the freshly washed black vehicles to a high shine while Aric Savage and Kalen Black were running around throwing wet, soapy sponges at each other. Nick exchanged an amused look with Hammer and the two of them stopped to watch.

"Gotcha!" Kalen yelled as his missile hit Aric's chest with a wet *splat*.

"Yeah? Take this!" The redheaded wolf shifter returned the favor, dipping his sponge into a bucket and then letting it fly, hitting the Sorcerer in the head.

"Oh, yeah? Die, mangy wolf!"

With that, Kalen waved a hand at his own bucket—and the contents shot from it, completely drenching Aric. Who sputtered, cursed, and laughed at the same time.

"You fucker! That's cheating!" He wiped soap from his eyes and gave Kalen an evil grin. "You're gonna pay, Magic Man."

Aric waved a hand at his own bucket, the sudsy water splashing on the concrete as he used his gift of telekinesis to hurl the entire thing at Kalen. Who immediately used his own magic to stop the bucket midair and send it straight back at Aric. Halfway to Aric, the bucket met with equal resistance and hung suspended between them.

"Stalemate," Kalen said dryly.

"Yeah. All the water's gone anyway."

With the ceasing of their power, the bucket fell unceremoniously to the ground with a clatter. Nick rolled his eyes and stepped forward. "Is that all you two idiots have to do today? I'm sure I can find jobs for you. Like cleaning the staff restrooms, for example."

The words apparently held no real heat, though, from the unrepentant grins he received in response. Aric answered, "Nah, that's quite all right. I'm sure we can find something to keep ourselves occupied, can't we, Goth Boy?"

"You bet, Red." Kalen plucked at his soggy T-shirt.

Hard to imagine that just months ago, those two were at each other's throats. Now they were horsing around like a couple of teenagers, all smiles. Who knew?

And how far would it set them and the entire team back once Nick was gone?

Nick shook his head to clear that thought. "Anybody know if the Huey's fixed?"

"The mechanic's still in there," Jax said, tossing down his polishing rag. "He was replacing a couple of parts last time I checked."

"Okay. I'll go take a look."

"You ever seen this guy before?"

Nick studied the tattooed shifter, who was rubbing his goatee thoughtfully. "Scott? Just met him earlier today when he interviewed with me. Why?"

"I don't know, but Tom really loved his job taking care of our vehicles. Guess it just doesn't sit right that he left without so much as a 'see ya.'"

"I thought that was weird, too," Nick admitted. "But Grant confirmed Tom's departure and vouched for Scott. He seemed competent enough when I spoke with him before."

"Never mind. I just thought it was strange the way Tom left without a word. That's all. And in our world, strange isn't typically a good thing."

Nick gave a soft laugh. "True. I'll keep an eye on him." And how the fuck was he supposed to make good on that when he wasn't planning on hanging around?

Aric nodded, attitude sober now. "We all will."

Leaving them to finish the SUVs, Nick strode into the hangar, Hammer still dogging his heels. It was rapidly becoming apparent he wasn't going to shake his friend anytime soon. Damn. He didn't know whether to yell or be grateful.

Forcing himself to focus, he crossed the expanse of the hangar to where Scott was working by the nose, grease-covered hands fiddling with some wires. At their approach, the man looked over and turned to greet them, pulling a dirty rag from his front pocket and wiping his hands.

"Hey, there. I think I've got her fit to hit the clouds again."

"Good to know." Nick studied Scott again, taking closer note than he had during their interview.

Scott Morgan was thirty-one, according to the employee profile Grant had e-mailed to him, and had plenty of experience working on aircraft. He wasn't overly tall, maybe five-ten or -eleven. Slight build, hands that appeared work roughened, as they should. His brown hair was clean but a little shaggy, falling into dark eyes, and his demeanor was relaxed. His expression was friendly. There wasn't a single thing the least bit disturbing about the mechanic.

Except that he'd replaced their regular man so suddenly, without warning. Nick was falling down on his job when it took his team members to point out a potential concern. The shame nearly consumed him. He wasn't doing anyone a favor by remaining here as their leader.

Time for that issue later. Nick gestured to the craft. "So, we can take her for a spin?"

"Absolutely. Whenever you're ready." Scott pulled

out his cell phone. "In fact, I can call Steven if you need a pilot."

Steven was one of the Pack's standby pilots who lived in the nearby town of Cody, Wyoming. He and a couple of others filled in to help out Aric when the team needed more than one pilot to go out on a call. The extra personnel was approved by General Jarrod Grant, and sworn to secrecy involving whatever they might witness on the mission. A must when Nick's team was made up of wolf shifters—and one panther—with special Psy abilities. Their job entailed battling the world's most lethal paranormal and human enemies, and anyone from the "outside" had to be trusted implicitly.

"That won't be necessary," Aric said, entering the hangar and approaching the group. "I can take everybody." His long red hair, T-shirt, and shorts were still damp, and he wore flip-flops on his feet. He looked more like he belonged in a rock band than at the controls of a helicopter. But he was a damned good pilot, even from before his time in the military.

"Oh. Okay." Scott put away his phone. "I can ride along if you all want. Make sure she's running smooth."

Aric smiled. "That's a great idea."

Nick knew that smile. It was the fake one the Telekinetic/Firestarter gave people he didn't trust, and Nick wasn't sure why the man was leveling it at Scott. In fact, his own PreCog abilities hadn't given him a single vision or even a vibe about the new mechanic. That in itself wasn't unusual or alarming. It wasn't like he saw *everything*. But he trusted Aric's instincts.

"I agree," he said. "If she's still doing anything funny, you can make some adjustments when we get her on the ground."

The mechanic nodded. "Sounds good."

Nick didn't add that even if there was something seriously wrong with the copter, it wasn't going to crash with Aric on board to set it down safely. Their Psy gifts came in damned handy sometimes.

If Scott had caught on to their wariness of him, he didn't show it as they boarded the Huey. Nick took the copilot's seat up front with Aric, while Hammer sat behind them with the mechanic. Aric hit a button and the roof above them slowly slid open to reveal the bright skies. The blades started with a whine and in moments they were lifting off.

The ground fell away, and Nick let himself enjoy the view of the mountains and valleys, the lush green forest below. He wondered whether he'd ever see it like this again, with the earth far below him.

Maybe, if battered old wolves were allowed in heaven.

The ride went without a hitch. After about an

hour, Aric brought the Huey around and headed back to the compound. Once they landed in the hangar, Aric shut off the copter and saw to refueling it while Nick and Hammer thanked Scott and said good-bye.

After the man left, Jax and the others who'd been washing and waxing the vehicles walked into the hangar, clearly curious as to Nick's impression of Scott. They were joined by Phoenix Monroe, a Pack brother who was a Firewalker in addition to being a wolf. Meaning, the guy could literally walk through fire without being burned—unless he purposely dropped his shields.

Hammer posed the question on all their minds. "You think Scott's legit?"

"Logic says yes," Nick said. "But I didn't get any visions."

"You tried to read him?" the big man asked.

"Yeah. There was just nothing."

His friend didn't appear pleased about that news. "My wolf's nose says he's human, at least. Not a shifter or a vampire."

"Mine, too. Unless he's somehow masking his scent."

Phoenix frowned. "How could he do that?"

"*He* couldn't, but someone could do it for him. Someone powerful could, like a Sorcerer, or perhaps there's a drug we don't know about that has the capability."

"That's a disturbing thought," Hammer put in.

"Which one?"

"Both." Hammer eyed him. "Have you actually heard anything about a drug that can mask scent?"

"No, but who knows what all is out there? Our own medical team is working on a drug to delay the negative effects of mating sickness. Nobody outside the compound, except Grant, knows about it."

"Say *what*?" Phoenix stared at Nick. "A drug that can delay having to mate? Who are they using for test subjects?"

Nick cringed inwardly at the sudden interest from the wolf. He thought of Noah Brooks, the human nurse who'd been waiting for Phoenix to claim him as his mate, and regretted mentioning it. "They've got a couple, from Sanctuary. They haven't mentioned needing more volunteers."

He sensed his attempt to deflect the wolf from the subject wasn't successful. Phoenix excused himself in a hurry, and Nick shook his head. Another fuckup to add to his growing list.

"Shit," he muttered, watching Nix's retreating back.

Hammer shook his head. "Hey, you don't make his choices, or anyone else's. If he breaks Noah's heart, or his own, that's on *his* head." There was a murmur of general agreement from the others.

"I know, but we can't afford to lose two good men." Nick ran a hand through his hair, which needed a trim. Like it mattered. "Anyway, about the testing. I was just trying to make a point."

"I got it," his friend said. "It stands to reason there are plenty of paranormal studies we don't know about, considering how many different groups there are. Either way, we'll keep an eye on Scott. Want us to watch him?"

"For the time being. If he's up to something, we'll find out sooner or later."

"Do we know where he's staying?" Hammer asked.

"His contact info lists a motel in Cody, supposedly while he looks for a place to rent. Also, call Tom and see if he'll shed more light on his departure."

"Will do, right after we're done at Sanctuary."

The others dispersed to tackle other tasks. Hammer stayed with Nick as he walked to the Sanctuary building, and Nick resigned himself to his friend's presence. Truthfully, he found the man's dogged persistence comforting. He wasn't half as annoyed as he tried to be.

They entered the lobby of the facility, and he stopped for a moment to admire the completed project. The place was like a high-end long-term-care home for shifters and other injured, sick, or displaced paranormals—except instead of coming there to receive comfort and care at the *end* of their lives, they were there to *begin* to live.

It was certainly a lofty goal, and though it hadn't been his brainchild, he'd been in full support of the project since its inception. Kira, Jax's mate, had founded Sanctuary. When she'd first come to live at the compound, she'd been horri-fied at the treatment received by the residents of Block R—the rehabilitation wing. In particular, she'd bonded with their Fae prince, Sariel, or "Blue" as some called him, who'd been depressed and uncommunicative. No wonder, as he'd been exiled from his realm, captured by the Pack, and was wasting away in the equivalent of a jail cell.

Kira had been passionate about having a real facility to treat paranormals, one that would use staff trained in delivering love and understanding rather than a punitive system that inspired fear. With Blue's and Noah's help, she'd put together quite the haven. That wasn't to say they didn't have their hard-core, sometimes dangerous cases that required extra measures, such as restraints or drugs, for everyone's safety. But they received bet-ter care than ever before.

The lobby was empty except for the receptionist and a lone shifter sitting in one of the oversized chairs, curled up with a blanket around her shoul-ders, staring out the window. A nurse hovered near her, tidying the area and keeping an eye on her charge.

"Been wondering about her story," Hammer com-mented quietly, eyeing the small tiger shifter. "She always looks so sad."

Nick kept his voice down. "Her name's Leila. She and her brother, Leonidis, were attacked while in Cody on some sort of assignment."

"What kind of assignment?"

"Not sure. She and her brothers are a pride of big-cat shifters, and they run some sort of detective agency. The one upstairs on the hospital floor was injured pretty badly and might not make it.

"Damn." The man cast a glance toward her filled with something like longing. "I'll ask her later if there's anything I can do to help."

"I'm sure she'll appreciate that."

Interesting. Nick pondered his friend's reaction to Leila as they got into the elevator. In fact, Hammer had been much more animated lately. Talkative. Very unlike the typically quiet guy Nick had known for so long. But he didn't want to point that out and cause the man to clam up.

On one of the residence floors, they exited the elevator and Nick asked around for Kira. Since he'd given Hammer the excuse of coming here to check on things, he might as well make good. He learned she was tied up on the phone in her office, and instead found Noah coming down the hallway toward them. The head nurse gave them a sunny smile, tired blue eyes at odds with his happy expression.

"Hey, guys. What's up?"

Nick stopped and studied the younger man carefully. He looked more than tired—vibes of sadness were coming off Noah in waves, though he probably didn't realize it. "Just checking to see how things are going over here. Any problems?"

"Ha! Is it a day that ends in D-A-Y?" he quipped, making a face.

Nick chuckled in spite of himself. "That bad, huh?"

"No—okay, yeah. But nothing we haven't been able to handle."

"Leo?" Hammer guessed.

Noah blew out a breath. "He's one issue in a string of them. He crashed two hours ago and we almost lost him. Between fighting to save him and fighting with his unruly family, I'm about ready to put in my notice. Go park my ass on a beach somewhere and sip fruity drinks."

"Except you won't," Nick told him with a half smile. "You care too much."

"Total personality fault," Noah assured him. "I'm working on it."

Nick clapped him on the shoulder. "Don't change a thing. You're doing great, a real asset to everyone here."

The nurse's face flushed and he looked pleased. "Well, thanks. I've got lots of help, though."

A familiar tingling sensation began in Nick's fingers where they gripped Noah's shoulder. It was one of the hallmarks of a vision coming on, though he didn't need to touch people or even be near them to "see" a glimpse into the future. His eyesight swam, and a buzzing overtook his brain. Then the corridor disappeared and the scene unfolded.

"He's gone?" Phoenix glanced around at his Pack brothers in confusion. "Where did he go? When's he coming back?"

"He left, idiot," Aric snarled, eyeing Nix in disgust. "Did you really think he'd stay after what you did to him in front of everyone?"

"I—I was going to apologize! That's why I'm looking for him!" His voice took on a desperate edge. "Is he staying in Cody? It doesn't matter. I'll find him and make him understand how sorry I am. I'll—"

"There's more," Jax put in, his expression grim. "Noah's been taken."

"Taken . . ." Nix uttered the word, obviously trying to make sense of it.

"He was kidnapped, by Jinn. I'm sorry, man. But we'll find him. I promise."

"No," he moaned in agony. His legs buckled and Aric grabbed him to keep him from hitting the ground. "God, no."

The vision faded, though Nick tried to hang on to it. He became aware of his surroundings again, and the other men's voices asking whether he was all right.

"I'm fine," he said hoarsely, trying to clear his head.

Here was the part that sucked about being a PreCog—the urge to tell people what was in store for them. His general rule, though, was to be vigilant but *never* to tamper with the future.

And who the hell was Jinn?

"You sure you're okay?" Noah asked, grabbing his wrist to check his pulse. "You're kinda pale."

"I'm good." He took his hand back and gave the nurse a reassuring smile. "Anyway, I was making a point. Never sell yourself short. The work you do here is tough, and it's important. Utilizing your team is essential to success, and that's something you excel in—which is why you're in charge of the nurses. Don't forget that."

Noah stood a bit straighter. "I won't. Thanks, Nick."

"We'll let you get back to work," he said. "Call if you need us."

"I will."

He thought about giving Noah a small pep talk about his would-be Bondmate, but decided against it for the time being. Besides, who was *he* to give anyone warm fuzzies on *that* subject?

As he and Hammer left the building, he said, "Listen, I'm going to go for a run. When I get back, let me know what you found out about Tom."

"I will."

But instead of veering off, his friend walked with him all the way to the back of the compound, where the forest began. When Nick stopped, Hammer was quiet a moment before he spoke.

"You get a vision back there?"

"Yeah." He debated whether to reveal what he'd seen. But what if he wasn't around to help the would-be mates through their trials? Someone should know. "Phoenix and Noah. They're going to have it rough for a while. Not sure when, but some bad shit is coming, too."

His friend frowned. "Like what? You talkin' in general, or something specific?"

"The bad shit is someone named Jinn, and he's going to kidnap Noah." He ran a hand through his hair. "That's all I know."

"Jesus," the big man muttered. "That's more detail than you've ever let me in on before. Why?"

"I just felt you should know."

"What for? What I am supposed to do that you can't— Wait." Then Hammer narrowed his icy blue eyes at Nick. "You've been trying to shake me off your tail all day, and now this. I know what you're planning to do."

"I don't follow." But he did, of course.

Hammer's voice was sharp as the crack of a gun. "Don't lie to me. Not to *me*, goddammit! I know you've been through hell. And I know you want out, but—"

"You have no fucking *idea* how messed up my head is," he shouted, jabbing a finger at his friend's chest. "Not a day goes by that I don't feel Carter Darrow's fangs in my neck! That I don't remember what it was like, *begging* that bastard to drain me dry! He raped my soul, and I don't know how to live with that."

"You had no choice," the other man emphasized. "It wasn't your fault. Vampires seduce their prey. That's how they operate."

His anger began to deflate, leaving him hollow. "I know that. But it doesn't make living with the nightmare any easier."

"And then there's Calla."

Nick's jaw tightened, his gut clenching. "What about her?"

"Man, I saw how you reacted to her at the party the other day," he said, studying Nick carefully. "You exchanged a few words, looked at her like she'd grown a second head, and lit out of there like your ass was on fire. She your mate?"

"Where'd you come up with that?" He swallowed hard.

"I'm asking. It's not that tough a question."

"Yeah, well, it's a tough answer." Nick sighed, looking away. His heart hurt like it was being scored with razor blades—proving he wasn't dead inside. Unfortunately. "Tell me what I'm supposed to do about having a Bondmate, one I can't stand the thought of touching me the way Darrow did. Seducing me, and feeding from me."

"Shit." Hammer paused. "You can get past it. I believe that."

"I wish I had your faith."

"One thing is for sure—I'm not going to stand by and watch you kill yourself. Not that I really believe you'll go through with it."

He gave a bitter laugh. "What makes you so certain?"

"You care too much," Hammer said simply. "About your daughter, about Noah and Phoenix, your whole team. Even the mate you don't want. You care, and you won't leave no matter how much you want to."

Misery clogged his throat. His friend was right, and he hated it. Turning, he looked out, into the forest he loved so much, and at the mountains beyond. The one place that had always given him comfort. Until recently. Now even his wolf didn't care whether they ran. He was curled up inside Nick, hurting deep in the core of his being.

He took a breath. "I've lived over two hundred years, and as a born wolf I'll live a lot longer. I've seen so many changes in the world. I've lost more than I ever thought I could and still be sane, much less alive."

"So why is what you've been through with Darrow any different?" Hammer pressed. "You lost your whole family and it didn't destroy you. You've survived a hell of a lot."

"Yeah. We all have. But I'm the commander of this unit. All the suffering the Pack has endured is my responsibility, and I don't know how much more I can stand. It's an accumulation of everything, to be honest. I got Selene back, and I'm beyond grateful we're mending things between us; don't get me wrong. But after Darrow . . ."

His friend remained silent, and Nick put it as simply as he could.

"I'm just tired, John," he said quietly.

It was several moments before the other man spoke. "I get that. Hell, I've been there, too. But you can't quit."

Turning, he faced Hammer again, taking in the worry on his face. "I'm so damned tired, all I want is for the world to wake up tomorrow without me in it."

Hammer shook his head. "Tough shit. Not going to happen. So, now's a good time to think of Plan B."

Nick laughed softly in spite of himself. "Maybe."

"Definitely." He held out a hand. "Give me the gun tucked in the back of your jeans."

"What if I run into a grizzly?"

"*He'll* run if he knows what's good for him. In fact, I'm positive you'll be the most dangerous predator out there. Gun. Now."

The man wasn't going to budge. Anger surged as he tugged the weapon from his waistband and placed it in his friend's hand, butt first. He tamped it down, though. Hammer—*John*—had always looked out for him. He wasn't going to stop, especially now that Nick was in a crisis.

Hammer's gaze softened. "Thanks. See you when you get back."

"Sure."

They both understood that if Nick was truly

done, no force on earth could make him stay. Many immortals—vampires and born shifters included—met their demise by their own hands sooner or later. Forever wasn't all it was imagined to be.

But as Nick stripped off his clothing and shifted, then took off through the forest, he knew his friend was right—Nick did care. Maybe too much.

Whether that would prove to be his downfall or his salvation remained to be seen.

Two

Calla Shaw swept through the corridors, fuming. *Gods! What the hell has that high-handed, arrogant brother of mine gotten me into now? Who does he think he is?*

Just because Tarron Romanoff was the leader of their coven—as well as prince of all the vampires in North America—didn't mean he had the right to tamper with her life. To destroy her hard-won peace.

Even their toughest guards had the good sense to move out of her way as they took in her murderous glare. She usually considered herself a calm, pleasant person, but that flew out the window with the phone call she'd received. Eviscerating her brother with a rusty spike sounded like a pretty good idea.

When she barged in, Tarron was seated behind

his desk in his office, reading some papers, head down, shoulder-length dark brown hair falling around his face. The door banged into the wall and his head snapped up, expression startled.

"Calla! What's wrong?" He stood.

"What's *wrong*?" She stared at him incredulously. "Are you serious? I get a phone call from the Russian vampire prince himself thanking me *very* enthusiastically for inviting him to our party, saying he's looking forward to *seeing* me, and you ask what's wrong?"

"Calm down and have a seat, would you?"

"I'll calm down when you tell me you aren't playing matchmaker." When he shifted in his chair, surprise turning to guilt, she marched up to his desk. "Way to throw me face-first under the bus, big brother."

"Rolan Stanislav is a great catch," he said defensively.

"That old fogie is nine hundred years old!"

"So what? We're over four hundred, which doesn't exactly make us spring chickens," he said evenly. "You know very well he's quite attractive, and any number of female vamps would kill to mate with him."

That, at least, was the truth. Rolan was tall, powerful, with long white blond hair and jade green eyes. She didn't know him very well personally, but he was widely considered kind and honorable. Admirable.

Unfortunately, he wasn't Stefano. The thought of replacing her dead mate made her sick with guilt, though it had been decades since he was killed.

She shook herself from taking that nightmare trip down memory lane. "Then they're welcome to him."

"Just one problem with that—he wants you. Has for ages, Calla, ever since he recovered from his mate's death. How long are you going to avoid him? Hell, not just him but the entire male population?"

"I don't care what he or anyone else wants! European vampires are stuck in the Middle Ages when it comes to just about everything, including their views on women." That wasn't necessarily true anymore, and it felt like the lame excuse it was. She crossed her arms over her chest. "I'm not mating with him and that's final."

"I'm not asking you to mate with him. Just *meet* with him, socialize a bit. Give him a chance, for me? He's a suitable match who would bring two vampire covens together as one unbeatable force. Nobody would mess with us then."

"Nobody would mess with us *now*," she insisted. "Except for Carter and his band of thugs, there isn't anyone who's dared in the past seventy years."

"I never take our safety for granted." His lips thinned in anger.

"Neither do I. But I'm sure there's another way to merge with another powerful coven besides selling me to the highest bidder."

At that, he looked shocked and hurt. "I would never suggest such a thing. Calla, I love you. I just want to see you happy again."

"And if you can kill two birds with one stone, all the better?"

"Yes. Is that so wrong?"

No, it wasn't. Her outrage evaporated like smoke as she studied her brother. Tarron truly loved her, and their coven. She had never doubted that. Every day, he put his own happiness on hold to make certain they were all safe and prosperous. He worked harder than anyone she knew.

And she suddenly noted something about him. There was a shadow in his eyes she'd never seen before. Perhaps it was worry, or melancholy.

Slowly, she lowered herself into a chair. "Do you have reason to believe we're going to be threatened?"

"Nothing specific," he admitted. "But I've been uneasy. There's a feeling of foreboding that I can't quite shake. As though Carter's death was too easy, and there's something waiting in the shadows. Like the old saying goes, if you kill one cockroach in the kitchen, there's a million more behind the walls. I can't explain it better than that."

His words gave her a chill, and she rubbed her arms. "We've got good allies in the Alpha Pack."

Unbidden, a mental picture of the Pack's sexy commander popped into her head. She tried to ignore it—and struggled not to think about how he'd spun on his heel and walked away after meeting her. As if she'd offended him with her presence. The dismissal still stung.

Tarron nodded. "Yes. And I'm glad about that. To be honest, I wouldn't mind having them around all the time, but Nick needs his men there. They've got a job to do."

"True, but their purpose isn't so different from ours. They fight to protect others from harm so we can all live peacefully. They're a family, like us."

"Yes, but they're not vampires."

"Elitist much?"

He scowled. "I didn't mean that they're less because they're shifters, just that they don't hold the same loyalty to us as our own kind would."

"That's your opinion, with no proof to support it."

Her brother merely shrugged. "I'm grateful for their friendship, and I know they'd come if we needed them. I just don't see the harm in our coven being bigger and stronger."

"How about 'the bigger they are, the harder they fall'? Ever heard that one?"

"Gods, you wear me out." He rubbed his eyes, then leveled a piercing look at her. "So, will you make nice with Rolan at the party?"

"Seeing as you're not going to let this rest until

I do, I'll agree. But only to be cordial, nothing more," she warned him.

Tarron gave her the brilliant smile that turned other females' knees to jelly. Calla had to admit it was pretty potent. Until she remembered what a jerk he could be sometimes.

Coming around the desk, he wrapped her in a hug. "Thank you. I promise the Russian prince will be a perfect gentleman. And if you really don't have any feelings for him, I won't push. Either way, it still won't hurt to have a strong ally."

"All right, I can't argue with that."

"Thank fuck."

Laughing, she pulled back and pecked him on the cheek. "Talk to you later."

Throwing Tarron a smile, she took her leave. It was hard to stay angry at her brother. But her amusement quickly faded as she replayed their conversation in her head. Even if she were ready to move on, to take another mate or even simply a lover, she'd never felt a pull toward Rolan.

Not like she'd experienced when she'd met Nick Westfall a few days ago. They'd been introduced and he'd taken her hand—and it was like she'd been pumped with a million volts of electricity. From the shock on the wolf shifter's handsome, rugged face, he'd felt it as well.

And he'd been none too pleased, if his hasty exit was any indication.

Sadness nearly overwhelmed her in that moment, tears pricking her eyes, and she wasn't sure why. She'd met the man for all of thirty seconds, and didn't know him from Adam. So why was there a gaping hole in her chest?

A desperate need to escape overwhelmed her. Sometimes the coven's mountain stronghold in the Smokies was more of a prison than a home. Going against her brother's standing directive, she used her gift of translocation to avoid her bodyguards and take herself away from there. *Far* away. She knew exactly where she wanted to be, and when she landed a few seconds later, she stood in a gorgeous copse of trees in the middle of the Shoshone National Forest hundreds of miles from the coven.

Home to the Alpha Pack. And the wolf commander.

What was this compulsion? This aching need to be near him? The last time she'd felt this way had been . . . when she met Stefano. Her throat burned with grief at the thought of what that might mean.

There was a certain peace in being cold and numb. In allowing every limb and organ to remain frozen so that the pain could never sneak in again. The idea of finally allowing the thaw was beyond her comprehension at this point. She wasn't sure whether she wanted to let another man inside her heart. Or whether she was capable.

She wandered for a while, enjoying the lush forest with its greenery. Insects buzzed and various birds chattered. The day wasn't too hot, a balmy breeze moving the leaves and branches. At last she came to a break on a rise and sucked in a breath at the beautiful Rocky Mountains in the distance. The sight was simply gorgeous.

But not nearly as breathtaking as the man sitting in the grass on the edge of the knoll, looking out over the vast expanse as though trying his best to ascertain the secrets of the world. His profile was strong and almost regal, with a square jaw and dark eyebrows arching over a straight nose that sat perfectly on his rugged face. His inky hair was touched with silver at his temples. He had a set of broad shoulders, and she remembered he was tall when standing, well over six feet.

One of his jean-clad legs was stretched out in the grass, the other bent at the knee. Compelled by some unnamed force, she approached and spotted a wicked-looking dagger with a pearl handle sitting on the ground at his side. Frowning, she studied it, then looked back to the commander. She could have sworn she scented blood—a sweet, heady aroma that she recognized was pure Nick. But she didn't *see* any blood.

Finally, he lifted his wary gaze and acknowledged her presence. "Calla."

"Hello, Nick," she said, glad her voice gave away no hint of how hard her pulse was racing at the sight of him. "Out for a run?"

"I let my wolf out earlier, but now I'm just out

for a walk and taking a break to do some thinking." He studied her intently. "You're about the last person I expected to see out here."

She shrugged, and decided to go for honesty. "I was drawn here. I'm not one hundred percent sure why."

Instead of addressing that, he asked, "Ditched your guards again, did you? Your brother will be pissed."

Moving around in front of him so she could see him better, she narrowed her eyes. "How did you know about that? Has Tarron been talking about me?"

One corner of his full, succulent mouth kicked up. "He didn't have to. I've seen you do it."

"What? When?" She stared at him in surprise.

"A few weeks ago, when the team and I stayed at your stronghold. Before I was . . ."

She didn't have to ask *Before what?* She knew he was referring to when he had been kidnapped by Carter, and tortured. She let it go for now, to his visible relief. "What was I doing when you saw me?"

"Pretty much the same. You were out for a walk in the woods, and you'd decided to sit by a pond for a while. I was in wolf form and I watched you until Tarron yelled, obviously upset and looking for you."

She blinked at his frank admission. "I'm not sure how to feel about you spying on me."

"I was just making sure no harm came to you," he said, then looked away. "And maybe admiring the view as well."

"Really, now," she murmured, a tiny thrill dancing through her body. Making a decision, she took a seat beside him on the grass, uninvited. "You could have at least made yourself known so I could've had the same pleasure."

A soft chuckle rumbled in his chest and he seemed to relax a fraction. "You don't mince words."

"Never saw the point." They were silent for a moment. Her gaze fell on the knife again and she nodded at it. "I'm not thinking a born wolf shifter needs a blade for an afternoon stroll. Were you planning to harm yourself? I smelled blood when I approached you."

His shoulders tensed. For a while she thought he wouldn't answer. Then he held out his arm and turned his wrist over, showing her a red line, the slice still a bit bloody. The implication washed over her like ice water.

"Why isn't it healing?" She couldn't hide the tremor in her voice.

"Silver blade," he said simply. "But if I wanted to do the job right, I'd have to drive it into my heart."

Truly alarmed, she placed a hand on his thigh, noting the hard muscles bunching under her palm. The spark of attraction threatened to ignite again, but she fought it down. This wasn't the time. Focusing on his emotions, she could see that anyone would think he was completely calm—if it wasn't for the desolation in his dark blue eyes.

She kept her voice gentle, nonjudgmental. "Why would you contemplate such a thing? Because of what Carter did to you?"

His eyes snapped to hers, piercing her to the core. "What do you know? Has Tarron given you the sordid details?"

"No," she assured him. "My brother and his men are not prone to discussing others' misfortunes, especially when it involves a mission or a battle. The only ones who are privy to everything are the ones who were there, or those who need to be told."

Dropping his chin, he blew out a breath. "That's good to know. Thank you."

"I'm here, however, if you want to talk." She paused, biting her bottom lip with one fang before admitting, "I've been where you are now. At the lowest point in my life, I was ready to give up."

That got his undivided attention again. Startled, he laid a hand over hers. "For God's sake, why? I can't imagine a woman as smart and beautiful as you having a reason to feel that way."

She gave him a sad smile. "Thank you. But I had every reason, or so I believed at the time. I lost my mate over seventy years ago, and I almost didn't survive his death."

"Calla, I'm so sorry," he said quietly. His tone and his expression were honest.

"Me, too. Stefano was a wonderful man, and we were very much in love. Do you know it's rare for a vampire to find his or her true Bondmate?"

"I've heard that, yes. Is that what you were to each other?"

"We were," she said. "Some vampires wait centuries and never find their other half. Many of them seek death when they can't stand the loneliness any longer. After I came of age, I waited two hundred years before we found each other, which seemed forever but is actually not nearly as long as most of our kind. We had more than a hundred years together, and then just like that, he was gone."

"Can you talk about what happened?"

The commander was so kind, and understanding. Tears pricked her eyes, and she sniffed. "One day, I'll tell you more about him, and what happened. That's not the point I'm making right now."

"What *is* the point?" He was still holding her hand.

She considered her words carefully. "There have been many times in the past seventy years I've wanted to give up. Sometimes the struggle just seems so overwhelming, like I can't take one more day. Some days I have to dig deep, and I survive for three reasons: First, Tarron would be devastated and I can't leave him with that burden. He'd blame himself forever, perhaps even follow me, and I'm not going to let it happen. Second, the bastards who ruined my life would win, and that's not acceptable, either."

"Those are damned good reasons. And third?"

"There's always a tiny bit of hope inside me that I'll find happiness again," she whispered. "What if I took myself out of the game too soon, when I only had to wait a little longer?"

"How come you make so much sense?" He tried a smile, but it didn't quite materialize.

Reaching out, she touched his face. She loved the manly stubble against her fingers, his lips and cheekbones. Even more, she was drawn to the kind, genuine man behind the steely demeanor. "I can see how sad you are, Nick. How weary. Whatever Carter did to you, I suspect that's not the only reason you're feeling down."

"You're right. It's not. It's just the latest in a string of blows."

"And yet you're still here. Don't you see? You don't *really* want to give up, or you would have by now. You're a bit lost, but you're going to find your way."

"You seem sure about that."

"I am," she said with growing confidence.

"And I thought *I* was the Seer."

Then Nick gave her the first honest smile she'd seen since they had met, one that reached his eyes, and it completely transformed his face. *Sweet gods, he's beautiful!* If she'd thought him handsome before, now she just about swallowed her tongue. Her long-neglected libido stretched and awakened, purring like the engine of a Ferrari ready to burn rubber.

With regret, she reined herself in. Neither of them was ready to move fast, were they?

"Would you like to go for a walk?" she asked.

"That's the best idea I've heard all day."

Nick lifted the right cuff of his jeans and sheathed his knife in the holster strapped to his ankle. Then he stood and helped her up, letting his hand remain wrapped around her smaller one for a moment before releasing it. She felt the loss of his touch immediately, and craved more. She would have to content herself with his nearness—for the time being.

"Tell me about your family," he said. "I got the impression there's only you and Tarron in the coven?"

"Yes, but we have a younger brother, Adrian, who lives in England. He doesn't prefer coven life; he's sort of a loner. He works for the Secret Service and loves it."

Nick whistled in appreciation. "I'm impressed. Do they know he's a vampire?"

"Only his handler and one close friend. Everyone else is discretionary, on an absolute need-to-know basis. He's good at his job, a real badass." She shot him a grin. "Sort of like someone else I know."

"Not so sure about that." But his expression was pleased. "Anyway, you sound very proud of Adrian."

"I am. I was blessed with wonderful brothers."

"What about your parents?"

"They died long ago, right after I reached puberty," she said wistfully. "Even though there were so many dangers that existed back then from human hunters, rogue shifters, and other paranormal creatures, that's not what got them. It was a simple accident. A log shifted and rolled from the hearth in the night and our little cottage went up in flames before we knew what was happening. They couldn't get out."

"I'm sorry." Reaching out, he took her hand again, stroking her skin with his thumb.

A pang lanced her soul, but Nick's hand wrapped around hers soothed it. "It's all right. I've had centuries to make peace with their deaths. Tarron got me and Adrian out, and has been taking care of us ever since. Well, mostly me these days. Sometimes I think he takes his role of substitute father a bit too seriously," she said to lighten the conversation.

"Let him. Family is everything, and at least he loves you."

Something in his tone made her wonder, and she decided to probe a little. "What about your family? I was introduced to your daughter and her mate when your team stayed at the stronghold. Then I met your brother at the party, but I don't know much about them."

He sucked in a breath. "Selene and I are just getting to know each other again after many years apart. Things were rocky at first, but I think mating with Zan has really grounded her. They're madly in love and I'm reaping some of the benefits of her softened attitude."

"Why did you and Selene spend time apart?" She shook her head. "From your expression I'd say that's upsetting to you. I'm sorry."

"It's all right. It's a long story, but the short version is that when Selene was eleven years old I made a mistake and broke Pack law. As a result, my brother, Damien, who you met at the party, took Selene from me and cast me out of our Pack."

"That's terrible," she said quietly. Her brain couldn't wrap itself around the thought of being rejected by her own family. The sorrow of such an act would probably kill her.

His hand squeezed hers. "The horror I recently suffered at Carter's hands doesn't begin to compare to losing my child. Only the hope that we might know each other someday, that she might forgive me, kept me going. It seems we're finally finding each other again."

"I'm so glad. And Damien?"

His jaw clenched. "He's an asshole. The bastard can rot in hell for all I care."

This might not be a good time to mention the intense longing on Damien's face as he'd observed Nick at the party. That his eyes had been filled with regret. Maybe once she and Nick were better acquainted, he'd be ready to hear it.

He went on before she could form a response. "We never had any other siblings, and our parents are dead also. My father was murdered by hunters thirty-five years ago, just before I met my mate, and my mother died of grief soon after."

Mate? What effing mate? She cleared her throat. "I'm so sorry to hear that."

"Thank you. It was a terrible time for the clan. My father was the Alpha, and was beloved by almost everyone. Damien took his place and there were the usual challenges to his leadership before he settled in." He paused. "Why are you looking at me like that?"

She stopped walking and leaned her back against a tree, studying him. "You mentioned a mate. Am I going to find myself on the business end of some alpha bitch's teeth and claws?"

He shook his head. "That mistake I mentioned before, the one that got me ousted from my Pack? My mate was killed as a result—by Carter Darrow. He saw an opportunity to come after me recently, and you know the rest."

"Not entirely, but I won't press you."

"I appreciate that. I'm sure I'll tell you the whole story one day, but not today."

"I'm sorry about your mate," she said sincerely. "What was her name, if you don't mind my asking?"

His lips curved up just a bit, and his expression was fond. "Jennifer. A name as sweet and simple as the woman. I wasn't looking for a mate, and one day she visited from a neighboring Pack. It was like being electrocuted."

He got the strangest look on his face, and she cocked her head. "What?"

"Nothing. Anyway, that's ancient history."

Time to lighten the mood again. "Speaking of ancient, how old are you?"

He laughed, showing off those straight white teeth—complete with a couple of canines that were slightly longer than a human's yet not as long as her own. The sight intrigued her.

"I'm two hundred sixteen. A mere baby next to you," he teased, blue eyes dancing with mischief.

"Oooh, that was a low blow, wolf." She narrowed her eyes, her tone playfully menacing. "Or should I say 'pup'? Perhaps you're too young and green to play with the grown-ups."

"Pup?" A feral gleam lit his eyes, coupled with humor. Moving in swiftly, he pressed his big body against hers, palm braced above her head. "Do I seem like a pup to you?"

Bark dug into her back, and she relished the feel of his hard muscles surrounding her. The thump of his heart. And there was nothing humorous about the hard-on in his jeans.

Their easy playfulness rapidly becoming something deeper. Nick continued to push against her, letting her feel his arousal. Then he raised a hand and stroked her face. Brushed a thumb over her lips.

"No," she admitted. "You certainly don't."

"You're beautiful."

She stared back at him, ensnared in his gaze. "Thank you."

Please, kiss me. I need—

His mouth covered hers and she whimpered, returning the kiss with equal hunger. Heaven. He was pure heaven, his heady scent and rich taste playing havoc with her hormones. Never before had a man *owned* her with a kiss like this one. As though he fully intended to possess every corner of her soul.

She wanted the contact to go on forever. Her vampire instincts surged to the fore, and she had to force down the desire to bite him. To claim her mate.

Mate!

Suddenly he pushed back, breaking the kiss. His chest heaved and he stared at her as though he'd read her thoughts. Maybe he had, somehow. And if so, he seemed less than happy about what he'd seen.

"I shouldn't have done that."

Not too promising.

"In case you didn't notice, I rather enjoyed it," she pointed out.

"So did I, but . . ." He ran a hand through his jet-black hair. "Look, I need to get back. I'm not ditching you, it's just that something tells me I'm needed."

He sounded sincere and she breathed a small sigh of relief. "I'll take you."

"You don't have to do that. My wolf can run fast."

"My way is faster." She held out a hand and waited. He hesitated only a second before placing his palm in hers. With a smile, she said, "Don't let go of me."

"Wouldn't dream of it."

Shifters didn't like traveling by translocation as a general rule. It tended to make many of them dizzy and sick to their stomachs. But there were times that it was the most expedient way to get where you were going.

Closing her eyes, she imagined the Pack's compound and let her gift take them there. The flight lasted merely a few seconds and soon she felt solid earth under her shoes again. Looking around, she saw that they were in the grassy yard area in the back where the party had taken place.

Nick staggered a bit, then leaned over and rested his hands on his knees. "God, that sucks."

"Are you all right?" She touched his shoulder.

"I will be." Gradually he straightened and gave her a rueful smile. "At least my lunch didn't make a reappearance."

"Thank goodness for small favors."

"Yeah."

"Nick!" The commander glanced toward the back of the building to see one of his men jogging out the door.

"Micah, what's wrong?"

Calla recognized the younger man with the scarred face as Micah Chase, Rowan's brother. One side of his face was like melted wax from being tortured months ago while in captivity. The evil scientist who'd held him and many other shifters had poured molten silver on him, ensuring the tissue would never heal. She shoved down the stirring of pity, sensing the young wolf wouldn't appreciate it.

"We got called out," Micah said, jogging up. "Oh, hi, Princess Calla. Sorry to interrupt."

"Just Calla, and no worries," she assured him. Seemed Nick's gut feeling that he needed to return had been spot-on.

"What type of call, and when did it come in?" Nick was all business now, standing straight and tall, his own problems forgotten. Every inch the Pack's Alpha wolf.

Secretly, it gave her a bit of a thrill to watch him work.

"About two minutes ago. There's a group of hunters attacking a coven of vampires about fifty miles from here. We gotta skate. They can't hold out much longer."

Nick turned to Calla, but she held up a hand. "Go. I'll be fine."

"Either stay here until I get back or go straight home," he ordered firmly. "I don't want you without protection with hunters running around here."

"I'll go home. Promise." She gave him a smile, and his face softened a tad.

"I'll talk to you soon."

With that, the commander turned and jogged with Micah toward the hangar. Calla was so intrigued by the sway of his tight ass as he ran, she hadn't noticed that someone else had joined her.

"Quite the sight, isn't he?" a woman's voice teased.

Calla turned her head to see Selene, Nick's daughter, observing her with humor etched on her angular face. Great, she'd been busted ogling the woman's father.

"He's passable enough." She shrugged.

Selene laughed. "Ha! You were staring at his backside like he was a nice juicy steak, so don't even try that with me. He seemed pretty into you, too."

"I don't know. Maybe."

The other woman's smile turned contemplative. Suddenly, she leaned toward Calla and sniffed.

"Holy shit, his scent is all over you. That old dog, he marked you good, didn't he?"

"M-marked me?"

"Yeah," Selene drawled. "Oldest shifter mating ritual on record, girlfriend, especially with born wolves. The male marks his female to warn off other guys. Guess which ritual is the second oldest."

Nick's daughter was fucking with her, and enjoying herself immensely. But that didn't make what she said any less true. Calla had heard about the marking thing—she'd just never encountered an example firsthand.

Calla drew herself up and looked Selene straight in the eye. She wasn't sure whether she was being mocked, or merely teased in a good-natured manner. "I like your father a lot," she said directly. "I'm drawn to him as well, and to be honest there could be more than mere attraction there. Is that going to be a problem?"

She'd said as much as she could to the woman without revealing she was pretty sure Nick was her mate. Nick deserved to hear those words first, when the time was right.

"Not at all," Selene said, dropping the teasing. Her expression was warm, and she seemed genuine when she spoke again. "I want nothing more than to see Dad happy. He's been on the edge of a cliff, and if you're the one who can pull him back, I'll be thrilled."

"Me, too. And thank you. I don't know what's going to happen, but it's good to know we have support."

"Always. Not just from me, either, but from everyone."

Impulsively, Calla pulled Selene into a hug. The other woman appeared surprised at first, then returned the gesture with enthusiasm. Then she stepped back and squeezed Selene's hand.

"Thanks, but I have a feeling your dad is going to prove to be a challenge. Marking or no marking."

And then there was Tarron and his damned matchmaking to contend with.

She wondered what the commander would think about *that*.

Something told her she'd better keep that tidbit under wraps where a certain possessive wolf was concerned.

Three

The ride to the site where they were to intercept the hunters was short—but it was long enough to recall every moment Nick had spent in Calla's company this afternoon.

Was this woman for real? All he could think was, *She's too perfect. Too beautiful. She has to possess at least one flaw.*

Then he'd lost his head. Pushed her against the tree and devoured her mouth like the starving wolf he was. Fucking hell, it had been so long since he'd felt such a strong connection to a woman. Like he had to have her or he'd go crazy.

His wolf hadn't been able to get close enough, either. Immediately he was rubbing all over her, leaving so much of his scent on her that every shifter within miles of her would know who the hell she belonged to. He had to mark her or lose his mind.

And then he'd felt her tense. As his tongue explored her delicious mouth, he'd actually touched one of her fangs as it lengthened. Her need to bite him became a palpable thing.

There was her flaw, he remembered.

Calla was a vampire. As such, she'd need to feed from her mate, eventually.

And she's my mate. If there was any question before, there isn't now. My wolf is howling with the need to be with her. To claim her for us. Then she'd have to claim me, too, as vampires do.

Sink her fangs into my neck. Drink from me.

Like Carter.

He couldn't let that happen. The very idea made his gut writhe as though filled with poisonous snakes. And yet, if he didn't claim her, he'd eventually get mating sickness. He was much older, could hold out longer than the turned wolves on his team, but not forever.

Had Calla saved his life for nothing, then? What was the point in living if he couldn't work past the horror of what Carter had done to him?

What am I going to do?

"We're here! Get ready!" Jax shouted.

Nick slid from his seat and grabbed the M16 off his shoulder. Sometimes a direct assault and good old-fashioned firepower was the best tactic. That was what they were doing with the hunters since there wasn't time to set down miles away and come in quiet. The coven that was under siege was out of time.

They flew in low, balls to the wall, and let the bullets fly. It wasn't too difficult to tell who the bad guys were—they were the armed ones shooting back. The humans were dressed in cammo, too. Real original. Bullets pinged off the sides of the Huey. One missed Nick's head, so close he swore he felt the heat from its passing.

He fired off round after round, hitting more than he missed. Hunters dropped like puppets with their strings cut, and he felt nothing. No sympathy. He thought of Rambo in the movie declaring they'd drawn first blood, and that was how he viewed the matter.

They started it. We'll finish it.

With Aric at the controls, the Huey Nick was riding in circled around, making another pass at the wide-open spaces between the buildings of the coven. Most soldiers who weren't dead were on the run, headed for the trees, guns slung over their backs.

Except one. Nick saw the bastard take aim in his direction a split second too late. A punch seared his chest and he was thrown backward, onto the cold metal floor. His weapon clattered from his hand. Hammer's shouts reached Nick's ears, but he couldn't understand what his friend was saying. He tried to push up. Couldn't move.

"Stay down!" Hammer's frantic face loomed over him.

"Vest," he gasped, trying to raise his arm. "I'm okay."

The big man shook his head, exchanging a panicked look with someone. "They had armor-piercing bullets. You're shot through. Stay still."

What? Raising his head a bit, he looked down at himself. His tan body armor was rapidly becoming soaked, turning a dark rust with his blood. "Oh, fuck."

His head swam and he dropped it back to the floor, staring at the roof. The motion of the Huey was making him sick. The craft executed a sharp turn and he knew Aric was taking him home as fast as the copter would fly.

"The coven," he rasped.

"The others stayed behind to wrap up," Jax said from somewhere near his head. "Stop worrying and save your strength."

His chest burned like the fires of hell. It was as though someone had pried open his sternum with their bare hands and then poured acid into the bloody cavity for good measure. He couldn't breathe. This wasn't right. He'd suffered gunshot wounds before—hell, all sorts of injuries—and he'd never experienced anything like this.

He sucked in a shallow breath. "Silver?"

"Maybe. You're not healing like you should."

Hammer laid a meaty palm on his shoulder. "We're close to the compound. Hang on, buddy."

That look on his friend's face, in his eyes. Nick knew in that moment he was in real trouble. This was a mortal injury, even for a born wolf. And Zander was still restricted from performing a healing of this magnitude.

"Calla," he managed.

"Tarron's sister? What about her?"

"Mate."

Hammer frowned. "I don't understand."

"Calla's mine," he wheezed. "She'll come."

"Shit! Got it." Hammer squeezed his shoulder. "We'll get her there."

"I don't have her number, but I'm calling Tarron now," Jax said.

Vaguely, Nick heard Jax shouting into his cell phone. He wondered what the vampire would make of his sister being summoned to save a wolf. And not just any wolf—her mate. Then he decided he didn't give two shits.

Calla was coming, and that was all that mattered. Could be he wasn't ready to give up, after all.

The copter started its descent just as his lungs gave up the ghost. Thrashing, he fought to take in air that would no longer come. His vision darkened, and regret consumed him.

Not yet. Can't give up.

Then he knew nothing more.

*   *   *

"Calla!"

Tarron's bellow thundered down the rocky corridor outside her room, and Calla jumped. The book she was reading tumbled from her hands and *thunk*ed to the floor, making her lose her place. Irritated, she crossed to the door and flung it open.

"Can you *ever* simply knock and say my name in a normal tone instead of shouting the mountain down over our heads?" She rested a hand on her hip and glared at him as he came to a stop at the door to her chambers.

Her annoyance went unnoticed and he appeared to be in a hurry. "I just got a call from Jax Law. He said the Alpha Pack was out on a mission and Nick was shot by hunters during the gun battle."

She gasped, holding on to the doorframe for support. "Oh, gods. How is he?"

"Not good. Jax said the bullet must be silver or something, because he's not healing. He wants you to come, says you're the only one who can help him. They're rushing back to the compound by helicopter as we speak."

"Of course! Let's go." She grabbed for his hand, but he held back.

"Wait a second. Why *you* when I could help him just as easily?" he demanded. "What's going on, sis?"

"I'll explain later. There isn't time right now."

"I'm not going to like this, am I?" His expression was grim.

"Later," she stressed.

"Fine, but I expect some answers soon."

At least her brother cared, as Nick had pointed out. That was damned hard to remember when he stuck his nose into every aspect of her life. Without waiting for Tarron, she transported herself to the Pack's compound, landing on the lawn again. Since she'd never been inside and didn't know the layout, it seemed the safest bet.

As Tarron appeared beside her, she looked around for anyone who might escort her to where she needed to go. She spotted Selene waving frantically from the back door and took off. As she stopped in front of Selene, she grabbed the woman's hand, heart thumping.

"Are they here yet?"

Selene's face was pinched, eyes red. "No, but they're only minutes out. Come on—we'll meet them at the new building. The hospital there has newer equipment and a much better setup than what we were using in the compound. That has to help Dad, right?"

"I'm sure it will," she said, hoping it was true.

But the reality was, Nick's team wouldn't have called in Calla if it wasn't absolutely necessary. *If you're a paranormal being and you need a vampire to save your life, you're in serious trouble.*

She and Tarron followed Nick's daughter to the new building she'd spoken of. Etched into the stonework itself was the word SANCTUARY. As they pushed through the glass doors and walked inside, she thought the name was fitting. Warm and inviting, this did indeed look like a place dedicated to helping others find peace.

There was no time to appreciate their surroundings or the important work being done there, however. They got on an elevator and rode it to the hospital floor at the top, then got off. A team of doctors and nurses was waiting for the helicopter's arrival, and none too patiently. A blond male nurse was pacing the hallway, clearly anxious. The second he spotted Selene, he trotted over to her.

"Was anyone else injured?"

"Phoenix is fine, Noah," she said. "Dad was the only one seriously hurt."

Noah winced, appearing guilty. "I'm sorry. It's just . . ."

"No need to apologize. Believe me, I get it. I was worried about Zan, too. But you can't let it get to you every single time they go out, or you'll go nuts."

"I know, but it's hard." His voice was quiet.

Was Noah mated to Phoenix? If not, the two were apparently close.

"It gets harder. Trust me."

That made him chuckle. "Thanks. Your pep talks are the bombdiggity."

Before Selene could reply, a rumble from outside came closer and closer, until the sound was almost like thunder. It was right above them, and Calla realized the new building must have a helipad for emergencies such as this one. Everyone mobilized, and another nurse urged a protesting Selene, as well as Tarron, to a waiting room down the hall.

"Come with us," a female doctor said to Calla.

She recognized the doctor from the party. Mackenzie Grant was mated to the Sorcerer/panther shifter Kalen Black. They had a cute new baby boy named Kai. Those facts rushed through her head, and she thought of how she'd been smiling and socializing with these people merely days ago. To be in the middle of a serious personal crisis of this sort with them now, especially involving Nick, was strange and disorienting.

But there was nowhere else on earth she'd rather be when he required her help.

The OR was ready when the trauma team filed in, every surface shiny and each instrument gleaming. They wouldn't stay that way for long, though. Calla clasped her hands to stop their shaking while they waited. Soon, heavy footsteps came down the hallway, moving fast. She heard a gurney being pushed along, orders barked.

And then several men from Nick's team burst through the OR's doors with their commander. She gasped at the horrible sight of his shirt and body armor soaked in blood, a gaping hole almost exactly centered in his chest. How could anyone survive a wound like that one? If he was human, he would've been dead already.

Dr. Grant moved aside for another female doctor, who immediately took charge. This one had shorter, straighter hair than Mackenzie, but it still brushed her collar. DR. MELINA MALLORY, her tag read. Calla recalled meeting the prickly woman before also.

Noah swiftly ran a tube down Nick's throat so the respirator could breathe for him. Then he removed the commander's vest and used a pair of scissors to cut his T-shirt up the middle. The ruined material was discarded and the nurse began to wipe the area. Dr. Mallory quickly assessed the damage.

Wearing latex gloves and grabbing some sort of probe, she began to dig inside the wound, which made Calla's stomach lurch dangerously.

"Single gunshot wound, one punctured lung. The bullet is still lodged in there, close to his heart, so I'll get that out before we attempt any healing."

Dr. Mallory's voice was so cold and clinical, it made Calla shiver. But the woman seemed good at her job, and she took a small amount of comfort from that. She watched, barely breathing, as Nick fought for his life. And he *was* fighting, hard. She sensed that even though they weren't Bonded, and it made her proud of him.

After what seemed an eternity, yet was probably only a couple of minutes, the doctor fished out a large bloody bullet. "Silver," she announced. "Those rotten bastards."

Calla couldn't agree more. Noah held out a container and the doctor placed the bullet in it.

Noah sealed the container and held it up. "Rush it to the lab for tests?"

"Absolutely. I don't like the looks of this tissue around where the bullet was sitting. It's dying too quickly."

Calla's hand went over her mouth. Only her desire to see Nick get well prevented her from running from the room. "My blood can't heal flesh that's already dead."

The doctor gave her a sharp look. "Of course not. I'm going to clean away the necrotized tissue first." Dr. Mallory continued her work, completely focused. Once she was done, she stepped back and nodded to Calla. "All right. Let's get some of your blood into him and speed along his recovery."

On shaking legs, she stepped up to the gurney and peered down at Nick's chest. Cleaned up, the wound didn't gape quite as much as she'd first believed, but then again, perhaps it had started healing now that the silver had been removed. In any case, he needed help. He was pale from blood loss.

Noah offered to make the cut on her wrist with

a scalpel. "It'll hurt less than using your fangs or something."

She nodded and allowed him to execute the cut, then quickly held her wrist over the commander's chest and let the life-giving fluid flow into the wound. The effects were immediate. The ragged flesh began to return to a healthy pink, and slowly knitted together from the inside out. Nick's face was still pale, his body still, but the worry that he'd die gradually drained away.

"Thank you," she said to whatever power had kept him alive until he got here.

Noah laid a hand on her arm, and gave her an understanding smile. "Why don't you wait down the hall with your brother while we finish up and get him situated in a room? I promise someone will come and get you as soon as possible."

It really wasn't a request. Now that the danger was past, they needed her out of the way. Reluctantly she agreed and, after taking one last look at Nick to reassure herself he was breathing, walked to the waiting room.

Tarron stood the instant she went inside. "How is he?"

Her voice trembled as the adrenaline left in a rush and reality set in. "He'll be okay. We almost lost him."

" 'We'?" Never one to miss a thing, her brother arched a brow. "He's a friend, but he's not part of our coven, Calla. Why 'we'? Who is Nick to you?"

She looked around the waiting area. "Where's Nick's daughter?"

"Her mate came for her and he insisted on taking her for a walk to calm her nerves. Now, tell me what's going on."

"Selene and Zan won't have gone far. This isn't really the time or place to—"

"Sit down. We're going to finish that discussion we didn't have time for earlier, and you're going to tell me what the hell is going on."

She knew that he loved her, and that he meant well. But right now he was taking the high-handed attitude of a ruler instead of the gentle caring of her brother. It seriously pissed her off.

"No," she said coolly. "I'm not. Frankly, there isn't much to tell at the moment, and even if there were, my relationship with Nick is none of your business."

Of course, he pounced on her slip. "So there *is* a relationship." He sighed, crossing his arms over his chest. "Damn, you never do anything by half."

"What's that supposed to mean?" She glared at him.

"He's a wolf, sis. They're totally different from us, and I don't mean that in an elitist way before you accuse me of that." He waved a hand to indicate the entire hospital, perhaps the whole compound. "They're warriors. They live dangerous lives, twenty-four/seven. Is this what you want for the rest of eternity? Constant terror for a man who might never come home?"

"Stefano was a quiet, cultured man who lived a peaceful existence," she said quietly. "But that didn't exactly save him from the hunters, did it?"

Her brother sucked in a breath as though she'd punched him. "I'm sorry. I'm just worried about you."

"I know." Her anger subsided and her heart swelled with love for him. Still, she had to be firm or he'd pry until he wormed the truth from her before she was ready to talk. "Worry all you want, but trust me, will you? Let me work things out for myself and then I'll tell you what you want to know."

"Just don't shut me out, please. That's all I ask."

"I wouldn't, unless you forced me to."

He opened his arms and she walked into them, thankful their disagreement hadn't turned into a bigger fight. She hated being at odds with someone she loved so much, especially Tarron.

Selene returned with Zan, and Calla related that all had gone as well as it could with her father in the OR. The woman slumped with relief against her mate's side and he put an arm around her, kissing her cheek.

"I don't know what I would do without him," Selene said softly. "He and I have had a rough time getting reacquainted, but I can't imagine him not being here."

"He told me a bit about it." When Selene's eyes widened, Calla thought maybe she should've kept her mouth shut. "He didn't go into all the details, just that he has a lot of regrets about the past. I know he's in a great deal of pain."

"He told you that?"

"Not in so many words, but his feelings were quite clear." Somehow, she couldn't bring herself to reveal to Nick's daughter and her mate that she'd discovered the commander thinking of shoving a dagger into his own heart to escape his agony—not just over his past, but also because of his recent ordeal.

That would remain between him and Calla unless Nick chose to share it.

Just then, Noah stuck his head in the door and addressed Selene. "We've got your dad in a room if you want to sit with him for a while."

"Yes! Thank you."

Zan hustled her from the room and Calla sat back with a sigh. It could be ages before she got in to see Nick, and it made her nerves coil in anxiety. Selene had every right to see him first, she reminded herself. Besides, if Calla acted more worried than a concerned friend, people would start asking questions she wasn't ready to answer, as her brother had already done.

After what seemed like hours, Selene returned and poked her head in the door, giving them a tired smile. "Dad's resting. They said he'd probably sleep until the morning, but you're welcome to see him if you'd like. You did save his life, after all."

"Thank you." Calla stood. "I'd love to check on him before we have to go home."

"He'll appreciate it when he wakes up. Just go down the hallway on the right, fourth room."

Taking Selene's hand, Zan led her away. Calla stood, and looked at her brother, but he opted to wait for her. She was glad he was giving her time alone with Nick. Maybe some of what she'd said to her overprotective sibling had gotten through.

At the doorway to Nick's room, she paused and took a breath before pushing inside. The sight that greeted her was definitely not what she had expected.

Instead of Nick, the man, lying on the bed, a huge white wolf was sprawled on the sheets, head on the pillow. She came to a halt, hand over her pounding heart, and stared. His fur was thick, as pure as the driven snow, not one other speck of color to be seen except for the black gumdrop nose on the end of his snout. She'd seen lion shifters with smaller paws. His head was big and so were his jaws, which looked strong enough to crush someone's bones as though snapping a toothpick.

Moving forward as quietly as possible, she took a seat beside the bed. Without a doubt, this wolf—Nick—could easily take down any opponent. And yet he looked so gentle, lying with his fluffy tail curled around his legs, snoring slightly.

Tentatively, she reached out and stroked the top of his head. Then his ears. He gave a soft rumble of unmistakable pleasure and nosed into her hand in his sleep, seeking her touch. Wanting comfort. She gladly gave it, rubbing all over his face and ears, the scruff of his neck. He was simply majestic, and being able to touch him as a wolf was a privilege she figured few had been allowed.

"Aren't you beautiful?" she whispered. "I'll bet shifting helps you heal, huh? Just sleep, Nick. I'll stay for a bit, and then I'll come back tomorrow."

The wolf let out a sigh, and slept on.

He never knew when she rose later and reluctantly slipped from the room.

Nick came awake gradually, blinking, eyes adjusting to the gloom. The sun was apparently just coming up, and the room was so dim he couldn't see where he was. Couldn't think straight.

It came back in snatches—the call to save the vampire coven from hunters. The Huey. Flying low, shooting.

Being shot.

He was alive then, if damned slow and stoned on whatever the doctors had pumped into him. Lifting his head, he saw white paws stretched in front of him. He didn't remember shifting. That was good, though, since it would help him get back on his feet much faster.

Just then, a sweet scent tickled his nose. It was

faint, whomever it belonged to no longer around, but it drew him all the same. Instinctively he whined, snuffling the covers on one side of the bed to try to make out more of the delicious scent. It seemed to be on his fur as well.

Both the man and the wolf knew the owner of it. *Calla*. She'd been here?

He wanted her to come back. His wolf wanted to leap from the bed and track her down. The man had more restraint. Barely. Besides, his strength wasn't up to par just yet.

Concentrating, Nick focused on his human form and made the change. The transformation wasn't quite as seamless as usual, and was a bit painful given his healing injury, but at least it was quick. Once the change was complete, he took stock of himself.

Lifting his hand, he carefully explored the puckered scar on his chest, and frowned. The fucker who'd shot him must've used silver, so the scar might never totally disappear. However, while that pissed him off to a degree, he had more important things to worry about.

As a distraction to said worries, the television mounted on the wall wasn't much, but it would have to do until they sprung him. He spent a while flipping back and forth between *Good Morning America* and the *Today* show, and knew he'd reached a sad state when he found himself engrossed in a story about Miley Cyrus's tongue and whether she'd donate it to science one day.

"Fuck's sake," he muttered, shutting off the TV in disgust.

"That bad?"

His gaze jerked to the doorway, where Calla stood smiling at him. He sat up straighter, or tried. Still quite sore, he winced. "Worse. Thank God you're here to save me, or I might have started with *Jerry Springer* next. I think they're discussing ticking internal clocks and exploding ovaries or something. Hell if I know."

She laughed, wrinkling her nose adorably. "Then it's a good thing I arrived when I did."

He studied the vampire, drinking her in like a man dying of thirst. She was gorgeous, as always, dark hair falling around her face and shoulders. A snug pink T-shirt with a V-neck emphasized her breasts, and nice jeans encased her long legs. She wore high-heeled strappy wedge sandals and her toes were painted to match her shirt.

He'd like to get a closer look at those toes. While kissing his way up those long legs. His wolf rumbled in agreement, and he cleared his throat to mask the sound.

"What have you got behind your back?" he asked, curious.

"You caught me!" She was clearly delighted that he'd noticed, and came to sit by the bed. From behind her, she brought forth a square tin and thrust it at him. "For you."

"Me?" Taking the tin, he stared at it, then at Calla. "A present?"

"Yep. Go on; open it."

"Nobody's given me anything in ages." Sad, but true. He didn't think anyone even knew when his birthday was, except maybe Hammer.

Eagerly, he pried open the lid, and inhaled with sheer bliss. "Holy shit! You brought me cookies? Chocolate chip and snickerdoodle, my favorites."

"I made them myself," she said proudly, clearly happy that he liked his gift.

Snatching a fat chocolate chip one, he took a large bite and moaned in ecstasy. "Mmm. Only thing better than this is sex."

"Very true. But the cookies will have to suffice, for now." Her eyes sparkled with humor, and a lot of heat, if he wasn't mistaken.

He almost choked on his cookie. His dick made a valiant effort to express just how very on board he was with the idea, but his body was still healing and not quite ready for acrobatics. He was glad, because the last thing he wanted was to embarrass himself in front of this woman.

Calla was special. A lady. He would treat her as no less.

"These are wonderful. Have one?"

"I already ate three before I came, but what the heck?" She took a snickerdoodle and joined him.

After a moment, she said, "There's another reason I came besides giving you cookies. Tarron's having a party next weekend and I'm hoping you'll come as my guest."

He hesitated. "As your date?"

"If you like. Provided you're healed." She shrugged, but something about her tone said his answer meant something to her. "And only if you want to."

"What kind of party is it?"

"Sort of a gathering of European acquaintances of my brother's. A boring, rubbing-elbows and ego-stroking event guaranteed to drive me mad, unless I have company."

"Vampire acquaintances?" he asked, trying to make his voice as casual as possible.

"Mostly."

Absorbing the implications, he tried not to break into a cold sweat. Did he want to attend a party literally stuffed full of unknown vampires and try not to think about how fast he could become dinner? Not hardly. But Calla wanted him to come, and that alone made his heart pound in excitement.

"Tarron's trying to shore up relations with the European vampires," she went on. "He thinks we're too vulnerable, in light of the recent problems with rogues and hunters."

"Well, he's got a point."

"It would be so much more fun if you were

there," Calla went on. "Plus, you could benefit from these contacts as well. And maybe if you're there, Tarron won't— Never mind. What was I thinking? Of course you don't want to hang around with my kind after what happened. I'm sorry. I'll just go."

Struggling to cover her upset, she started to rise, and he caught her wrist. "Wait. If I'm there, maybe Tarron won't do *what*?"

"Nothing. Forget I mentioned it."

Damn. Now she's clammed up. Probably thinks you don't want to spend time with her. Great job, dumbass.

"I'd love to go," he said softly.

Her eyes met his and the pain there vanished. "Really?"

"Yes. But a few of my men will accompany me, if that's all right."

"Of course. No leader attends a party full of other powerful leaders without some backup." She smiled. "I'm glad you're coming."

"Any excuse to spend more time with you." That part wasn't a lie. He wished he didn't have to attend the party in order to see her, but for some reason it seemed really important to her, so he'd manage his fears. Somehow.

"Thank you. I can't wait."

When she leaned over and gave him a lingering kiss, warmth filled him.

Perhaps, for once, he'd done the right thing.

Four

"Do they suspect?"

"No, Master."

The vampire studied his Sorcerer, who was kneeling before him in supplication. As it should be. Quite a coup to have a powerful creature such as Jinn under his complete control. Such a rush.

That was what love did to the victim—it blinded. A fatal flaw, in the end.

An emotion he would never allow into his heart again.

"Good, my pet." He stroked the soft hair on the bowed head, let his fingers linger at the nape. "We will continue to blend in, to infiltrate their ranks, learn their secrets. I want you to find me one who we can turn to our purposes. Can you do that?"

"Absolutely, Master. I have one in mind who I've learned craves power among the vampires."

"His name?"

"Graham, a guard. He'll do nicely."

"Fine."

Jinn looked up at him. "About Tarron's gathering. We'll still attend?"

"Of course. I'm invited, and no one will recognize you as your true self. Ironic, isn't it?"

"Very much so." Jinn hesitated, then said solemnly, "Master, I'm going to help you make them all pay for what they've done. Every vampire in Tarron's coven, and every one of their wolf allies. I swear to you."

For a split second, something like warmth fluttered against his icy soul.

"I know you will. Now, rise and see to it."

"Yes, Master."

Jinn pushed to his feet, turned, and left in a swirl of his black cloak. The vampire took a moment to appreciate the Sorcerer's fine form, then exited the room himself to attend to other business. First, he was ravenous.

Steps quickening, he descended the stone steps to the basement. Then down a dank, torch-lit corridor to one of the cells therein. Using his key, he turned the lock and walked slowly inside. Took stock of his trembling, terrified blood slave and smiled.

"Hello, Tom," he said pleasantly. "Just dropping in for a quick bite."

*   *   *

Nick hadn't seen Calla since she'd brought him the cookies a few days before, and that didn't set well with him. At all. He found he missed her company—and her kisses.

Cookies. His heart warmed all over again as he recalled the gesture. He couldn't remember the last time anyone had done something so thoughtful for him. It made him miss her even more.

Why the hell hadn't he thought to get her cell phone number? Even vampires had them. He could call Tarron and ask for it, but that would mean a bunch of explanations neither of them was ready to give. Tarron would likely question him about his sister inviting Nick to the gathering as it was. Dammit!

The party was tonight, though, so his wait was over. He'd chosen to concentrate on Calla and not on the fact that he'd be surrounded by dozens of the elite of her kind. Or that was how it was *supposed* to work. His suit chafed against his skin, so uncomfortable he felt like stripping it off and going dressed in his jeans, a black T-shirt, heavy boots, and a few weapons strapped on for good measure.

But that probably wouldn't bode well for diplomatic relations.

Not that he cared what anyone else thought— just a certain vampire princess. He'd endure the whole thing for Calla, and maybe he'd find out why it was so important to her for him to be present. He knew she liked him, but he sensed there was something more behind her invitation.

With a sigh, he made one last adjustment on his tie, then left his quarters and made his way to the recreation room. Jax, Hammer, Aric, and Micah were supposed to meet him there, where they'd be picked up by the coven's guards and teleported to the stronghold. All of them except for Hammer, whose Psy gift happened to be teleportation. A handy skill. As disorienting as that form of travel was to shifters, it beat hours in a plane or helicopter.

Nick walked into the rec room, and all eyes fixed on his attire. Predictably, the comments were teasing but good-natured.

"Jesus, who's having a funeral?" Ryon cracked.

"I didn't even know he owned a suit," Zan said.

From his position sprawled on the sofa, Kalen eyed him. "Nick, is that *you*? Hey, you clean up okay."

"Well, *I* happen to think he looks rather handsome," Mac said in his defense, bouncing baby Kai on her hip. That earned her a frown from Kalen, which she ignored.

"Thanks, Mac," Nick said, then rolled his eyes. "Christ, people, haven't you ever seen a guy dressed up before? We need better entertainment around here."

Snickers sounded and he ignored them. The heat was taken off him when his chosen men for the evening walked in dressed in similar dark suits. Another round of razzing ensued, followed by verbal heartfelt relief from those who weren't chosen to go.

"Sounds boring as hell, making nice with a bunch of uptight, prissy vampires," Kalen said. "Have fun with that."

"Their bunch *can* be pretty snooty," Ryon put in.

Zan arched a dark brow. "So, you're taking one for the team in the name of political alliance? That's your story?"

"And I'm sticking to it," Nick confirmed.

A few knowing grins and glances were exchanged, but he didn't rise to the bait. Let them think what they wanted. They probably weren't far from wrong.

Their escort showed, appearing outside and knocking rather than popping into the room. A common courtesy observed, same as not barging into the house of someone you don't know very well.

"We've been invited to stay overnight as Tarron's guests," Nick told him as they walked out. "So don't wait up."

"Be safe, dear," Kalen called out. "Use protection!" The others laughed.

"Idiot," Nick muttered.

As much as they annoyed him sometimes, though, there was a time not so long ago when his men hadn't felt comfortable enough with him to joke around. Except for Kalen, they'd all served under the team's late commander, Terry Noble, and the teasing meant they'd come a long way toward accepting Nick since Terry's death. He had to admit it was kind of nice.

Outside, the vampire guards were waiting and each one took hold of one of their arms. Even Hammer, though the big man protested. Apparently, Tarron's men took their jobs seriously.

After a few disorienting seconds, they appeared in a gigantic ballroom Nick hadn't seen on their previous stay at the vampire stronghold. The space was stunning, with crystal chandeliers hanging overhead, glittering crystal glasses of every type of liquor, not to mention crimson liquid his wolf could smell was blood. Either donated or purchased through a blood bank, of course.

Long tables were filled with food at each end of the room because vampires did have to eat, same as anyone else. Pleasant music—and he used that phrase loosely—was being piped in through hidden speakers, but there was also an area set up for a live orchestra to perform later. Likely more elevator music.

Idly, Nick wondered what they would do if he found the sound system and blasted in a little Alice in Chains or Slipknot.

Before he could be seriously tempted, Tarron spotted him and headed over, a welcoming smile on his face. He stuck out a hand and Nick shook it.

"Commander, so glad you could come! Calla told me she invited you and some of your men to join the festivities. A bit of PR between species never hurts, I say."

Nick wasn't here for the damned PR, but wisely refrained from saying so.

"Right."

Tarron greeted Nick's men and shook their hands as well before turning back to him. "You're completely healed, I hope. You had us all worried last week." The vampire studied him with genuine concern.

"I'm good as new. Thanks for asking." Just then, a waiter stopped by and held out a tray loaded with beer, wine, and champagne. Nick snagged a glass of beer and the man hurried off. "Is the waitstaff all vampire?"

"Mostly, with a shifter or some other creature thrown in here and there. For events like these, I always have to hire some staff from the outside, and there aren't many humans I trust."

"I hate to break it to you, but there are plenty of our kind that aren't trustworthy, either."

"True. But at least if things go south, the fewer humans in on our secrets, or in the line of fire, the better."

"Also true," Nick conceded. He couldn't stop himself from searching the crowd as they spoke.

"Looking for my sister?"

"Is it that obvious?"

"Probably only to me." There were questions in the vampire's eyes, and hovering on his lips. That much was obvious, too. But either he'd decided to respect his sister's wishes on prying further, or he'd given up on getting answers before they were ready to be given.

"So, why don't you introduce me to some of your friends?"

Tarron accepted the change of subject gracefully. "I'd love to. Though I wouldn't call most of them friends," he said under his breath, for Nick's ears only. "Present company excluded."

Nick flashed him a smile. He wouldn't exactly call Tarron and himself friends yet, either, but the potential was there. As long as the man didn't drain him dry for messing with his sister.

That brought a host of unpleasant memories and he fought to retain his hard-won calm. He fought to forget where he was, and among whom. His men were here, and between all of them they could put up a good fight if need be.

That didn't stop the cold sweat from breaking out underneath his dress shirt. Or his heart from racing like he'd been jacked with speed. *Fuck's sake, calm yourself or they'll sense your fear. And then what? Converge on you like a pack of rabid dogs?*

Here, at a social gathering in which almost everyone hoped to gain something, and were all under Tarron's protection, that was highly unlikely. Nick told himself that until it sank in and he finally began to breathe easier.

In truth, most of the vampires he met were friendly and entertaining. Some downright boisterous. One in particular, a teenage vampire named Daegan, whom Nick's team had rescued from rogues a few weeks ago and brought to Tarron, was charming and funny, putting everyone around him in a good mood. The young man had adjusted well.

"Nick, I'd like you to meet Prince Rolan Stanislav, from the Russian territory," Tarron said smoothly. "Rolan, Commander Nick Westfall, of the Alpha Pack team here in America. Those guys are great allies to have, my friend."

Rolan nodded, giving Nick a small smile and holding out his hand. "It is nice to meet you," he said in a heavy accent. "I don't believe we have met."

"No, but same here. Good to meet you." Nick eyed the tall platinum blond prince. "Russia . . . that's a hell of a long way."

The prince shrugged. "Not so long when we can teleport. Though it does take several minutes rather than seconds to cross such a long distance."

"So, how do you know Tarron?"

"We met perhaps sixty years ago at a gathering similar to this one, but in my country. We have kept in touch. Unlike myself and his beautiful sister." The Russian turned to Tarron. "Where *is* Calla hiding?"

Nick's wolf began to growl, low and dangerous, and he silenced it with an effort.

"She's here somewhere— Oh, here she comes," Tarron said.

They turned and watched Calla weave her way through the crowd toward them. Nick nearly swallowed his tongue at the sight of the princess.

She wore a classic sleeveless little black dress with a plunging neckline that showed a hint of the swell of her breasts. The hem stopped a few inches above the knee, and his gaze automatically traveled the length of her slender legs all the way to her strappy high heels.

Holy Mother of God.

Her attention went straight to Nick, and she gave him a wide smile. "Hey, there! You made it."

She walked right into his arms and hugged him close, although briefly, and turned her head so he could place a kiss on her cheek. Not quite the claim he would have enjoyed staking for everyone to see, but it was early days yet. He hadn't missed how she'd had eyes only for him, and that soothed him and his wolf somewhat.

After letting him go, she turned and greeted Prince Rolan, but not nearly as warmly as she'd greeted Nick, he noted with satisfaction. However, he didn't miss how the prince's face lit with pleasure at her attention.

"Calla, you're looking radiant," the prince said, taking one of her hands in both of his. "How have you been?"

"I'm doing well, Prince Rolan. And you?"

"Better now that you have graced us with your shining light." He kissed her hand. "Would you do me the honor of taking a walk with me?"

Shining light? Nick thought sourly. *The vampire can't be just handsome, titled, and rich? He has to be fucking Shakespeare, too?*

And his wolf was growling again. Thankfully nobody heard.

"Um, well . . ." Calla caught her brother's eye and he nodded. "All right. I suppose a brief stroll would be good exercise."

Rolan's smile was pleased. "Very good. Shall we?"

Anxiety joined the party along with the slow burn of anger. Possessiveness. The vampire was gazing at Calla in naked interest, as though *she* was the reason he'd come tonight—not stuffy politics. He was more than happy to leave his colleagues behind to enjoy a "stroll" with Calla.

She threw Nick an apologetic look as they walked away, which mollified him a little.

"I invited him," Tarron said ruefully.

"What?" He rounded on the vampire.

"I asked him to come because Rolan has been interested in Calla for ages, but the timing has never been right. I thought they'd make a good couple."

"Well, *I* don't fucking think they would," Nick snarled.

"To clarify, however, I invited him *before* I got wind of something going on between you and my sister." He pinned Nick with a glare of his own. "I'm not that manipulative or dishonorable."

"Good to know." Fists clenched, Nick looked away, still pissed.

Tarron's voice grew hushed. "You wouldn't blame me if you knew how truly sad and alone she's been these past few years. I just wanted to help."

"Understandable," he replied evenly. "But she doesn't need *his* help—in any way."

"Try that attitude on her and you'll get not an inch further than I ever do. Trust me on that. If she digs her heels in, you're done."

Dammit, the man made too much sense.

"Come on. I'll introduce you to more of the guests."

That was the very last thing Nick wanted to do— socialize while Calla was alone with the fanged Casanova. But he gritted his teeth and endured while Tarron made more introductions, and he answered curious questions about what his team of shifters did to protect citizens. That, at least, was a subject he could warm to, and that part wasn't so bad.

"Nick, this is Ivan Cardenas, from Barcelona, Spain," Tarron said in introduction. "Ivan is an old acquaintance we haven't seen around here in some time. He'll be joining the discussion in the dining hall later with the other leaders."

"Hello," Nick said, shaking his hand. "I'm sure that will be a fascinating talk, won't it?"

Cardenas chuckled. "I'm sure it will. It's good to meet you."

"You, too."

Nick was grateful when the Fates intervened and Tarron was pulled into a debate on whether blood banks were sufficient to feed their population, or covens should be allowed to feed on death row inmates or some shit. Nick excused himself and nobody noticed when he found a corner, held up a far wall, and finished his beer.

Except for one man. "Haven't seen you around," a voice said idly.

Nick eyed the dark stranger standing in the shadows. Reaching out with his PreCog senses, he found the walls surrounding this man to be nearly impenetrable. That bothered him more than he cared to admit. "Can't say I've seen you, either. You know Calla or her brother personally?"

"Not really. You could say I'm gate-crashing." His smile was feral. "Friend of a friend. You know how it is."

Something about the man put him on edge. "I'm Nick Westfall, com—"

"Commander of the Alpha Pack. Yeah, word gets around. Nice gig if you can get it."

What the fuck was that supposed to mean? "Sometimes it's not all it's cracked up to be."

"Most times, things aren't."

Nick got a good look at the guy to be sure it wasn't anyone he'd ever met. Tats on both arms peeking from underneath his long-sleeved black shirt, with scrollwork, dragons, and other symbols etched in black. Expert work on the artist's part. The man had wavy dark hair, just to his shoulders. He was slender, but with some muscles he appeared tough as well. His dark eyes were glacier cold. Like a man who didn't get fucked with often, or he would make you pay. Strangely, he was eating a square of cheese from the buffet table as if he hadn't a care in the world.

He seemed familiar, but Nick definitely would've remembered him.

"I didn't catch your name," Nick said.

"I didn't say." He polished off the cheese, eyeing Nick. "But it's Jinn."

"Jinn . . . ?" he prompted.

"Just Jinn. No last name."

Inside him, Nick's wolf shifted and rumbled in warning. *Just Jinn*. The name from his vision, he realized with a start. Possibly the man who would abduct Noah. "And how is that?"

Moving closer, he got a whiff of Jinn's scent and found he wasn't a shifter, or a vampire. He wasn't Fae, human, or anything from this world at all, it seemed.

The man—creature—laughed, showing off straight white teeth with very large incisors. "Did you know that in Arabian mythology, the Jinn are the third creation of God, after angels and humans? It's said that we're made of smoke and fire, can take human form, and travel between dimensions. And we can be either good or evil, as the mood strikes us."

"Is that so?" Nick tensed, ready for battle if need be.

Jinn shrugged, grinning. "Some call us genies. But you can't believe everything you read, right? I simply consider myself more your garden-variety Sorcerer."

He wished Kalen, or even Sariel, were here to check this guy out and give their own opinions. Being Sorcerers, and Fae, they had a much better radar for magical beings than anyone else.

"Interesting," he said with a half smile. "Never met a genie before. If I rub the top of your head, will you grant me three wishes?"

Jinn blinked at him for a second and then laughed out loud, causing a few vampires to turn and stare. Nick noticed that the humor still didn't seem to reach the Sorcerer's eyes.

"Points to you, wolf. You're not the first one to make that joke about me. But you *are* the first one to ever say it to my face."

"How did you know I'm a wolf?" he asked casually.

"Someone must've told me."

"Who did you say you came here with?"

"A friend. Nobody you'd know." He pushed away from the wall. "It was nice talking to you, Nick. See you around."

"Sure." Brows furrowed, he watched the Sorcerer start to make his way through the crowd. Before Jinn got too far, though, he stopped and turned, looking back at Nick.

His lips were curved in a half smile, his eyes flashing with some dark, dangerous emotion. A very real current of malice hit Nick square in the chest, so blatantly physical he gasped from the wave of blackness.

Then Jinn was gone.

And Nick knew, without a doubt, they would meet again. He just didn't know when.

Shaking off the sudden chill, he put the encounter out of his mind and made a sweep of the entire room. A few minutes later, he realized Calla and Rolan still hadn't returned from their walk. And that they'd damned well been gone long enough.

Blood heating with anger, he slipped from the party and out a side entrance. Once under the cover of the trees, he discarded his clothes and let his wolf free. Picking up Calla's scent, and the vampire's, was easy.

But ripping out the bastard's throat if he'd touched what was *his* would be a sheer pleasure.

*   *   *

The sun was setting as Calla joined Rolan on their walk, the play of light and shadow over the mountain making the scenery stunning.

Her companion was an interesting man. Cultured, refined, genuine, and, yes, sexy. Casting a surreptitious glance at him, she took in his tall form and regal bearing. His ice blue eyes were compelling. His long, white blond hair practically begged to be explored by a woman's fingers.

Just not by *her* fingers.

The prince, as good of a catch as he seemed, did nothing for her. He didn't make her breath catch, or her heart pound. He wasn't dark and brooding, didn't have black hair laced with silver, and midnight blue eyes. Nor was he a rare white wolf.

He wasn't Nick. Her mate. The man she'd stupidly left behind in order to be polite to their guest. She'd have to fix that right away.

Still, Tarron had invited the prince here for a reason that was no longer valid, and she had to set him straight. She just hoped he took it well and things didn't get too awkward.

"You and Tarron have made a good life here for your coven," Rolan was saying. "That is commendable."

"Thank you. We had lots of help, though." Walking beside him, she picked her way down the path leading to the pond.

"I remember when all of your coven lived in the castle in Romania. It was a shame you had to leave."

That hit her in the gut. "It was no longer safe for us there, as you know."

Appearing stricken, he grabbed her hand and pulled her to a stop. "I'm very sorry. I was not thinking."

"It's all right." He moved close, and she noted that he smelled good. Sort of spicy.

Before she realized what he intended, he closed the remaining distance between them, framed her face in his hands, and took her lips in a gentle kiss. Taken by surprise, she did nothing at first, thinking he would release her right away.

He didn't, and deepened the kiss, likely taking her silence as permission to continue. In truth, she wondered how the prince's kiss would be different from Nick's. Whether she'd feel a spark for Rolan that she hadn't previously. But as his tongue explored her mouth, she knew her earlier assessment was true.

Rolan wasn't her mate, and his touch did nothing to inspire her fantasies.

Urgently, she began pushing at his chest—and then heard a low, ominous growl coming from the path to the right of her and Rolan. Calla shoved back from the prince and locked eyes with a large white wolf. An extremely pissed-off wolf.

"Nick," she breathed. "This isn't what it looks like."

Rolan's eyes widened as he stared at the massive canine. "Nick Westfall? The commander?"

"Yes." Her heart pounded as the wolf's glare centered on Rolan.

The wolf crept closer, ears flattened back against his skull. His lips curled up, revealing an impressive set of sharp teeth, and he appeared more than eager to use them to rip the prince apart limb from limb. He placed his body between Calla and Rolan, driving them farther apart, snarling, and asserting his claim—and his challenge—quite clearly.

Rolan held his palms up in surrender and spoke calmly to Nick. "I won't lie—I've wanted Calla for a very long time. But after that kiss, I can see her heart is elsewhere. She isn't my mate, wolf. I knew that the instant our lips touched, and I would never attempt to take what isn't mine."

At that, the wolf's threatening stance eased the tiniest bit. His body no longer appeared poised to spring, and he raised his head a bit. To Calla, it was a message to Rolan to retreat while he could. But the vampire turned to her instead.

"I am very sorry for the drama I have caused," he said with real regret. His eyes were sad. "I had hoped for a different outcome between us, but I see that I have been nursing a false hope for a very long time."

"I'm sorry, too. But you didn't cause any drama." She gave him a tentative smile. "I hope we can be friends, as trite as that sounds."

"That means a lot to me. Thank you. I hope we can as well." He shot a wary glance at Nick. "I'm going back to the party, then to the meeting before I head home. Be happy, Calla."

"You as well. You deserve someone special."

Instead of teleporting, the vampire gave Nick a nod and started up the path, alone. Calla felt sad that things had gotten so awkward between her and Rolan, and she couldn't help but wish Nick hadn't come along so she could've handled it by herself. Now she had an angry, possessive wolf to deal with.

She frowned down at the big wolf. "I had that handled, you know." This earned her another low growl. Eyes widening, she put a hand on her hip. "Oh, no, you didn't! You did *not* just growl at *me*! You've got no claim on me yet, Cujo. Not technically. So until you do, I'll thank you not to butt into my business!"

She swore the wolf looked shocked as she whirled and headed up the path toward the wading pool. Of course she felt terrible about Nick finding her and Rolan locking lips. She also understood that as a shifter, his possessive nature would always take over in a situation like that. But she'd be damned if he would show his fangs and growl at her in anger!

As she reached the pond, a sharp tug on the back of her dress brought her up short. Turning, she made a sound of frustration and grabbed the material of her dress, trying to free it from the wolf's teeth.

"Let go of me," she hissed.

He did—and reared up, planting his two big front paws in her midsection and knocking her off balance. Losing her footing, she hit the ground on her ass with an *umph*. Immediately, he took advantage of his much greater weight and bore her to the ground, pushing her flat on her back as he settled himself on top, paws on her chest and his muzzle right in her face.

"Get off of me, you big fur ball." She shoved at him, but there was no way she could dislodge his bulk.

He didn't move a muscle, and she found herself peering into very familiar midnight blue eyes. Eyes that were filled with remorse. This time, when his ears flattened against his head, he let out a soft whine. He looked completely pitiful, his expression the classic portrait of a canine who'd been caught being very bad.

It melted her heart into a puddle of goo. But she wasn't ready to give in.

"Oh, you're sorry, huh?" She scowled at him. "Change into a man and tell me yourself."

Another whine. Then a soft pink tongue snaked out and began licking her face and neck. It tickled and she shrieked in spite of herself, then started laughing even as she commanded him to stop. That only encouraged him more, and he had her wriggling to get away.

"Nick! Stop it!"

Finally, the licking stopped and he gazed into her face again. This time, his expression was . . . hungry. There was no mistaking the arousal in those eyes. *Uh-oh.*

"Um, Nick—"

Lowering his muzzle, he carefully took the strap of her dress in his teeth—and ripped it in half.

"Whoa! Wait a second!"

He ripped the other one, then met her gaze in challenge before he started on the bodice.

"Nick! *If* we're doing this, we're sure not doing it with you as a wolf," she said firmly. "I'm no prude, but I don't do furry."

At that, he snorted. Then his body began to waver. Re-form. He never moved off her, and in seconds she found herself partially undressed and covered head to toe with a sexy, delicious man. A yummy *naked* man.

"Is this more like it?"

Oh, hell, yes.

Five

Nick's deep voice, the raw desire on his handsome face, made Calla shiver. Reaching up, she swept a lock of black hair from his gorgeous eyes. "Yes, that's much better."

His mouth took hers in a deep kiss. A kiss of possession and passion, nothing at all like the poor excuse of a kiss she'd shared with Rolan. It wasn't the prince's fault, though. Nick was the man who pushed her buttons, made her body sing. His touch was electric, sparking every nerve ending and leaving her panting for more.

Levering himself up, he broke the kiss and used one hand to finish destroying the front of her dress. The fabric gave as he ripped downward, leaving her breasts exposed. He made a sound of appreciation deep in his throat as he stared, realizing that she hadn't been wearing a bra.

"You're beautiful."

"Thank you." She ran a hand down his back, smoothing her palm over one taut ass cheek. "So are you."

His cock hardened against her bare thigh, driving the hunger between them even higher. She wanted to feel every inch of him sliding inside.

"Please," she said. "It's been so long."

"For me, too." His finger traced her lower lip.

"Really?"

"Yes. I've sought companionship, but I haven't wanted—*needed*—anyone, until you."

She didn't want to think of him finding sexual relief with other women, and yet still being lonely. Instead, she focused on the blossoming joy that he was admitting to wanting something more with her.

"I need you, too," she whispered.

Flashing her a brief smile, he lowered his head and took one of her nipples between his lips. It tightened instantly, reacting to the multiple pleasures of his tongue and the wet nub being exposed to the evening air. She arched into him, stroking his hair, loving the silky texture as he laved her breasts.

It soon became clear he wanted the rest of her outfit gone. Impatiently, he split the rest of the offending garment down the middle and parted it, letting the material flutter to the ground. Bared to his heated gaze, she wore only a skimpy pair of lacy black thong panties.

"All for me."

"Yes," she agreed. Suddenly he moved off her and held out a hand. Puzzled, she took it and let him pull her up. "Where are we going?"

"Over there."

He pointed to the wading pool, which was fed by a twenty-foot waterfall. The rocks and lush greenery around it made for a stunning setting to make love in, and she grew even more excited. He led her into the pool, and she shivered a bit at the change in temperature. It was cool, but her vampire temperature adjusted quickly. She figured being a shifter, it didn't bother him much, either.

"I want to see you like this," he said in a husky voice. Then he showed her what he meant, backing her into the very edge of the waterfall's stream.

Her back was braced against a smooth section of rock, not uncomfortable. Then he took her wrists and lifted her arms above her head, instructing her to grab onto the small lip of rock there.

"Spread your legs." She did, and he stepped back, admiring her with a feral smile. "My very own water nymph. Can't wait to see if you taste as good as you look."

Naked and spread for him in the water's stream, she'd never felt more decadent. She took the opportunity to stare right back, nearly salivating over the sight of her mate.

Clothed, he was gorgeous. But naked, he was a

work of art. His muscled chest was sprinkled with dark hair, which tapered into a fine line leading to his naval. More dark hair made a perfect nest around his cock, which stood proudly at attention. His erection was long and thick, roped with veins and flushed deep red. Heavy balls hung underneath, and she wanted to savor them in her mouth.

"Soon enough." His lips quirked upward.

"You read my mind?" she asked breathlessly.

"Wasn't hard, the way you were devouring me with those pretty eyes. You'll just have to wait your turn, baby."

"Baby"? She liked the endearment, a lot. It made her feel rather cherished as he stepped up to her and began a gentle assault at the curve of her neck and shoulder with his teeth. She shuddered as they scraped there, her mating instinct strong. She longed for his bite. Craved it. He needed to sink his teeth deep into her flesh and take what was his.

But he only teased, alternating the small nips with kisses. Then he worked down to her breasts again, giving them more loving attention before venturing south. The rough pads of his fingers slid over her belly, to her hips. Claws emerged from his fingers and she watched, fascinated, as he used them to slice through the tiny straps of her thong. The claws retracted and he tossed away the scraps.

Next, he skimmed through her neatly trimmed

bush. His fingers dipped between her legs and rubbed her clit, and she moaned helplessly, spreading even wider. He made a very male sound of satisfaction, bending to use his tongue as well.

"Oh, Nick! More."

"Don't worry. I'm not done by a long shot."

His talented mouth loved on her clit, licking and sucking. Along with the dual sensation of the water cascading over their bodies, she had to fight not to come too soon. It was incredible.

Finally she couldn't stand not to touch him a second longer. Releasing her grip on the rock, she buried her fingers in his wet hair and held on for dear life as he ate her slit. Worked the tender flesh with his tongue, plunging it into her depths. She rocked with him as he tongue-fucked her, desire spiraling upward. Nearly taking her to the breaking point.

And then he stood, leaving her bereft.

"No!"

"Face the rock for me, baby, and spread yourself again."

She did, eagerly. Murmuring words of praise, he ran a hand down her back, over her ass. Then used his fingers to spread her sex and brought the head of his cock to her entrance.

"Tell me you want this, so there's no question," he rasped.

"I want you. Make love to me, Nick."

Needing no further encouragement, he began

to push inside. His girth stretched her opening, causing delicious friction as he inched deeper. He was big, but she was plenty wet enough to take him and pushed her ass out to get him as far in as possible.

He sank to the hilt, filling her impossibly. Their fit was perfect. Pleasure shot through every cell as he began to pump in and out. Stroking inside her, making the fires burn almost out of control.

Her fangs lengthened and her aggressive vampire nature took over with a vengeance. Hunger tightened her gut—hunger for the blood of her mate. She could barely keep the urge contained as he fucked her thoroughly. She longed to put his back to the rock face and bury her fangs in his throat. Drink until he came all over her belly from her feeding alone.

One day, she would do just that.

That fantasy, and the reality of now, pushed her over the edge. Her orgasm hit with brutal force, and she screamed, uncaring whether anyone heard. Pure joy washed over her again and again as Nick buried himself as deep as possible and jerked inside her, filling her womb with liquid heat.

Never had sex with any man been so raw. So explosive.

"Oh, my gods," she whispered. "I can't wait for us to make love while I feed on you. I want to taste you so much right now."

Against her back, he stiffened. And as her brain began functioning properly again, she realized she'd said exactly the wrong thing. He slipped from her body and pulled back. Quickly, she turned to face him, taking in his pale cheeks and the fear in his darkened eyes.

"I'm sorry. I wasn't thinking. Of course you need time—"

"No."

That word, so cold and final, struck fear in her soul. She reached for him. "I know what you've been through, and I won't push for more than you can give."

He laughed, and the sound was bitter. "And what if I can never give you more than a good fuck?"

That hurt. But she knew he was afraid. "I don't believe that. You need time, and I promise I can be patient."

"Don't you *understand*?" he asked, chest heaving. "Darrow ruined me. I can't stand the thought of a vampire's fangs piercing my skin. Even yours. The idea *repulses* me, Calla."

"Oh." The word escaped as a soft sound, as though she'd been stabbed. Tears flooded her eyes and suddenly she wanted nothing more than to get away. From him, and this place that should've been so special to them.

She stood frozen as he gathered the remnants of

her clothing. Couldn't breathe as he pulled her from the waterfall and back onto dry land. He handed her the bundle, his expression stoic.

"Wouldn't want anyone to find these," he said. "No telling what they might think."

"It doesn't matter what they think. You're my mate." Her bold declaration was met with a grim stare.

"And you're mine. But I'm not fit to be your mate. Not now, maybe not ever."

She tried to hold back the tears, but they fell anyway. "You're going to run from me without even trying? Is that it?"

"Not running," he insisted. "I just need time. Time to think. I don't know if I can be the man you need."

Her voice broke. She couldn't help it. "I know you already are. But *you* have to know it, or we won't work out."

For a moment, he looked like he might take her in his arms. Instead, he nodded toward her mountain home. "I won't leave you out here alone. Go, before your brother or a guard comes looking if they haven't already."

It wouldn't do any good to stand here and argue with him. Not with their emotions so raw. As much as it hurt, he was right—he had to come to terms with what Darrow had done to him before he could accept his place as her mate. And accept her as his, with all that entailed.

"All right. But this isn't good-bye, Commander. Not by a long shot." Wiping her tears, she pinned him with a determined look. "I don't give up easily and I don't think you do, either."

"Until later," he said.

"I'll hold you to that."

Lifting her chin, she teleported away, leaving him standing there looking as lost as she felt. Seconds later, she was in her private quarters, alone. Without Nick. Not the ending she'd imagined after the wonderful lovemaking they'd just enjoyed.

Tossing the bundle of tattered clothing on the floor, she walked to her bed and sat down, staring at a picture on the wall. Not just any picture, but one of her and Stefano, taken decades ago. They'd been so happy, so in love.

After his murder, she had never hoped to find another mate. She hadn't wanted anyone else, ever. Then she'd met Nick at that party, placed her hand in his. Looked into his eyes, and was gone. She'd known instantly what he was to her. Or what he could be, if only. Now it seemed as though fate had gifted her with another mate, but one so damaged he might never open himself to happiness.

She'd lost Stefano. She might lose Nick before they began.

Unable to hold back the flood, she let herself indulge in a good, hard cry. She sobbed until she was hiccupping, finally cried out. Though she felt better, crying solved nothing.

She was still alone, and to make matters worse, she was hungry. The burning in her gut wouldn't be denied. Though she didn't want anyone but her mate, she had to feed or be sick. At least they hadn't officially mated yet, or she'd be forced to starve.

With a shudder, she dressed in comfortable sweats and a T-shirt. Screw it. She wasn't going back to Tarron's gathering. Once she was clothed, she used her cell phone to call one of her favorite guards, who was always happy to serve as her donor. She would survive, day by day.

Nick would be hers. Somehow, she would help him through his nightmare so they could be together.

She was sure of it.

From the safety of the trees, the vampire watched the commander fuck his fiery princess.

He'd been careful to make certain he stayed downwind, to avoid being detected by the wolf's superior sense of smell. Picking his way soundlessly after them, he'd remained hidden as the wolf had pressed Calla to the ground. Even *he* was shocked, thinking the wolf intended to take her in animal form.

Actually, he was disappointed when the wolf had shifted back. Damn his own kinky black heart.

Disappointment was quickly forgotten, however, as the two had proceeded to the waterfall to engage in a scorching scene he was surprised hadn't boiled the water. When Westfall had turned the woman to face the rock and plunged inside her, the vampire's own cock had turned to steel in his pants.

Oh, he watched. Every thrust and moan. Every single cry of pleasure. He stood there panting with equal parts longing and hatred, until the commander reached a magnificent finish, emptying himself inside the one who was, quite possibly, his mate.

Then he listened to every word of their postcoital conversation and smiled. Trouble in paradise before the mating even happened? Fucking perfect. He couldn't have hoped for a better scenario. The best revenge of all had fallen right into his hands, and he hadn't lifted a finger.

After the couple had gone, the vampire freed his rampant erection. Gripped it in a tight fist and stroked himself quickly to orgasm, his seed pumping onto the grass. It was a cold, lonely release.

And the blame rested on the commander and his wolves. On Tarron and his men as well.

He'd pay them back for destroying what was his. Very soon.

As he tucked himself back in and zipped his pants, he heard a noise coming from the trail. Seeing that it was Jinn, he stepped from his hiding place.

"I've been looking for you," Jinn said, eyeing him. "I saw Westfall walking back inside, but he didn't see me. Did you learn anything?"

"Oh, yes, I did."

Quickly, he outlined what he'd seen and heard—especially the enlightening chat between the lovers at the end. Then he instructed Jinn on what course of action they would take next.

"I know I can trust you to carry out my wishes," he said gravely.

Jinn nodded. "To the letter, Master. I won't fail you."

"See that you don't. And keep your involvement a secret, for now. No need to tip our hand too soon."

"As you wish."

"Let us rejoin the gathering. Separately, of course."

"Yes, of course."

Resisting the urge to shake his head, the vampire left the Sorcerer standing in the path and made his way back to the stronghold. He could practically feel Jinn's eyes burning a hole in his back, his devotion palpable. Yes, that was what love did.

It left you alone, and miserable.

With any luck, for Jinn that message would hit home far too late. After he'd served his purpose.

Nobody noticed when he slipped back into the

party. Nobody particularly cared about his presence. But that would change, and they would all wish they'd paid more attention.

Especially when he and his men laughed at their screams and bathed in their blood.

Carter trailed a finger through the red liquid on Nick's bloody back and brought it to his lips. Tasted. Nick fought to remain conscious. Knew he'd have to fight to survive what was still to come.

"Delicious blood. Born shifters taste so exquisite, not even the finest red wine can compare to the full-bodied richness."

"Get off me, you freak," Nick hissed, yanking against his bonds.

"Don't be so dramatic. After all, you're going to love the next part."

"What are you talking about?"

"Remember what I said before? Your mate loved what I did to her. . . ." Darrow moved close, into his captive's back. Ran a palm down his shoulder and side, rested his chin at the crook of his prey's neck as a lover might do.

"No," Nick whispered. "Don't."

"Oh, yes. I'm going to feed from you, wolf. And you're going to love every moment of it . . . right until you breathe your last."

"You twisted motherfucker—"

Nick's words were cut off as Darrow struck, sliding his fangs into the curve of his captive's neck. He cried

out, his body tense . . . and then he relaxed, letting out
a hoarse moan. At last, he was defeated. Broken.

With a dark laugh, Darrow pulled their bodies to-
gether tightly, Nick's back to his front, and began to
feed slowly. With long pulls and the occasional lick,
nuzzling his prey's neck, then repeating. His captive
sank further under the wicked spell, unable to stop
what was happening. Past caring.

Seduced.

"You're mine now," Darrow murmured against his
skin. "Say it."

"I'm yours."

"What do you want, wolf?"

"Drink from me. Take it all."

"Patience. I'll do as you wish. After we've enjoyed
this fully."

Nick jolted from the nightmare, heart thumping
in his chest, slick with sweat. No, not a nightmare—the *memory* of what Darrow had done to
him. Day and night, the horror never left him. The
shame.

The shame most of all, because he'd given in.
His worst enemy had seduced his body, fucked up
his mind. Even though he could still see Calla's
stricken face at the waterfall days ago, even
though he wanted to make it right, this was the
reason he couldn't.

He didn't know how to get past this.

After taking a few deep breaths, he settled in

again and tried to sleep. It was a long time coming, but eventually he slid back into dreams.

The mountain fortress trembled with the onslaught.

Acrid smoke clogged his lungs and his nose. Fire surged to the ceiling, consuming everything it touched with its greedy fingers. All around him, death and destruction rained down, claiming his men. His friends and allies.

Calla? Where was she?

"Calla!" he yelled. "Calla!"

If she'd fallen, too—

"Noo."

Nick came awake again, and sat on the side of the bed. Running both hands through his sweat-soaked hair, he blew out a tired breath and tried to make sense of the vision. Or was it simply a nightmare?

Usually, he could tell the difference. But not this time. That was probably because even though he was a PreCog, his gift didn't extend to being able to see his own future—only that of those around him.

Calla's future intersected with his, so perhaps this was why he'd been given a glimpse of hers. Was this the fate that awaited his mate if he didn't get his act together? For her to be lost to him forever?

Or was his stress simply manifesting itself in his dreams? He wished he knew.

A glance at the clock showed it was just after five in the morning. Early but not so much that he cared to fight for sleep any longer. Rising, he padded naked into the bathroom and turned on the shower. While the water was getting hot, he brushed his teeth. Then he stepped under the spray and groaned as it pounded on his sore muscles.

He ached from the punishing workout he'd given himself in the gym the evening before. He'd hoped to exhaust himself into oblivion, but it wasn't to be. Now the water made him think of Calla's sleek, naked body under the waterfall and his cock lifted to half-mast. The memory of her spread and ready for him, of sliding himself deep into her channel, wrung a groan from his lips.

What would it have been like if he'd allowed her to claim him? That was such a natural step for Bondmates, and his wolf rumbled in agreement.

Taking his steely rod in hand, he relished the feeling of the water cascading over his dick as he stroked. In his fantasy, Calla faced him and pressed her breasts against his chest, a gorgeous water nymph ready to take him to heaven.

She kissed his lips, tangled her tongue with his. His palm worked faster, his cock swelling as he pictured her attentions moving to his jaw. His neck.

There, she teased his skin with the tip of her tongue. Just there, over the vulnerable artery. One fang grazed the spot where she would claim him—

And her body became hard. Male.

Carter.

Fear seized his chest and he gasped, opening his eyes as his erection suffered a swift death. As dead as he would have eventually been in Carter's hands.

Disappointment enveloped him like a shroud. He couldn't even fantasize about what should be a beautiful act between mates without the awful memories ruining it. For a moment, he rested his head on the tiles and tried to get his shit together.

He would put this behind him. Things *had* to improve, right? Getting out of the shower, he dried off and dressed in jeans, boots, and a T-shirt, and headed for his office. The kitchen staff wouldn't have breakfast ready to serve until six, so he had plenty of time. Maybe some paperwork would provide the distraction he needed.

Halfway there, his cell phone vibrated in his pocket. Pulling out the device, he scowled at the screen. Damien, again. What the fuck did that asshole want, and so early in the morning? And why the hell didn't he just take the hint and fuck off?

But no. It was like some Mexican standoff. Damien was determined to speak to Nick, and in turn Nick was equally as determined to ignore him. As he tucked his phone away again, guilt pricked his conscience. He *had* told his brother, or implied, that he would at least try to be open to communication between them, perhaps reconcile someday. That couldn't exactly happen if they didn't speak.

Yeah, he'd call Damien later. After paperwork. Phone calls. Breakfast. Scrubbing his toilet.

In his office, he proceeded to tackle some of the tasks awaiting his attention. There were more shifters on the way to Sanctuary, being sent by Grant. They needed more beds in their empty rooms, so he set about ordering those. Next was a report Grant had e-mailed him about rogue vampire activity, which had decreased with Carter's death but was still problematic. The report contained surveillance on where a few known pockets of them were hiding, and Nick made notes, planning for the team to make several strikes in the coming days to eradicate them.

Then there was another report on human hunters, who killed innocent vampires right along with the bad ones. The bastards were vigilantes. Radical, dangerous. They caused more problems than they solved, leaving vampire families torn apart. Activity involving hunters had increased by leaps and bounds, and Grant wanted to know the source. So did Nick.

Reports on the hunters' various locations weren't as numerous, which was frustrating. The fuckers were good at lying low.

His stomach rumbled and he closed his laptop, heading for the dining room. A few of his team were already there, loading their plates with pancakes, bacon, eggs, and sausage. The cooks here rivaled the best ones at any great diner, and this pack of hungry wolves rarely missed a meal if they could help it.

Spotting Hammer, he joined him at a table. The big man eyed him as he took a seat, grabbed a plate, and began loading it with food.

"You look tired," Hammer observed. "Not much sleep?"

"None to write home about." He didn't get into why. His friend didn't ask.

"So, what about that meeting Tarron held with all those fancy-ass vampires? Think anything good will come of it?"

Nick shrugged and slathered butter on his pancakes. "Hard to say. The name of the game is to have something everyone else wants. With that bunch, it's the power of sheer numbers. Everyone wants that, and they can give a measure of safety to each other. Maybe it'll work."

"If one coven is under attack, the rest will come to help? Right." He snorted, clearly skeptical.

"That was the agreement they made. We made it, too. Though I hope we never need to test their honor."

"Yeah."

"Any word on Tom?" Nick asked. Their inability to reach the former mechanic was becoming a cause for concern, and his friend's next words did nothing to alleviate it.

"None. In fact, I was getting ready to tell you that Rowan and Aric made a trip to his apartment in Cody, and he didn't answer the door. They made the decision to gain entry, and found that his furniture and other household items are still there, but a lot of his clothes are gone."

"He could've taken a trip."

"Maybe," Hammer said. But his frown indicated he didn't necessarily agree.

The topic was dropped when Jax and Micah joined them and sat, muttering their good mornings, and then diving into the food. They talked for a while about mates, babies, and Sanctuary, until Micah looked at Hammer and changed the subject.

"So, you knit, right?"

Hammer eyed Micah, as though determining whether the guy was making fun of him. Some of the others gave him no end of shit about it, despite the fact that he could take any of them apart with his bare hands if he wanted.

"Yeah. Why?"

"My granny knitted." Micah paused. "No offense. Not saying only grannies knit, man. Just heard you did and it got me curious about why you do it."

Hammer paused. "Stress relief."

"Really?"

"Yep. Helps clear my mind of all the bad shit. You should try it."

"Hmm. I'm not very talented with things like that. You know, making stuff."

"You don't have to be." Hammer shrugged. "Read the directions. It ain't fuckin' rocket science. Then you'll be able to give useful gifts, especially when your friends start having kids."

Jax grinned. "Is that what you've been doing? Making baby blankets?"

"Yeah. So?"

"Nothing, Hammer. That's just really cool."

There was a beat of silence, and then Hammer spoke one word. "John."

Whoa. Nick's mouth fell open. He couldn't believe Hammer—John—had finally opened up. Would the rest of the team get what a monumental act of trust this was for the former agent? Activity around them stilled as the others listened, and Jax frowned at John, chewing a piece of bacon.

"Say what?"

"John. That's my name," he said quietly. "Former FBI special agent John Ryder, reportedly deceased. And it needs to stay that way, if you get my drift. Spoken outside of these walls, that name could get my ass toasted."

Nick grinned. That was probably more sentences strung together than anyone on the team besides Nick had ever heard him utter. John—he could finally let himself think the man's real name so he didn't accidentally speak it in front of the others—had finally decided to let his team into his world.

Jax's bacon dropped to the plate. "Wow, man. That's just . . . I'm honored you decided to trust us with sensitive information like that."

There was a general round of agreement, and John simply flashed a quick grin.

"Yeah, well, I know you've got my back."

And that was it. No fanfare, though the news was cause for a bit of excitement in the building for the rest of the day. Rowan enjoyed smugly informing everyone she had already known, because John had told her months ago. Clearly, they all needed to get out more.

For a while, John's revelation served as a distraction from how badly Nick missed Calla. Being away from her, his wolf grew more anxious with each passing day. Keeping the beast's foul temper in check was a daily struggle. As a man, he wanted to get to know her better—her mind and heart, not just her luscious body. What time they'd spent together wasn't nearly enough.

And yet. She was a vampire.

The memory of Carter's seduction weighed heavily on his soul. The vampire had tortured him as well as fed from him, and the events were stuck on a horrible loop in his head.

"Stop it, you pussy," he muttered, shoving from his office chair.

He needed to clear his head of the bullshit. Get some perspective. He went straight to his quarters and changed into some loose basketball shorts and a T-shirt. Then he made his way to the gym, strode inside, and picked up a basketball from the rack.

"Who's up for a game?" he called to the few guys who were getting in their workouts.

Ryon grinned. "Bring it, old man!"

"You're on."

If he couldn't gain some insight, at least he'd be too tired to dream tonight.

He hoped.

Calla paced her bedroom and brooded until she couldn't stand it anymore. Until she was sick of her own company.

Hiding out and waiting for Nick to come to her obviously wasn't going to work. The commander's issues ran too deep to simply disappear because they'd enjoyed fabulous sex at the waterfall.

No, she needed a plan. But what, she didn't know.

What she needed was a distraction. After dressing in a pair of black pants and a nice casual blouse, she headed for the stronghold's school. Vampire children were not great in number, given that most vampire pregnancies didn't survive to term, but the ones they were fortunate enough to call their own required schooling. Public school being out of the question, that meant they had to handle education internally.

Calla didn't hold a teaching certificate, but their actual teachers did. Their staff studied at major universities, remaining under the humans' radar until graduating and returning to the fold to teach the coven's children.

For Calla's part, she loved children. She liked to be productive, and substituting two or three days per week to give the other teachers time off suited her just fine. The kids would definitely help take her mind off her troubles.

She stopped in at Lora Hart's room. Lora taught the first through third graders in one area, and was always thankful for a break. Calla popped in and smiled at the chorus of happy greetings from the sweet faces that looked up from their work.

"Hey, guys," she called.

"Miss Shaw," Lora said with a smile, greeting her that way for the kids' benefit. Calla insisted the teachers not use "Princess Calla" when she came to take over. It might be too distracting for the young ones to process the difference between "princess" and "teacher."

"Mrs. Hart, would you like a break? I saw Mr. Hart earlier and I thought you might like to have a late lunch with your mate."

Pure gratitude flooded Lora's face. "Are you sure? I mean, if you don't mind, that sounds lovely!"

"I'm positive, or I wouldn't have offered. Just show me what you guys are working on today and I'll take it from here."

Quickly, the teacher showed her the plans and where she'd put the materials for the art project the students were going to make. Calla assured Lora she and the kids had things under control and not to worry about hurrying back. The grateful woman fled, as though Calla might suddenly change her mind.

With a chuckle, she got to work. The children proved to be the very best medicine that afternoon. The day wasn't without its challenges—a boy peed his pants, one threw up, and one spilled paint all over the floor. But there wasn't a dull moment, and she didn't think of Nick once. Until Lora came back two hours later.

Calla said good-bye to the kids, with the promise to come back later in the week and stay all day. Her heart tugged as she left. Wistfully, she thought of having her own children someday. Pregnancy wasn't in the cards for too many vampire females, but maybe the Fates would bless her.

But that wasn't going to happen if her mate wouldn't come near her.

Marching to her brother's office, she pushed inside and shut the door with enough force to make him jump.

"We need to talk."

Six

"I f you want me to stop bellowing for you in the hallways, then you might stop barging into my office without knocking," Tarron pointed out in annoyance.

"This is important." Calla threw herself into one of the stuffed chairs and ignored his scowl. "I need for you to help me come up with a way to put me and Nick together for an extended period of time."

"Are you serious?"

"No," she said, deadpan. "Because I'm totally fine with me and my mate living hundreds of miles apart in separate states. It's all good."

"Your mate?" Sitting back in his chair, Tarron exhaled a breath. "Well, that solves *that* little mystery."

"I'm sure you suspected, given our talk before."

"Will you be angry if I admit I'd hoped it was a passing thing? Infatuation?"

A tiny shard of hurt speared her stomach. "Why would you hope that? Don't you want me to be happy?"

"Of course I do! I just— Look, I'm not going to beat a dead horse. You know my reasons for being skeptical of a wolf-vampire union. But if you're *certain* Nick is your mate—"

"He is. I pretty much knew it the moment we met."

"Does *he* know?"

"Yes. We've discussed it, but only briefly," she admitted, biting her lip. "He ran. And that's the problem—how can we work things out when we're so far apart?"

"All right. I'll do all I can to support you," he said gently. "You can trust me."

She relaxed, some of the anxiety dissipating. "I know. Thanks, big brother."

"Let me think about it, okay? Maybe I can suggest some type of training exercise for coordinating during emergencies." He paused and added thoughtfully, "That might not be such a bad idea, anyway."

She beamed at her brother. "Genius! Get them here for a few days and I can do the rest."

He shook his head with a laugh. "I like your confidence."

"More like optimism."

"Same thing."

Pushing to her feet, she went around her brother's desk, threw her arms around him, and hugged him tight. He hugged her back fiercely and kissed her temple.

"I only want you to be happy. Nothing else matters."

"Thanks. Love you."

"Yeah, yeah," he said affectionately. "Out of my office, brat. I've got a million things to do."

"Oh, whatever. I see that Candy Crush app minimized on your tool bar, you slacker."

"Damn."

Giggling, she let him go and made her way out, feeling a whole lot lighter. Tarron would schedule the training, and Nick wouldn't be able to avoid her. It was a win-win all around.

What to do now? She would go back to the school area, except classes were done for the day. She might as well go for her daily walk. In fact . . . Yes. She'd go back to the waterfall—hers and Nick's—and relive every single moment of their rendezvous. That sweet memory would keep her going until they met again.

On the way out, she was confronted by a guard. To her annoyance, she couldn't dissuade him from accompanying her, no matter what she said.

"Graham, come on. I've been walking the mountains and forests around here for quite some time, and I've never encountered a single problem. I won't tell my brother that you didn't go with me if *you* don't. He'll never know." She gave the guard her best winning smile. It fell upon stony ground.

"Princess," he said, arching a brow, "*I* would know. The hunter problem is rampant, and it's dangerous. Are you going to allow me the pleasure of your company, or should I inform your brother?"

Annoyed, she uttered a very unladylike curse under her breath. With no choice but to give in, she huffed, "Fine. Suit yourself."

Graham was like a sticky burr on her sock the entire way to the falls. His presence "seriously sucked," as the teenage students would say, and she snorted to herself. She'd been hanging around with kids far too long when she started thinking in their slang.

Being with Nick would fix that!

She picked her way down the path, doing her best to ignore Graham and focus on the beauty around her. After more than four hundred years, there was still wonder to be enjoyed and she counted herself fortunate she felt that way. So many of her kind had soured on their existence long ago and sought peace in death.

For years after Stefano's murder, she had wished to join him. But over time, she began to face the fact that he would want her not only to survive, but to embrace life again. Hell, she was no Disney princess, and she had plenty of bad days, but the good outweighed them.

Besides, what sort of example would she be to the young ones if she gave up?

Feeling content, she picked a rock by the edge of the wading pool and used it as her seat. Across the pool, the falls were shimmering with the golden afternoon light. Letting her mind roam, she relived the moments she'd spent there with Nick. She knew without a doubt it would always be one of her most treasured memories.

Graham settled on a log a few yards away and started playing on his phone. She guessed it was pretty boring watching her stare at the pool and didn't blame him for playing a game or checking his messages. Then again, he'd insisted on tagging along, so if he was bored, it was his own fault.

She wasn't sure how long she sat there. But the sun was starting to dip behind the trees and shadows lengthened across the earth when she decided she was ready to go inside.

Just then, she heard a cry of surprise, and she spun on her rock, thinking the guard must've somehow hurt himself. Instead, she was shocked to see him struggling with a human dressed in a camouflage shirt and pants.

A hunter!

Graham went for the gun stuck in his waistband, but was too late. The hunter brandished a dagger and plunged it into his shoulder, and the guard went down.

"Graham!" she yelled.

But he was slow getting to his feet, and the hunter stabbed him again. Panic exploded in Calla's chest. She couldn't abandon the guard. But she wasn't much of a fighter. Should she go for help?

Yes. She needed to alert Tarron. It would take only seconds—

From behind, strong arms grabbed her and something heavy was snapped around her neck. She screamed, and her hand went to the collar. Iron! Oh, gods, no!

"No! Let go of me!"

"Shut up, vampire bitch!"

A fist cuffed the side of her face, and pain reverberated in her skull. She was tough, but incapacitated this way, she knew she was in serious trouble. The iron collar severely hampered her natural defenses against abuse, and she couldn't teleport away. It weakened her immediately.

The man began dragging her away as his companion wiped his knife on Graham's shirt. She didn't know whether the guard was alive or dead, and a wave of remorse hit her hard.

"Help! Tarron! Somebody, help me!"

"I said, *shut up*!"

Another blow to her face made her head swim. She couldn't form a coherent thought, and came very close to passing out. When the bastard picked her up and slung her over his shoulder like a sack of potatoes and ran, bouncing her stomach again and again, she had to fight not to be sick.

After several minutes, the man stopped. He roughly yanked her off his shoulder and thrust her toward the open side door of a dark van. Two more men were waiting inside, and pulled her in, shoving her to the dirty carpet. Her arms were pulled behind her back and one picked up a roll of silver duct tape, wrapping several layers around her wrists. Another piece was slapped over her mouth, and the man who'd abducted her jumped into the passenger's seat.

The van took off with a lurch, and her heart pounded in terror. What the hell was going on? *Hunters don't kidnap their victims. They kill them outright.*

They must want her as a hostage. To trade for . . . something. Had they taken Tarron as well? The thought made her go cold.

Oh, Nick. Help me. If only they'd mated already, she could've communicated with him telepathically. As it was, he'd learn she was missing after Tarron and his men did—and how long would that take? They would search, but her scent might be gone by that time.

"That's one fine bitch right there," one of the men drawled.

His companion snickered. "Yeah. Too bad she's a bloodsucker."

Calla angled her head to see them. The first speaker was a shorter, bulky man with a graying buzz cut and pockmarked skin. Military, maybe. But more likely military wannabe than the real thing. The second man was younger, skinny. Dark hair, mean dark eyes. He reminded her of a rodent.

Buzz Cut spat near her head. "I'll bet she can suck this just fine," he said, crudely cupping his crotch. "I'll find out soon enough. But if she bites, I'll take a pair of pliers and pull those teeth out."

The idea made her sick. The agony, she'd heard, was indescribable. Survivors of this sort of torture were forced to feed by drinking from a cup. They could never bite their mates again. A horrible fate.

"What do ya think, honey?" Rat said, pushing a lock of hair from her face. "Think you can Hoover my cock with nothin' but your gums?"

"Shut up back there, both of you," the man in the front passenger's seat growled. "You're making me sick, going on about sticking any part of you in some filthy vampire. God knows what you'd catch."

That was ironic, considering vampires didn't get diseases, and humans were technically the dirtiest creatures on earth. That man was the one who'd taken Calla. She couldn't get a look at him in her position. The driver huffed a laugh, but didn't add anything to the conversation, such as it was.

Rat seemed fascinated with her hair, and kept touching it. Drawing back, she tried to hiss, flashing him a deadly glare. If her mouth weren't taped shut, she would've used her fangs to rip an artery open by now. He knew that and enjoyed taunting her about her helplessness.

"Ooh, you wanna bite me, doncha, pretty bloodsucker? So bad you can taste it?"

His smile showed teeth that seriously needed brushing. He smelled bad, too. Like old piss and beer. She wouldn't have fed off this piece of shit if his were the last blood source on the planet.

She tried to convey that with her glare, but the message was lost on the stupid oaf.

Buzz Cut slapped her arm. "Just keep that attitude going, missy. That's the way we like 'em—feisty."

They continued to talk more nastiness, but the humming between her ears finally got the best of her. The earlier blows to her face were making her loopy, and she could barely keep her eyes open.

She must've fallen asleep—or, rather, passed out—because the next thing she became aware of was the van coming to a stop. Doors opened and footsteps crunched on the ground outside. Then she was unceremoniously dragged from the vehicle and shoved forward, being ordered to walk.

It had gone fully dark, but for a vampire night vision wasn't a problem. She could see a modest log cabin just a few yards ahead, and two more vehicles. She couldn't fathom why so many hunters were involved in kidnapping one lone vampire. It didn't make much sense.

Walking ahead of the men, she stumbled up the porch steps and into the cabin, whose door had swung open at her approach. A couple more men waited in the living room, giving her satisfied smiles as she stopped.

"Who's this?" one asked. He had a prominent beaklike nose, so she dubbed him Beak. "I thought we were supposed to grab Romanoff first."

Fear clogged her throat. They *had* wanted Tarron, after all.

"Opportunity popped up," Rat said. "This one's just as good, if not better. According to our source."

"She'll draw the rest of her kind, as well as those mangy wolves, to us. That's all we care about."

The others smirked. Fear coursed through her anew. She was to be used as bait? No. Tarron and Nick would come for her, but they would realize they were being set up. They wouldn't fall into any trap, no matter what these Neanderthals tried to do.

They pushed her down a dim hallway to a door close to the end.

"Put her in here," Beak said, throwing it open.

Buzz Cut flung her into the windowless room and gave her a feral grin. "You get comfy, now. Be back before you know it."

Her venomous glare said what her mouth couldn't. A huge "fuck you" that she wished she could voice. The door slammed and she heard the sound of the lock clicking into place. Taking stock, she peered around in the darkness.

There wasn't one stick of furniture in the room. No junk lying around, nothing she could use to sever the tape on her wrists. She was standing in a suffocating box with no way out.

Legs shaking, she put her back against the far wall and slid down it until she was seated on the dirty floor. Tears threatened but she refused to give in to them. She wasn't going to give these animals the satisfaction of seeing her cry.

She didn't think she could sleep in this horrible place, but eventually exhaustion took its toll. Slumping sideways, she settled down and let her eyes drift closed.

And she lost the battle to stay awake.

Tarron was nearly finished with his evening meal in his private chambers when his cell phone rang. Picking it up from the table, he studied the display.

The head chef? Why was the man calling him?

He answered politely. "Hello, Anders. What can I do for you?"

"I'm sorry to bother you, Prince Tarron," the chef said. "But I was wondering whether to save the princess a plate. We're getting ready to close."

He frowned in confusion. "I don't know. You mean, she didn't come to dinner?"

"No, sire. I even asked around and nobody has seen her at all," the man said, his worry obvious. "It's not like her to miss a meal, and when she does, she always lets us know what her plans are."

A prickle of dread shivered along Tarron's spine. "Go ahead and save something for her. Just put it in the fridge, and when I see her, I'll let her know it's there if she gets hungry."

"I'll see to it right away."

"Thank you, Anders."

Tarron hung up and immediately punched in Calla's number. The phone rang multiple times on the other end before he gave up. Ending the call, he rose and paced the floor. Calla was always telling him that he worried too much, and if he summoned the guards to search for her only to find her tucked away in some corner of the stronghold enjoying some privacy, she'd let him have it.

On the other hand, what if . . .

Quickly, he made another call, to the head of his guard. Jareth answered on the first ring.

"Prince?"

"Find out if anyone has seen my sister. I last saw her this afternoon, an hour or so before dinner. And find out if anyone was seen with her."

"I'm on it, sir. I'll call you back in a few minutes."

Tarron hung up and left his quarters, jogging through the corridors in search of his sister. He started with her chambers and knocked. When there was no answer, he used his key to let himself in, something he'd never do under normal circumstances.

It took only seconds to ascertain she wasn't there. Taking a quick look around, he saw there were no clues as to where she'd gone, either. His bet was that she wasn't on the premises at all, and the thought chilled him.

If Calla wasn't inside by now—

No. He wouldn't think that way yet. Just then, his phone rang and he answered.

"Jareth. Have you got anything?"

"She was with Graham earlier," the guard said. "Witnesses saw them head outside, and it seemed she planned to take a walk. She wasn't too happy he insisted on going, it seemed."

"What about Graham? Has anyone seen him?"

"No, Prince. As far as we can tell, neither of them has returned. I've already sent several groups of my men to comb the grounds."

"Check the wading pool and the falls area. It's her favorite place."

"Heading there now, sir."

Tarron was already running as he tucked the phone into his back pocket. If anything happened to Calla, he wouldn't survive it. Stones and dirt slipped under his feet as he navigated the path too fast, belatedly realizing he could've teleported. He was too panicked, not thinking straight.

Jareth and two other guards were already at the waterfall when he arrived. Jareth and one guard were crouched over a prone form on the ground while the other guard stood watch.

"Is that Graham?" Tarron managed as he stopped next to them.

"Yes," Jareth said grimly. "He's alive, but quite severely wounded. It appears he was stabbed."

Tarron crouched by the bleeding guard. Graham was unconscious. Tarron cursed, knowing they'd get no answers from him for a while. "Take him to the infirmary."

The two guards grabbed the injured vampire and teleported away. Jareth stood and walked the area, eyes on the ground. Tarron joined him in looking for evidence that Calla had been here, and it wasn't long before they found something.

"Is this her phone, sir?" Jareth asked. He bent and picked up the object, handing it over to Tarron.

He unlocked the screen and nodded, heart sinking. "Yes. It appears she's been taken." It was all he could do not to crush the device in his hand. "Let's head back inside and then we'll decide our next course of action."

Which would be eviscerating whoever had kidnapped his sister.

This time he had the presence of mind to teleport, and appeared in his office seconds later. Mind gone cold, he made a call.

Nick answered on the second ring. "Tarron, what can I do for you?"

"Commander, it seems I'm being forced to ask for your team's assistance much sooner than I'd planned."

Instantly, the wolf was on alert. "What's happened?"

"It's Calla," he ground out. "She's been kidnapped."

There was a beat of silence. Then, "I'm on my way."

Boots thudded on stone, Nick's entire team on his heels as they marched toward Tarron's conference room.

The prince had sent his guard for them, and he was grateful. The faster they arrived, the faster he could find Calla. Fear almost overwhelmed him, but he wouldn't give in. Getting her back was the only thing that mattered. He could fall apart later. When she was safe.

Giving only a cursory knock, he pushed open the door and strode inside. His team filed in and took places around the room, none bothering to sit. The prince's guards took up the spaces at the large table anyway, not that he cared.

"Nick, all of you, thank you for coming," Tarron began. His face was taut with stress, mouth pressed into a grim line.

"I wouldn't be anywhere else."

"I know," Tarron said softly.

The vampire held his gaze for a moment—and

Nick realized he meant that he *knew*. Tarron knew exactly what Calla was to Nick, though he didn't say so to the room at large. Now wasn't the time or place.

Nick got to the crisis at hand. "Has anyone claimed responsibility for her abduction?"

"Not yet."

"Are you expecting someone to step forward?" he asked.

"It's possible. Hunters don't take prisoners, as a rule."

"How do you know it was hunters?"

Tarron said, "Because one of my guards, Graham, was with her at the time. They were down by the wading pool when the humans surprised them. Just moments ago, he was able to tell this to Dr. Archer, who relayed the information to us."

"Okay," Nick said thoughtfully. "If hunters take a prisoner, which they almost never do, then what are they after? Ransom money? Some kind of political leverage?"

"My guess is they're after money. Not to mention the thrill of having a prominent vampire at their mercy," Tarron said with anger.

"Money and sheer brutality, then." He could imagine what they were doing to his beautiful vampire, and shoved the thoughts out of his mind. "We need to move. I'll take half of my men and we'll track her scent, as well as the bastards who took her."

Tarron's expression was grateful. "In the meantime, I'll—" On the table, the prince's phone buzzed. Everyone went quiet as he checked it. "It's a text, from a blocked number. Looks like the link to a Web site."

"That's all?" Nick asked. "May I see?"

Tarron handed him the phone, and Nick clicked on the link, which was just a series of letters and numbers that didn't spell anything. The device switched over to the Internet browser and the Web site popped up on-screen. He frowned.

"It's a room that's empty except for a chair sitting in the middle of the floor." Turning the device around, Nick showed the screen to the prince.

Tarron stared at the picture for about two seconds, then turned to one of his men. "I'm going to get my laptop from my office. Get Teague in here to record this and run a trace."

"Yes, Prince."

The man hurried away and Tarron disappeared. Nick and the others fidgeted restlessly until Tarron returned a couple of minutes later with the laptop. Looking at his phone, Tarron typed the link to the site and pulled it up. The mystery room on the screen was still occupied solely by the chair.

But not for long. Several men came into the frame—and one shoved Calla hard into the chair. She stumbled and almost fell over it, hands bound behind her back; then she righted herself and sat in it as ordered. Her glare spoke volumes about what she'd do if she were free and able to speak, but her mouth was taped as well. Nick silently cheered her courage, even as terror gripped him anew.

"Hurry up with that trace," Tarron snapped at his tech man as the guy hurried into the room.

Wires were hooked into the laptop, then stretched to another computer Teague had brought with him to run the trace. Nick didn't know how to help with that part, so he kept his attention on what was going on with Calla.

The hunters secured her ankles to the chair with more tape, and then moved behind her to do the same with her wrists to the chair slats. Then they left and she was alone in the frame for a few minutes. To psych her out, he guessed. *And us, too. They want us to suffer along with her.*

A tall figure finally moved slowly into the frame. Any hope of identifying him withered as he turned to face the camera, and it was revealed he was completely cloaked in black from head to toe. Nothing showed, not even his eyes.

"Fucker's wearing one of those mesh mask things," one of the guards spat. "He can see out, but we can't see in."

Nick tried to gauge his height, but without a point of reference other than Calla seated near him, it was hard to say. Six feet or a little over, maybe. The black cloak concealed his build, too.

"Are you all watching? Prince Tarron and Commander Westfall, I think you'll find this presentation particularly interesting."

The man's deceptively calm voice was a jolt, shattering the stillness in the conference room. The voice was distorted electronically, which had exactly the intended effect—it chilled Nick and everyone else to the core.

"Somehow, he knows about you and Calla," Tarron said quietly to Nick.

They exchanged uneasy glances and turned their gazes back to the screen as the cloaked fucker went on.

"If I don't have your attention now, I will soon enough." He paused. "You have no idea how I've suffered because of your actions. All of you."

"What the hell is he talking about?" Tarron asked hoarsely.

Nick shook his head. He had no idea.

"How can I make her suffer? How many ways can I make her bleed?"

"The trace," Nick growled to Teague. "Do you have it?"

The tech banged a fist on the table. "They've got the IP address blocked. Dammit!"

Sidling close to Calla, the figure leaned over, putting the front of his mask close to Calla's neck. Then he raised the mask just enough to expose his chin and mouth—and then he struck, burying his fangs in her flesh. She cried out, arching against her bonds.

Vampire. Nick stood there, fists clenched, his wolf surging inside him, demanding to be freed. Anger boiled, and he desperately needed to rip out the bastard's heart for daring to touch his woman. To put her through the same torture Nick had endured at Carter's hands. He was vaguely aware of Tarron shouting his anger at the monitor.

But when a slim blade slid from the sleeve of the assailant's cloak, his blood ran cold.

"Our sweet princess won't bow to my persuasion. Perhaps this will remind her who is in charge around here." Reaching out, he ripped the tape off her mouth. "Let them hear you."

Without further warning, he plunged the blade into the top of her thigh. Calla screamed in agony, head thrown back.

And Nick could take no more.

He ran from the room, from the stronghold. He bolted straight to their pond, the last place she'd been seen. Once there he stripped and shifted, and wasted no time sniffing the entire area to pick up her scent. He found it on a rock, and her sweet aroma almost knocked him to his knees. He would get her back, and then this bastard had better watch out.

"Nick!" John called.

Turning, he saw his team racing down the path

after him, John in the lead. When they reached him, the big man stopped and scowled at him.

"You're not doing this alone," he reminded Nick. "I suggest half of us help you track her on the ground. The other half should go back to the compound and retrieve our air transport because we can't always rely on the vampires to get us where we need to go. Ryon will go with our group on the ground so he can communicate where you are to the rest of the team, and they can rendezvous with us. Sound good?"

Frustrated with himself, Nick nodded. He should've thought of his team, but instead had gone off half-cocked. They couldn't function if their leader couldn't keep his head.

"All right," John said to the group. "How about me, Ryon, Kalen, Micah, and Jax go with Nick? The rest go back for the transport and be prepared for a rescue. They can take Tarron with them if he wants. Does that work?"

The others agreed, seeming a bit awed by the typically quiet man taking charge. Nick knew the truth—John's personality really wasn't that quiet or shy. He simply felt much more comfortable taking the reins now that his identity wasn't a secret and he no longer felt like he had to blend into the woodwork. It was good to see this side of his old friend that had been sleeping for years.

Those going back for the helicopters left. The

rest began to strip their clothing for their shifts—
except for Kalen, who, as a Sorcerer, didn't need to
remove his clothes to change into his panther.
Lucky bastard. But he was good to have around
when the rest of them needed to change back to
human form and had left their clothes far behind.
His magic had also saved their asses in more ways
than Nick could count.

Once his group had shifted, they joined him by
the rock to imprint her scent on their brains.

There were other scents, too, ones Nick didn't
recognize. In one spot blood was pooled on the
ground, and he investigated. This scent probably
belonged to the guard who'd been injured. He and
his team filed that information away as well.

From the rock, he followed Calla's and her captors' scents across the open area and down the
path, away from the stronghold. The trail led to a
dirt road, several miles away, where there were
tracks from an unknown vehicle that had pulled
in, turned around, and drove off again. There, the
scents were drastically reduced.

They'd taken her away by car. He could've
howled his anger, but forced himself to remain focused.

Pushing himself harder than he ever had, Nick
ran. On and on, hour by hour, his team flanking
him. Though he eventually grew tired, he stopped
only to allow his team water from the streams and
lakes they came across.

He had to find Calla, refused to think it might already be too late.

And he made a vow—if she was spared, he'd step up and grow a pair of balls. He was going to be a mate she could count on and be proud to call hers.

Or die trying.

Seven

If there was a place on her body that didn't hurt, she couldn't locate it.

Calla slumped against the wall in the little box she thought of as her coffin. Weakness weighted down her limbs and her vision was blurry. She couldn't see very well anymore, but her hearing was still fine. She heard the rain pattering outside the cabin, trickling off the roof and onto the ground. *Pat, pat, pat, pat.*

It sounded a whole lot like her life ticking away its final hours and minutes.

She could also hear the bastards in the other room laughing about what else their boss had in store for her. More draining of her blood, more cuts to her body. Maybe a beating or two thrown into the mix.

"That stingy vamp better let me have a go at her

pussy before he sends her to hell," Buzz Cut said from somewhere in the cabin.

"Think she's still nice and tight after a few centuries?" This from Rat.

"She'd better be, or I'll skin her worthless hide with my Buck Knife."

Shivering, she huddled and wrapped her arms around herself, trying to make herself smaller. Conserve warmth. That was easier to do since they'd removed the duct tape from her wrists, though it didn't help much. It was so cold and tomblike in the dank room—or that feeling could be the blood loss.

The vampire would return soon.

There was something slightly familiar about the voice of the sick bastard hiding beneath the black clothing, but she couldn't be sure. Did it really matter whether she recognized him? Nick and her brother would figure out the vampire's identity and make him pay for what he'd done. But she might be dead by then.

As sad as she'd been the past few years, she wasn't ready to give up. And she didn't deserve to have her life taken by some megalomaniac with a twisted idea of revenge. He seemed to think her brother and his allies should know what his acts were all about. Whatever it was, the vampire was past anger—he was insane with an emotion that went much deeper than rage. She hadn't been able to pinpoint what it could be, but the cold, methodical way he was capable of doling out his torture was frightening.

In the other room, the vampire's arrival signaled the end of Buzz Cut and Rat speculating about all the nasty things they'd do to her. Chairs scraped the floor as they apparently scrambled to attention, deferring to him.

"Fetch her to the video room again."

That was all he said, as though he had no emotion. But she knew better. She'd heard the tension, felt a shift in the air. It was in his voice, a certain kind of excitement or anticipation. Not pleasure, no matter what he claimed. Calla's torture was a means to an end, she realized.

That made him the most dangerous enemy of all. One with a point to drive home and nothing to lose in doing it.

The vampire's two main lackeys unlocked the door and Buzz Cut grabbed her arm, dragging her out. She stumbled to keep up with his long, hurried stride.

"Damn shame," he mumbled. "Waste not, I say. But he's calling the shots."

That chilled her to the marrow of her bones. She was about to die, then. Tarron and Nick would be searching, but they weren't going to find her in time. This was it.

Tears pooled in her eyes, but she refused to let them fall. She thought of her brothers, whom she loved so much. With Adrian off living his own life,

Tarron had been her rock for so long, even before
their parents had been killed. He was the best man
she knew, until Nick came along.

How unfair that she'd been lucky enough to
find a second true mate, only to have any shot at
happiness ripped from her grasp. With a start, she
realized Nick would be the same—he would lose
a second mate without having experienced what
might have been.

That decided her. She would hold on as long as
possible, for her brothers and the man she could
love if given the chance.

Her entire body shook as they yanked her into
the box of horrors and over to a steel table that
had been brought in. She stood beside it, wishing
with all her heart she could teleport. The iron collar was heavy around her neck, her death sentence.

"Take off your clothes," said the cloaked figure.

She stared at him, processing the horrid words.
"What? No."

"I said strip." The tone was more menacing.
"You have no choice."

Sniffing, she lifted her chin. "Do it yourself,
coward. You're going to kill me anyway, so I'm
not doing anything you say."

Quicker than she could blink, his hand shot out,
the silver blade flashing. Using one hand, he
grabbed the front of her blouse in a fist, then used
the other to slice the material. It parted like butter

and he roughly ripped the shirt from her body. Her bra was subjected to the same treatment.

Her throat burned with shame, humiliation. Unshed tears had never hurt so much, but she still refused to allow them freedom, even when her pants and panties followed suit. He was careless in his impatience, and the blade left some shallow slices on her skin. Dully, she noted that like the others, these weren't healing properly.

"Ain't she a beaut?" Rat said, then whistled between his teeth.

"Shut up," the vampire said coldly. "Or I'll cut out your stupid tongue."

This wasn't sexual, then. It was about exposing her shame to her family, and to the wolves who were their friends. To show that *he* was superior and wouldn't hesitate to take what he wanted from them.

What she didn't know was his motivation.

"Why are you doing this?" she asked softly. "How have we hurt you that you would do this to me? To my brother?"

"Get her on the table."

The vampire was immobile as the hunters did his bidding, and didn't answer her question. She hadn't really believed he would, but had hoped he'd be angry enough by her asking to slip. Soon she was on her back, and the burning began.

Shoulders, arms, back, legs, calves, feet. Hot, as though she was being scalded—which was precisely the truth. "The table is silver!" she cried, pulling against her bonds. "Let me off!"

Her skin crackled as though roasting over an open flame. She barely heard the order to start the video feed. Then the blade flashed, the figure in black standing over her. The cutting began, on the soft part of her abdomen. Slices that wouldn't hurt nearly as much had the blade not been silver. The skin parted, warmth pooling on her belly, rolling down her sides. Her thighs followed.

She writhed, struggling to control the pain, to find someplace to go in her mind, away from the torture. But peace was nowhere to be found and she lost the battle for silence.

Her screams echoed off the walls. In her brain. She was nothing but blood and bone, and terror. Her body was being baked alive. Her life stolen inch by agonizing inch. Cell by cell.

Then suddenly there was a howl, a repeated crashing noise. The sound of a door bursting inward, being ripped off its hinges and banging into the wall. Snarls and shouts.

Turning her head, she blinked through sweat and blurred vision. Cursing, the vampire vanished in a swirl of black robes. The human hunters he left behind weren't so lucky.

A white wolf led the charge into the video room, and Rat was the unfortunate first target of his black rage. *Nick*. He launched himself at the man and barreled into his chest, taking him to the floor.

Rat's scream was cut short as the white wolf tore out his throat.

Calla didn't bother to look away from the carnage. The hunters were getting what they deserved, and she would die knowing justice had been served. They would catch the cloaked vampire as well. She knew it.

With a sigh, she closed her eyes, too tired to scream any longer. Finished. She couldn't even be embarrassed about being naked and bound in front of Nick's men. The pain had lessened to a throb. Shock kicking in as a false relief.

"Calla? Baby?" Nick cried hoarsely. "Open your eyes, sweetheart."

The bonds were cut, the tension disappearing from her wrists and ankles. Strong arms lifted her, carried her out of the room. She was placed on something much softer. The sofa.

"Found me." She tried to smile.

"I did." A warm kiss touched her lips. "I'll always find you. Hang on for me, okay?"

"Home."

"Yes. We're going to get you home, and you'll get well," he said, voice breaking.

"Tried. So hard. Didn't want to leave." It was important he know that.

"You won't. Tarron and the rest of my team are on the way right now. They're almost here, so I want you to focus on breathing." His big hand stroked her sweat-soaked hair. "Just breathe."

"Try."

"You do that," he whispered, kissing her forehead. "Keep trying."

"Don't leave me?"

"No. I'm not going anywhere."

"Good."

After that, a buzzing started in her ears. She could tell Nick was speaking to her more, but had no idea what he was saying. There was more activity, then Tarron's voice reaching out and demanding that she hold on.

"Bossy," she murmured. Or thought she did.

Next she felt the brief sensation of teleporting, though that might have been her imagination. But now Tarron was yelling and she was being rushed at a dead run down a long, long corridor. She could hear boot steps clomping on stone.

Home. She was home. Didn't have to open her eyes to know it.

Hold on. She would try. For her brothers.

For Nick.

The image was burned into Nick's brain.

Calla, writhing on the table. Screaming herself hoarse, covered in blood. The scent of burning flesh. He'd tasted the hunter's blood, and his team had finished off the rest. It was a poor retribution in his eyes. He wanted to capture the vampire bastard and tie him to the same table. Then rip his flesh apart piece by piece.

He would tear out his beating heart and feast on it.

Now, though, his only focus was Calla. He begged her to hang on until Tarron arrived, and he was proud of her for fighting so hard. She was stronger than any woman he'd known.

Kalen used his magic to spell clothes on Nick and the team. His talents didn't extend to healing, however, and Zan was still on strict orders not to attempt something this serious. They were forced to hold out for what help Dr. Archer could provide for her at the stronghold.

Tarron's absolute horror and rage matched Nick's as he ran through the door ahead of Nick's team.

"Calla," he shouted, dropping to his knees beside the ragged sofa. Wasting not one second on useless words, he grabbed both his sister and Nick. "Hold on to me."

The teleportation was usually disorienting, but this time Nick didn't notice. In seconds, they appeared in the corridor that Nick recalled led to the coven's hospital area. Tarron's landing was a bit off, but at least they were there. Nick scooped her into his arms and ran toward the infirmary's entrance.

"Viktor!" Tarron yelled. "Viktor!"

Nick burst through the double doors, and the young vampire doctor ran out to meet them. His eyes widened in alarm as he spotted Calla and noted her rapidly deteriorating condition.

"In here," he ordered. Then he led them to what

Nick guessed was their version of an OR/trauma room. "On the table, on her side. Carefully."

This table was padded, unlike the torture device she'd been lying on earlier. Tarron helped Nick get her situated, and stood back looking devastated. Helpless. Viktor examined the shallow cuts on her body.

"Silver blade. This was done to bleed her slowly. She also has some bruising from an apparent beating. These would be easily treated, but . . ."

Walking around the table, he sucked in a breath as he saw her backside. Nick swallowed hard, and Tarron groaned. Her poor skin was red, bubbled, and blistered, as though she'd been boiled in oil.

"This is bad," he said quietly. "She would heal on her own if she hadn't already been so weakened. Her body won't be able to pull through this unless she feeds. Even so, she's too weak to do that on her own. She'll need to be tube fed."

It shamed Nick to the core that he sagged with relief. He wanted to be a good mate to her and put his fears behind him, but the thought of letting her bite him still made him shiver. This, however, he could do.

"Take my blood," he told the doctor. "I'm the best candidate you've got to heal her fast."

"How's that?" Viktor frowned.

"Because she's my mate." His voice was sure, and brooked no argument.

The doctor glanced at Tarron, who nodded. "It's true. All of that can be addressed later, but for now, just do what must be done to save her."

Nick was grateful Tarron already knew he and Calla were mates.

Viktor's eyes were kind and understanding. "I'll do everything in my power, Your Highness. For now, I need to get Nick's blood. Wait outside, please, and he'll join you momentarily."

A nurse stepped forward and gently touched Tarron's arm. Nick hadn't even noticed her presence before, he'd been so focused on Calla. Reluctance etched on his face, Tarron allowed the nurse to lead him from the room. Then Nick held out his arm.

"Take as much as you need. Take it all, if that means the difference between life and death."

"A generous offer," the doctor said with a knowing look. "But as you're mates, that will be unnecessary. Your blood will be much more potent with healing antibodies than anyone else's in the world. Nurse?"

Another nurse went about tying a rubber strip around Nick's arm. Then she found a good vein, slid a needle into it, and drew several large vials of blood. Nick's head swam a bit by the time she was done, though he hardly cared. He'd meant what he said. Calla was his only concern.

With Calla remaining on her side, the nurse inserted an IV and then hooked the vials to a pole by the bed and started the flow of Nick's blood into the vein.

"I thought you said she would be tube-fed?"

"That, too. The intravenous feed is extra insurance."

He was all for that. A tube was pushed down her throat and he winced, wondering whether deep down she felt any pain or discomfort from that or the burns on her back. She was out cold, so he didn't believe so.

"She's already breathing easier," Viktor observed.

"Thank God." He closed his eyes briefly. When he opened them again, a female nurse was smoothing a white ointment all over every part of Calla that had touched the silver table. Including her buttocks. Nick's wolf growled, but was calmed by the knowledge that the person touching her was female, and had only her healing in mind. Even though the doctor had the same intentions, Nick doubted the wolf would have cut a male the same slack. Good move on the doc's part.

Calla was still pale as they finished cleaning her up, and got her into a hospital gown, then settled her in a fresh bed with warm, clean sheets. He followed when they wheeled her to an empty room.

"You were supposed to go outside with Tarron," the doctor said.

"Yeah, well. You'll find out that I'll never follow orders where my mate is concerned, except when it involves her well-being and immediate safety. Just so you know."

"I understand. Just don't get in the way of my treatments, and we'll never have a problem."

"I won't."

That would never happen in a human hospital, but their world wasn't normal by a long shot—if "normal" even existed. The paranormal world was frightening, often brutal. Mates were a gift and nothing was allowed to interfere with that bond.

Nothing.

With a nod at Nick, Viktor and the nurse left him to sit with Calla. He would go get her brother in a few minutes. Right now, he was content to sit here, hold her hand, and watch. Make sure every single breath continued to get easier than the one before. That her cheeks pinked and she was no longer knocking at death's door.

He was a lucky wolf. He'd almost lost Calla today. His new lease on life. The reason he'd be glad to wake up every day from now on and embrace it.

Deadly determination seized his gut. He was going to find and rip apart the vampire who'd done this. No matter how long it took.

In the meantime, he was going to make good on the promise he'd made to himself.

He would get his shit together. Calla deserved a whole mate.

No, he wasn't perfect and never would be.

But he *was* falling for Calla Shaw like a ton of bricks.

Calla came awake slowly.

She listened to the sounds around her, unsure what to make of them. They were soft noises—beeps, talking from somewhere nearby, steady breathing. The talking between two people didn't sound like her captors. In fact, the male voice sounded like Viktor.

Am I free? Home?

Bits and pieces came back. Nick and his team arriving at the cabin as wolves. The white wolf leading the charge and decimating the human in his path. Trying to get to her.

She was lying in a comfortable bed, she realized. Her rescuers had succeeded. She could've wept in joy at the realization but she didn't have the energy. She settled for opening her eyes to determine the source of the breathing and discovered Nick, sleeping in a chair by her bed.

Her mate must be exhausted. His chest rose and fell evenly, and his body was loose-limbed in his awkward position. There were dark smudges underneath his eyes and his clothes were rumpled. She didn't want to wake him.

She watched him for a while, and as she did, emotion swelled in her chest and began to grow. He'd come for her, just as she'd known he would. She hadn't expected to survive long enough to see him again, but she never had a doubt that he'd find her.

Nick shifted in his chair and stretched with a groan. He tried to work out the kinks, rolling his head on his neck and arching his back. Then he finally opened his eyes and looked directly into hers.

"You're awake," he said, immediately scooting his chair close to grab her hand. His face was anxious. Haunted. "How do you feel?"

"Wiped out," she admitted. "But overall, much better than I did last time I was conscious. I don't hurt as much and my head is pretty clear."

"Thank God." Raising her hand to his lips, he kissed the back of it. "You gave me quite a scare."

"Sorry."

"No. It's me who's sorry," he said quietly. "This is all my fault. If I had manned up in the first place, you wouldn't have been captured. Forgive me, please."

Such torture in those dark blue eyes. Pain. It wasn't right.

"Nick, you are *not* responsible for what those animals did. Not you, my brother, or anyone but those bastards and the monster they work for. Let's not place the blame anywhere but where it squarely belongs, all right? Because as long as we're all sitting around beating ourselves up, they're in control."

After a moment, he gave her a tentative smile. "I have a smart woman for a mate. I'm lucky."

"So you truly acknowledge me?" Her heart pounded in excitement.

"Yes, Calla." Leaning over, he brushed his lips over hers. "We're mates. I'm sorry I didn't stay to talk it over with you before, at the falls. I'm yours, just as much as you're mine. I feel it, and so does my wolf."

Taking a shaky breath, she nodded. "What do we do now?"

"Well, mates are almost always stronger together than they are apart. I suggest I remain here with my team while we're battling this new threat to your coven. We take the time we need to cement our bond. Then, when things settle down, we can decide where to live."

The last part gave her pause. One of them would have to move away from family and friends. Calla or a guard could teleport Nick back and forth to work at the Alpha Pack's compound, but he should probably live on-site. That meant—

"You're thinking too hard." Smiling, he ran a finger down her cheek. "One step at a time, okay?"

"Sounds like the best solution." She tried to relax. "So, when are you busting me out of here?"

"Patience, baby. You just woke up after a pretty serious scare, and the doctor needs to clear you before I take you back to your chambers for complete bed rest. No arguments."

"You're quite the hard-ass, Commander," she teased.

"And don't you forget it." He paused, growing serious again. "I have to ask. Did they touch you, sexually?" The last word was soft, as though he'd forced it out.

"That wasn't on the leader's agenda. The hunters planned on it, though, but never got the chance. You rescued me before that happened."

He practically slumped in relief. "Okay. I'm sorry. I just had to know. If they had, I wanted to make sure you got help. Counseling, something."

"Thank you. But it didn't happen, so I want you to forget that part. I have a question of my own, though."

"Whatever you need to know."

"Did you and Tarron . . ." She swallowed, pushing down the dread of his next answer. "Did you see the videos of wh-what they did to me?"

His blue eyes darkened with anger. Sorrow. "Yes. I'm sorry. I ran out to start tracking you while that monster was torturing you the first time, but I watched the rest of the recordings with Tarron a short while ago."

"Why?" she whispered, the shame rushing back.

His reply was gentle. "To see if we could get any evidence off the recordings."

"Evidence? Didn't you guys get the vampire? Is he dead?"

"No," he said, voice betraying his frustration. "He got away."

That news filled her with terror. "Any idea who he is?"

"Not yet. But we *will* figure it out, and when we do, he's going to die. Painfully." He looked so fierce, she had to give in to a small smile.

"I'll cheer when you get him."

"Bloodthirsty mate."

"Literally." Nick paled. She must've said something wrong—shit. "I'm not a danger to you, or to anyone I care about. I could never hurt you, ever. Please believe me."

"I do. It's just hard for me to shut out what Carter put me through and move on." He shook his head. "I believe you. *In* you. I just have to get past the mind fuck he left for me, and I'm going to do it."

"That's a good attitude, but don't rush yourself," she advised. "He put you through a terrible trauma. That's not something a person just *gets over*, like they're suffering from a cold."

"Do vampires even get colds?"

"No, and quit trying to distract me while I'm lecturing you." She frowned at him, and he laughed.

"I'd never presume. I'm looking forward to an eternity of listening to my beautiful mate."

"Ha! You'll listen, but will you heed what I say?"

He arched a black brow. "If it's in our best interest as mates, yes. If I feel you're clearly wrong,
then no."

"I see how this is going to be." She sighed.

"That's what you get for hooking up with the
Alpha of the Alphas. You don't buy steak expecting bologna." His grin said he was very much enjoying their small bit of sparring.

"Good grief," she murmured, rolling her eyes.
She liked his teasing as well. "Get me out of here,
please? If I have to rest, I'd rather do it in my own
bed."

"Anything for the *princess*."

His tone when he said "princess" wasn't mock-
ing, but rather lightly teasing, so she let it pass. A
short time later, she was released with strict in-
structions to rest for at least two days. Then Nick
seated her in a wheelchair, over her strenuous pro-
tests, and rolled her to her chambers, where he
lifted her into his arms and carried her to bed.

"I kind of like this part," she told him, resting
her head on his broad chest.

"Me, too. But next time I'll be carrying you to
bed for a much happier reason."

The idea made her hot inside, flushed and feverish. She wanted him again. Couldn't wait for
him to claim her. She just hoped he allowed her to
do the same, because if he didn't—

No. That didn't bear thinking about. And she
wasn't going to tell him, either, and have him feel

guilty. Nick had to allow it of his own free will. She wouldn't accept him if he was afraid or felt coerced.

Once she was settled, he leaned over and kissed her. "Rest."

She didn't want to, but had no choice. Her eyes closed and she surrendered to healing sleep.

When Calla awoke the next morning, she was alone.

She didn't much like it, and wondered where Nick could be. Probably working with Tarron and his team to locate the rogue vampire and the hunters helping him. That alliance made no sense yet. But Nick and her brother's men would learn the reason if it took weeks or longer.

Rising, she pushed from the bed and took stock. She definitely felt better, though she was hungry. Blood was on the menu this morning and it pained her that it couldn't be Nick's. He could donate it to her in a cup, but that wasn't what she wanted. She'd drink from her mate's vein or not at all.

A donor it would have to be, then. Picking up the phone, she called for a pint and grimaced. Taking any blood from a mug was disgusting to her, but now that she had a new mate-to-be in her life, there was no chance she'd drink from other male and rouse his protective instincts. His jealousy. An angry, possessive mate was never a good thing.

The pint was delivered and the guard at the

door took a sip to make sure it hadn't been tampered with. After a moment, he deemed it safe and left her alone. This was a new measure and she hated the necessity, but after recent events she was hardly going to argue.

Curling up on her sofa, she sipped the lukewarm blood and flipped through a magazine. Try as she might, it didn't take away the heavy knowledge of today's significance. The anniversary of the day Stefano was kidnapped. Sorrow crept in, softer and more muted than in years past, not quite as debilitating. Because of Nick, the loss was bearable.

As if she'd summoned him, there was a knock on the door just before the commander stepped inside and closed it behind him.

"Hey," she said, tossing the magazine aside. "Where have you been?"

"In a meeting with your brother and our men." He crossed the room in a few strides and sat, gathering her into his lap. "Are you all right?"

Leaning back, she cupped his face and kissed him. "What makes you ask?"

"Tarron told me what today means to you." His expression was one of concern, not jealousy or anger.

She swallowed hard. "Yeah."

"Is there anything I can do, baby?" He stroked her hair.

"I'm okay. It's gotten a bit easier over the years."

"But it never goes away," he told her. "I understand, believe me. When Darrow murdered Jennifer, I thought my world had ended. And in a very real sense, it had. For a long time I just wanted to follow her to the other side, but something held me back."

"Hope," she guessed. "Somewhere, deep down, you hoped to reconcile with your daughter one day."

"I like to think that was it, and not that I was too big a coward to end it."

"I don't believe that." She fell quiet for a moment, and then asked, "What was the mistake you made? Will you tell me now?"

His heart pounded under her palm as she laid it on his chest. He held her gaze as he responded. "I knew it was wrong to try to change the future. But I used my power as a PreCog to save Selene from being murdered by a rogue vampire—Carter Darrow. All it accomplished was turning his attention from my daughter to my mate. I saved Selene but caused Jennifer's murder in her place."

"Oh, Nick. I'm so sorry."

"Selene blamed me for years, thinking I'd actively and purposely killed her mother, and came here not too long ago intending to kill me. She met Zander then, and her plans didn't quite turn out as she'd thought they would."

"At least you've reconciled."

"For the most part, yes." He nuzzled her neck.

"But enough about me. What about you? Do you want to talk about it?"

"There isn't much to say," she said sadly. "Stefano was caught by hunters during what should have been a simple trip to town. He just vanished into thin air. Eventually the hunters responsible couldn't resist sending me a taunt in the form of a lock of his hair and a ring I'd given him. Then a finger."

"That's sick." His anger was palpable.

"It was. Tarron and his men scoured the countryside, and they found him eventually. But it was too late. He was chained to an iron bed frame, dead of starvation. They just left him there to die slowly," she finished in a whisper.

"I'm sorry. I'll never understand how people can be so cruel, and evil."

"We are not undead." She shook her head. "We're living creatures. We're born, we fall in love, we bleed, and we can die. Yet we're less than human to them. Less than nothing. They had no right to take my mate from me, but it's done and can't be changed. A part of me will always love him, but I want you to know that I'm glad I found you."

"We found each other." He traced her face with his fingertips, his touch gentle.

"Yes."

Climbing off his lap, she stood and held out her hand. This man and his wolf were her future.

It was time to lay the past to rest. For both of them.

Eight

Nick pushed to his feet, anticipation making his pulse skip. Calla sensed his unspoken need, and reflected it. When she took his hand, he went willingly, following a step behind as she led him down the hall to her bedroom. Then she turned and placed her palms on his chest, their warmth branding him through his T-shirt.

"Make love to me, Nick. No mating rules, just us."

"Making love involves no rules between mates anyway. It's whatever feels right." He kissed her lips. "I won't push you into anything you're not ready for."

"*This* feels right, with you. I say we play the rest by ear."

"I'm all for that."

She tugged at the bottom of his shirt and pulled

the material up, over his head. He helped her, smiling as she tossed it aside and went for the button on his jeans. She unzipped his fly and parted the material, pushing at the denim until his cock sprang free.

They were together. He and Calla. That knowledge thrilled him almost as much as her tongue flicking out to capture the tiny bead weeping from the slit of the spongy head. He groaned as she took him in her mouth, surrounding him with wet heat. Threading his fingers through her hair, he fed her his cock, guiding the length down her throat, watching it disappear between her lips.

"God, yes," he breathed. "I need this. Your mouth on me feels so damned good. I could fuck you like this all day."

The pure pleasure was too electric, zinging little shocks of delight to his balls, through his belly. He wouldn't last long this way, but he wasn't ready to give up the feeling just yet. With her on her knees, sucking him and taking his less than gentle thrusts with obvious enthusiasm, he had no trouble believing he could die happy just like this.

He was going to love being her mate.

"Stop, baby. I don't want to come yet." She pulled off his cock with a moan of frustration and he smiled. "Don't worry. We're not done by a long shot. Undress for me."

He held out a hand for her and helped her

stand. She bit her lip, looking vulnerable. Was she having second thoughts already? Did she want to back out? Then her expression cleared, became more confident, as she held his gaze and slowly peeled off her blouse, dropping it. He feasted his eyes on her full breasts, the rosy nipples pouty, begging for his teeth.

Untying her pajama bottoms, she pushed them past her hips and down, taking the lacy scrap of panties with them. She stood naked before him, skin pale and creamy, a dark triangle of curls at the apex of her thighs begging him to explore.

She reached for him, and he took her hand, gesturing to her big, comfy bed. "I want you up there, on your back, knees bent and feet flat." He was pleased by the hunger in her eyes as she arranged herself on the covers. "Now spread your knees wide so I can see all of you."

Again, she did as he asked. Her thighs parted, revealing her pink slit, already wet. More evidence that she was turned on by his taking control and was eager for more. He toed off his boots and pushed his jeans the rest of the way off, then sat on the bed near her feet.

"Good girl. Look how pretty you are, already wet for me. Now I want you to touch yourself."

"Nick," she said, voice husky. Her pupils dilated and her breasts heaved with desire. His wolf could smell her heightened scent and growled in approval.

"Do it for me, honey. Finger yourself. Let me see you get excited."

For a second he thought she might argue, but instead her fingers slid down her belly and through the curls. The pad of one finger touched the small nub and began to work it in slow, rhythmic circles.

"You're so beautiful," he praised, glad he could still speak. His erection strained, demanding he take her. But not yet. "Now lower. Spread that sweet cream all over your slit, and then finger-fuck yourself."

No hesitation this time. She was getting into their play, preparing herself for him. Her thighs were spread and relaxed, tension gone, her posture completely open to him. Her slender fingers began to massage her slit, dipping into her channel, fucking herself as her hips arched off the bed. The sight was so naughty, so provocative, he nearly came just from watching.

"Ooh . . . Nick, please!"

"Tell me what you need, beautiful," he encouraged, moving closer.

"Nick, fuck me! Please!"

"Anything for my mate." Moving between her thighs, he positioned his cock at her opening, cupped her bottom, and lifted her, then sank into her slick channel.

"Oh! Oh, gods, yes," she cried.

He started with slow thrusts, angling deep.

Watched his rod impale her again and again, until a warning tingle began at the base of his spine and his balls tightened. Wouldn't be long.

Lowering her bottom, he covered her body with his and gathered her to his chest, wanting this closeness when they came together. The sense of completeness. He fucked her hard and fast, their breaths mingling. Drove them higher.

"Claim me," she gasped. "Make me yours!"

His wolf roared at the words they'd both been waiting to hear. "Are you sure?"

"Yes!"

She offered her neck, and his fangs lengthened faster than they ever had.

"Ah, fuck!" he yelled, every muscle locking down as he pumped his load inside her. He could stand it no longer, and struck, clamping his jaws onto the curve of her neck and shoulder, burying his fangs deep. She cried out and clung to his shoulders, riding out the wave, milking his cock. Bathing him with heat.

Suddenly, he felt them being enveloped in a brilliant white light. It grew, swelled, so intense he thought his body might explode. And then the light burst into a million stars, wringing a fresh orgasm from him, which he pumped into her channel.

From the stardust, an invisible golden thread spanned between them from Nick to his new mate, wound itself tightly between their two souls. Bound them as one in the way of his kind.

"I feel that," she gasped. "It's incredible."

"Me, too. And, yes, it is." He kissed her face, any part of her in reach.

When the last of their spasms subsided, he carefully released her shoulder and collapsed over her, sweaty and panting. And more satisfied than he'd been in decades. "Thank you," he whispered. "So much."

"It felt right."

"Yes, and it *was* right."

She gazed up at him, and there was such raw emotion on her face as she asked the question he'd known was coming. "Can I claim you, too? I want that so much."

A vampire's fangs. In my flesh.

A cold chill seized his heart, but he took a deep breath and said, "I want that, too."

Excited, hopeful, she rose up a bit and leaned over him. He closed his eyes, just letting himself feel as she began to place soft kisses on his face and neck. She stroked his chest, playing with a hard nipple, something he loved. The touches sent tiny little shocks of pleasure through his body, and he thought maybe he could do this. For Calla, and himself.

Pleasure warred against the fear. Nick cocked his head, presenting his neck, and tried to ignore how his blood pressure shot through the roof.

"Relax," she said, smoothing a palm over his chest. "Your heart is racing and I can practically scent your fear."

"I'm all right. Just do it."

A frown creased her brow. "My claiming you shouldn't be something you have to endure."

"I know, and I'm fine. Go ahead." He gave her a half smile.

She smoothed a finger over his jaw, her expression so tender he could've wept. "Nick, I can't do this when you're obviously not ready. My claiming should be done with joy on both our parts—"

"Calla, I said I'm fine—"

"No, Nick. This isn't the time."

Oh, God. Did she have any idea how emasculated he felt right now? How ashamed? He kissed her gently and slid from the bed. "I'm going to see Tarron, check on any progress with catching the vampire who took you. I'll see you later."

Disappointment clouded her pretty features. "How much later?"

"I don't know."

"Stay, please? Just for a while?"

She knew he was lying. It was there in her eyes, the hurt he'd caused. He could stand anything except being the cause of her pain.

"I have to go."

With efficient movements, he dressed and left before he could change his mind. He needed time and space to figure out how to get past his fear.

Dammit, Nick, you stupid asshole.

He'd ruined a perfect morning. He'd make this up to his mate. Somehow.

*   *   *

Nick stalked to Tarron's office and knocked sharply. He waited for permission to enter before striding inside to find the prince in a meeting with two men—Teague and a vampire Nick had never met before.

"Glad you're here," Tarron said with a genuine smile. He indicated the new vampire. "Nick, I'd like you to meet Ian Lockwood, my best friend and right hand for more years than I care to remember. He's been in England for the past few months, taking care of some personal business, and I for one am pleased to have him back. Ian, this is Nick Westfall, commander of the Alpha Pack."

"Years? Try a couple of centuries." The vampire stuck out his hand. "It's good to meet you. I've met some of your team as well and they seem like first-rate warriors."

Nick couldn't help but puff his chest out a little as he shook the offered hand. "They are, every single one. They make me look good."

"The best of men always do," Ian acknowledged.

Nick sized up Ian. The big vampire seemed openly friendly, and yet Nick sensed a strength about him. A steely determination that hinted he'd protect what was his. Nick didn't get any visions, but he didn't have to in order to know the vampire would need that strength in the days to come.

Tarron leaned back in his chair and addressed Nick. "Speaking of our men, some of them went back to the cabin where Calla was held. They're searching for more clues and will bring us anything more they find."

Annoyance surged inside him. "I should've been with them. I could be helping the investigation."

"Right now, you're helping my sister, and that's more important." Tarron's gaze telegraphed just how much weight that carried as far as he was concerned.

Nick wasn't sure how much good he was doing his new mate, considering, but wisely refrained from saying so. "She's my first priority, too, which is why I want this bastard of a vampire and his minions found and destroyed. I don't want them coming after her again, or you, for that matter."

Tarron's expression was grim. "We'll find him and he'll be *so* fucking sorry he messed with my family. In the meantime, we need to trust our guys to bring us the information we need to locate him."

Nick blew out a frustrated breath. "You're right, but it sucks waiting around. Who the hell is this asshole and why does he have such a hard-on for all of us?"

"That's the big money question."

Just then, there was a loud knock on the door. Tarron called for whoever it was to enter, and the door swung open. A few of Tarron's men, along with Micah, Aric, and Nix, strode into the room. Nix was carrying a laptop that he placed on Tarron's desk.

"We found this hidden in one of the dead hunter's bunks," he said. "We'll need someone with hacking skills to get inside and tell us what sort of secrets might be on there. Hopefully the kind that gives us answers."

Teague stepped up. "That would be me. Let me take a look and see what you've found."

Those around Tarron's desk gave him room. Pulling up an extra chair, the computer expert flipped open the lid and went to work circumventing the password-protected screen.

"Most people would be appalled at how ridiculously easy it is to get into their laptops," he said, without any smugness. "That part is child's play. The real question is, does the vampire heading up this band of misfits know what he's doing?"

"In what way?" Nick asked, curious.

"Mainly, will he have taken the precaution of coding his messages and hiding the IP address he's using as his home base of communications? Will his identity be hidden?"

"Seems like it could go either way," Nick replied. "He hid his identity on the video, but he probably wasn't expecting us to locate the cabin, either."

Teague worked for a few minutes, head down,

focus intense. After a while, he grunted in displeasure. "Unluckily for us, he's not that big of an idiot. The IP address is rerouted several times, so it's going to take a while to track. His messages to his followers were all done by an instant-messaging program and he used the screen name 'Executioner.'"

Aric snorted. "*That's* original."

Nick hovered over his shoulder, trying to read the print. "What do the messages say?"

"The spewing of hatred that you might expect. He's going to make us all pay for what we did, but no mention of what that was. If we knew what he's blaming us for, it would go a long way to figuring out who he is." Several others muttered agreement and Teague went on.

"There are plans on here from before he had Calla taken. They were waiting on an opportunity to get Tarron, but seized the chance to get her when it arose. Hmm, there's some disagreement among the ranks as to whether that was a good idea, especially since that group was caught."

Tarron's eyes gleamed with malice. "So, they're still using this messaging thread to discuss their plans?"

"They were, but shut it down a few hours after Calla's rescue." The hacker paused, scanning over the rest of the transcript. "Looks like the Executioner was talking with them about their next strike, when and where it would be wise to carry one out, when one of his men pointed out they should change to another thread because of the cabin raid. Damn!"

Nick couldn't agree more. Such a good break, only to have it vanish in an instant. "Can you find them again?"

"I'll try. In the meantime, I'll trace the Executioner's IP address, as well as the others on the list, and see what I can find."

"Thanks," Tarron said. "And bring me a print-out of their conversations before this thread was shut down. Nick and I will read over it thoroughly to make sure there's no hidden clue we're missing."

"Right away, my prince."

Teague took the laptop and headed out to complete his job. Nick and Tarron dismissed the rest of their men and Nick took a seat. For a moment, they sat in brooding silence before Tarron broke it.

"So, you and Calla have Bonded?" His tone was reserved, his gaze watchful.

"I've claimed her." He didn't offer more, and the other man's eyes narrowed.

"That should be cause for celebration. And yet I detect a note in your voice that suggests it's anything but."

"It's not that simple." He pushed his fingers through his hair. "I swear to you I'm doing my best to be the mate she deserves. It's just taking some time. Let me work this out with her before I end up speaking out of turn. This is between Calla and me."

"All right, I'll butt out—for now. But mark my words: Friend or not, you hurt my sister and you won't have to worry about battling some mystery vampire or anyone else."

"I know."

"Good. And furthermore—"

The ringtone of Nick's cell thankfully broke into his new brother-in-law's lecture. When he glanced at the screen, however, he wasn't so glad for the interruption. The call was from General Grant, which was rarely a good thing.

"Jarrod," he greeted the other man upon answering. "What's up?"

"We've got a basilisk loose in downtown Dallas, Texas."

"A basilisk?" Nick repeated. His blood chilled. "Not Belial."

"No. Mackenzie reports that Belial is safe and sound at the compound, trying to seduce one of those tiger shifters at Sanctuary into sleeping with him."

Thank God. The thought of the enemy getting to anyone under Nick's care and thrusting him into danger, forcing the team or himself to kill him, made his gut churn. "Casualties?"

"Five dead, ten injured at last count. There's

some sort of drunken celebration going on down-town because of a big sports win, and now the scene is total chaos."

Nick shot to his feet. "Fuck, that's a disaster! We'll be there as soon as we can."

He ended the call, mind racing. This was a complete clusterfuck. The one thing they feared more than anything was a paranormal getting loose in a situation so big the entire world would find out they existed.

"What's wrong?" Tarron asked, rising.

"We've got a basilisk loose in downtown Dallas. Five dead, ten injured—probably more by now. Shit!"

He started out the door, Tarron following. The vampire exclaimed, "A *basilisk*, you said? Those things really exist?"

At any other time, the irony of that statement would have been funny. "We have one living at the Pack's compound, in fact. Belial is being rehabilitated."

"You don't think—"

"No. It's not him," Nick said, hurrying down the corridor. "They're lethal yet solitary creatures typically, which begs the question of how one got deposited into the middle of a championship celebration in one of the largest cities in the U.S."

"Foul play?"

"That's my guess. I think someone put him there on purpose, and we're dealing with a frightened shifter who has no idea what's happening and is about to become just as tragic a casualty as his victims." The prospect was a grim one.

"That's all kinds of fucked-up."

"Tell me about it. But it won't be the first time something similar has happened."

"I don't envy you that job. Although I suppose I'm involved now, since we're family, and my warriors will be sent to assist yours."

Nick came to an abrupt halt and faced Tarron. "No. I can't ask you to risk your men in battles that aren't theirs. Your people likely resent our presence enough already."

"You're kidding, right? We were allies first and now we're family," Tarron said staunchly. "We're bound and you have our loyalty. There's nothing we wouldn't do for you, especially after you and your men have come to our aid in a fight that isn't yours."

Nick knew Tarron wasn't going to budge, and relented. "All right. I'm grateful to accept any help you want to send; just know I don't expect it or take it for granted."

"Noted."

After taking a moment to send an urgent text to his team, Nick continued on to the grand foyer in the entrance to meet them. They were fast, as usual, every one of them waiting before him in moments, ready to fight. Quickly, he outlined the situation, much to their shock.

"I'm not taking everyone, in case this is an attempt to make us leave the stronghold unprotected." He made a fast decision. "Kalen, I need you and your Sorcerer's talents with us. We'll need some major damage control."

"Yes, sir."

"John, Ryon, Aric, and Micah, you're also with me. The rest of you stay here and protect the stronghold."

Tarron chose his men and then turned to Nick. "We've been to Dallas. We'll teleport you to the city to save valuable time."

"Thank you." Quickly, Nick tried sending a mental message to Calla.

Baby, I'm sorry but our team has been called out. Your brother and some of his men are going with us. I'll be back as soon as I can.

He didn't know anything about shifter-vampire bonding, but he hoped she could hear him the way a human mate could. Even so, what if she couldn't answer until he'd allowed her to claim him in return? Another thing to feel guilty as hell about, denying her a basic right of mates—to be able to communicate freely.

There was no answer, which could mean several things, none of them good. With a heavy heart, he joined his team and the vampires, psyching himself up for the battle with the basilisk.

"A few last things," Nick told the group. "Don't shift. We've got enough trouble trying to cover up a mythical snake, much less a pack of wolves and a panther. Next, don't look him straight in the eye. His gaze will immobilize you; then he'll kill and eat you. Last, take it alive if you can. We need information."

"Jesus, as if," someone muttered in response to the last directive.

Then they were off. Landing, they found themselves in the heart of the city, in someplace called the West End. There were trendy restaurants and shops lining the streets, which were mostly empty except for a few screaming people rushing past, presumably in the opposite direction from the big snake.

"That way." Nick pointed.

He took off and the others joined him, following the ominous sounds of crashing, and a high-pitched bellow that made his hair stand on end. As they rounded a corner, a terrifying sight met their eyes. The basilisk was almost as big as Belial, but not quite. Even so, it was huge, rearing up high, whipping its great head from side to side, screeching, snapping at everything that moved. A barricade of police vehicles surrounded the beast, the police taking cover, some firing. Their bullets bounced right off the tough hide and served only to frighten and piss it off more.

The beast slithered toward one of the vehicles and slammed the hood with its nose, ripped at the metal with its fangs. The officers retreated, and the snake released a stream of liquid from its mouth, hitting one of the cops in the leg as he ran. The man let out a yell of pain and his pants leg sizzled, but he didn't stop running.

"To hell with this," Aric shouted. "Let me torch it!"

"No." Nick pointed at Kalen. "Can you neutralize it? Put it to sleep or something?"

"If you can distract it long enough for me to work, yes," the Sorcerer said, eyeing the snake. With a flick of his wrist, his Sorcerer's staff was in his hand, glowing with power.

"Okay, let's go!"

Nick led the group down the street and they fanned out to surround the beast. They danced around it on the balls of their feet, waving their arms and shouting to get its attention. They did a pretty good job of keeping it off guard, but it still managed to hit Ryon with its venom.

"Shit! Fuck!" He rolled on the ground, clutching his bleeding, scorched arm with his other hand. A couple of Tarron's men rushed in and carried him from the line of fire.

Nick pushed his concern about Ryon to the background. Glancing at Kalen, he saw that the man was standing with his arms out, chanting a spell. The basilisk must've felt or sensed what Kalen was trying to do, because it suddenly lunged in his direction. Nick and Aric moved to intercept it, Nick palming a medium-sized blade. Rushing in, he drove the blade between two scales and winced as it screeched loudly enough that nearby windows shattered and car alarms went off everywhere.

"Nick, run!" someone yelled.

He turned, but the beast came at him. It slammed him with the side of its head, knocking him clear off his feet and hurling him several yards away. By the time he hit the pavement and skidded to a halt, it was on top of him, head lowering, eyes red and jaws gaping.

Red eyes.

Nick froze in the act of peddling backward, unable to move a muscle. *Oh, God. I looked into its eyes. I'm fucked.*

Mesmerized, he watched as the beast took one of his thighs in its mouth, clamped down, teeth shredding his skin. He couldn't move, couldn't shout his agony as the venom broke the skin and began to move through his blood. Burning. On fire.

He could only watch as it lifted him off the ground, and then dangled him helplessly upside down as he waited to be devoured. All around him, his team and Tarron's were shouting at Kalen to hurry.

And then the creature stilled. Slowly, Nick was lowered to the pavement until he was lying on his back, his leg still in the creature's jaws. The basilisk's eyes drifted shut and its body relaxed in sleep.

"God," Nick gasped, pulling his leg to try to free it. "Get it off me."

People swarmed him, Aric and Micah dropping to his side. Aric gripped his shoulder and spoke in a soothing tone. "Easy, boss. John and the vamps are gonna pry your leg loose."

"Tell Kalen to wipe the humans' memories. Everyone he can. Kill the cameras and cell phones. The few that got away, nobody will believe them."

"I'm on it," Kalen told him from a few feet away. Then Nick lost track of him.

The pain was incredible. His injured limb felt like it was being boiled in acid from the inside out. The fire spread up to his hip, and he writhed in agony, groaning.

"Fuck." Sweat beaded on his face, rolled into his hair. The fire reached his chest, and his heart seized. His eyes widened and he met Aric's worried gaze. "Can't . . . breathe."

"Prince Tarron!" Micah shouted. "We need to transport him!"

Hands grabbed Nick, and he was traveling through the abyss. Back in the stronghold, he wished he could lose consciousness as the men rushed him through the corridors. He was dragging air into his lungs by sheer force of will, so hot he was sure he'd fry before the doctor could help him.

The rest came in disorienting snatches. The agony. Dr. Archer, barking orders. An IV being inserted into his arm, several shots of medicine going into the line. There was some relief as the burning lessened. His breathing became easier.

Then Dr. Archer leaned over him and said, "I'm putting you under while we clean out that leg and repair some of the damage. You're in no shape to shift just yet, and I've got to get to those thigh muscles before they're too far gone to heal. Just relax."

And those were the last words he heard for a while.

"Calla? Calla!"

"I'm coming!" As Calla jogged to the door, her heart leapt into her throat. She would recognize her brother's anxious voice anywhere.

She'd been on pins and needles since Nick's voice had unexpectedly pushed into her head, saying he was being called away. To hear Tarron sound like that spiked her fear.

Throwing the door open, she felt the blood drain from her face. "What happened?"

"Nick's in surgery," Tarron said. "But he's with Viktor, so he's in good hands."

Her knees went weak and her brother steadied her. "Why? Tell me what's wrong with him!"

"There was a basilisk loose in Dallas and we went with his team to help. He was distracting it so Kalen could spell it to sleep when the creature knocked him down and got his leg in its jaws."

Staring at her brother, she tried to process all of that. "He was bitten? By a basilisk?"

"Yes. The venom was nasty, but Viktor swears he'll be all right."

Calla felt faint. "Take me to Nick."

All the way to the infirmary, she fought panic. How the hell had a basilisk gotten loose in a crowded city? That shouldn't have been possible.

And now her mate was paying the price for simply doing his job.

Nine

"First of all, he's going to be okay," Viktor told Calla the instant she hurried into the lobby of the infirmary.

Most of Nick's men were there, hovering. For their benefit he added, "Both Nick *and* Ryon will be fine. Basilisk venom is nasty business and can be fatal, but they were both lucky. Either the creature's venom wasn't as strong as older ones, or she was only acting in self-defense, not trying to kill them."

"She?" John said in surprise.

"Yes. I had a look at her before she was taken to your compound, and the basilisk is definitely female. And in human form, a small, scared one at that."

"Huh." Aric snorted. "She seemed pretty fucking big on the street."

"How did she end up where she did?" Calla asked.

"We don't know," John answered. "But I'm going to question her while Nick is recovering."

"I'll go with you," Micah put in. The others wanted to go, too, but John limited the group to three—himself, Micah, and Aric—so as not to scare the shifter even more.

Personally, right now Calla couldn't care less whether the creature was frightened. What happened might or might not be the basilisk's fault, but still, she'd put Calla's mate in the infirmary. That would be tough to forgive.

Calla moved up to Viktor and got in his face. "This is all very interesting but I want to see Nick."

"The nurses are getting him settled, Princess," he said gently. "Give them a few minutes and one of them will come and get you."

"His injuries?"

"His right leg was bitten and the muscle torn, which I repaired in surgery. In a day or two, when he's stronger and able to shift, that will finish his healing. The venom, as I said, was painful but not lethal in this case. I anticipate no complications from his ordeal."

"Thank you." Sagging in relief, she was hardly aware of Tarron assisting her into a seat. She was so lost in her thoughts, she didn't realize he'd spoken to her at first. "I'm sorry?"

"I said, Nick told me that you two mated. I suppose congratulations are in order."

She couldn't blame him for phrasing it as a question. Things hadn't gotten off to a smooth start for her and Nick. As protective as her brother was, she wasn't about to tell him that she hadn't been able to claim her mate in return. He might finish the job the snake had started.

"We have some challenges to work through." That was an understatement. "But things will be all right, eventually."

"I know," he said with a smile, squeezing her hand. "But I'm here for you, whatever you need. Nick, too."

"Thank you."

One of the nurses appeared as promised, and took Calla to Nick's room. He was awake when she went in, but groggy.

"Hey," she said, sitting down to take his hand. "How are you feeling?"

"Like I got hit by a bus. How's Ryon?"

"Viktor said he'd be fine, so don't worry. Just get well." She brushed a lock of black hair off his forehead.

"Plan to." He yawned. "Where's the basilisk? Did they take him to Sanctuary?"

"Her, and yes, they did."

He blinked. "The creature is female?"

"Apparently so. Plus small and frightened, according to Viktor."

"God," he breathed. "Has she talked?"

"I don't think so, but John and a couple of others are going to question her."

He frowned. "You know, I was half expecting an ambush. I could have sworn she was a lure."

"Maybe that's what you were supposed to think. Then when you're wrong, you'll relax your guard next time you go out on a call and they'll hit you when you don't expect it."

"Smart woman. We'll just be extra careful, then." His eyes drooped and he tried to stay awake. "About earlier, leaving the way I did . . . I'm sorry."

"Hush. Get better and we'll deal with the rest as it comes."

Her heart ached as she watched him succumb to sleep. He had so much responsibility on his shoulders, had been hurt more than once protecting his team, and yet he was worried about her feelings.

She sat with him for a while, until hunger forced her to seek something from the kitchen. Reluctantly, she left Nick's side, knowing solid food would only temporarily stave off the need for blood. There wasn't anything else she could do, though. Her stomach would reject any other blood—she knew that by the ominous sickness that roiled just thinking of drinking from anyone but her mate.

The cook made her a roast beef sandwich, rare.

Calla devoured it and felt queasy afterward, but at least it stayed down. She thought she had things under control, and then her brother chose to make an appearance, sitting down beside her and giving her a piercing look.

"Are you all right?"

"I'm fine," she said, trying a smile. It didn't quite convince him as he eyed her in suspicion.

"You have dark circles under your eyes and you don't look well. Not what I'd expect when I see my happily mated sister. Or *is* the mating happy?"

"My mate was just injured, in case you forgot, and that doesn't thrill me. Besides that, we're still working things out. Of course things aren't perfect yet."

"In what way?"

"That's really none of your business."

"Since when?" He leaned forward, his worry apparent. "We've always been honest with each other and I can sense you're not being straight with me. What's going on?"

Shaking her head, she pressed her lips together. Telling him the whole truth felt like she'd be betraying her mate, even if that wasn't really the case.

"Sis, your lips are slightly blue," he continued in a low, ominous tone. "In fact, you look like you haven't had blood lately. Why don't I see if Nick's feeling better so you can feed?"

"No." Her voice was quiet and miserable. "I can't do that to him."

Her brother was clearly confused. "Why not? He's your Bondmate now, right? I mean, who the hell else are you going to feed from?"

"I'm *his* Bondmate, yes." She took a deep breath. "But he's not mine, officially. Not yet."

He scowled. "What the fuck does that even mean? You're either Bonded or you're not!"

"Nick claimed me, but I haven't claimed him yet," she hissed, frustration and sorrow warring with each other. "I can't, until he's free of his demons and can allow me to claim him freely, and share my joy."

"Share your *joy*?" he repeated, voice rising even though she tried to shush him. "Does he realize that by being claimed you can no longer feed from anyone else, vampire or human? That you'll fucking *starve* if he doesn't allow you to claim him?"

"No, and you're not going to tell him," she ordered furiously. "So help me, I won't speak to you again if you do!"

"Why the hell not?" he yelled. "This is your life we're talking about!"

"I won't have my mate coerced into Bonding!" Bolting to her feet, she slammed a palm on the table, making the dishes jump. A couple of other coven members who'd been dining on the other side of the room quickly cleared out. "You will not interfere in this. Do you understand me?"

"Calla." He was gutted; she could tell.

"I'm sorry. I know you're trying to help, but I

need you to stay out of my mating. He'll come around under his own steam, or not at all."

"But if he doesn't, you could— No, you *will* die."

"It won't come to that." She hoped. Tarron appeared so lost, she relented some and went around the table. Putting her arms around his neck, she gave him a hug and was immediately enveloped in his embrace.

"I love you, sis," he said hoarsely. "Don't let this go too long. You and Adrian are my only family, and you're everything to me."

She kissed his cheek, love swelling in her heart. "I won't. And I love you, too."

A twinge of hunger gnawed her belly as she made her way back to the infirmary.

Nick awoke the next morning, restless and irritated with the constant pain in his injured leg. *To hell with this.*

Seeing that he was alone for the moment, he made quick work of yanking out his IV line and ripping off every one of those damned itchy little stick-on circles connected to the heart monitor. Then he shucked his ugly gown and let his wolf free.

The shift was fast, due to centuries of practice. His wolf circled around on the bed, then flopped down with a sigh of contentment. Just when he got settled, a nurse rushed in, followed by Dr. Archer.

"You could've waited instead of scaring my nurse," the doc scolded. Then he smiled. "But I'm glad to see you're on the mend. I'll check on you in an hour or so; then most likely you'll be ready to go."

The doctor left. Nick dozed for a bit, letting his shifter's system heal the rest of his injury. He didn't sleep very well, though, because he kept jerking awake and wondering where Calla had gone. Was she upset with him for leaving the way he did before they were called to Dallas? She didn't seem as though she was when he last saw her, but his heart still ached at the thought.

The door opened and his mate pushed into the room. He raised his head and caught the full force of her smile, and the sight of her went straight to his soul. His wolf let out a happy chuff as she sat beside him and began to scratch his ears.

"Viktor told me you were sort of naughty," she said.

Not as naughty as I'd like to be, he thought.

Her eyes widened in surprise. "You really spoke in my head! I almost thought I'd imagined that before, when I heard you tell me you had to go out on a call."

Nope. All shifters can communicate with their mates once they've Bonded. It's a nice perk.

"But I'm not a shifter. Will I be able to talk back to you?" She looked intrigued, and somewhat worried she wouldn't be able to.

I don't know, he admitted. *I've never known a mated shifter-and-vampire couple. Try.*

Furrowing her brow, she concentrated on what he guessed was sending a message. When he didn't receive one, he shook his head.

It might develop later on your end, after you claim me.

Her tired eyes widened slightly. "Oh, Nick, are you ready for me to claim you? I'm not pressuring you. It's just that I want you so much. It'll be so wonderful, honey; you'll see—"

I want it, too. I do. Soon. I promise it won't be much longer.

Her shoulders slumped ever so slightly. Suddenly, he realized she didn't appear well. *Are you okay?*

"I'm fine," she said, giving him a half smile. "And I see you're feeling better."

Changing the subject?

"Stating a fact. Viktor should be here to let you go soon."

His reply was interrupted by a knock. Tarron, Ian, Teague, and John walked into the room without waiting for the go-ahead, and their expressions told Nick something had developed. He let the change flow over him and reverted to human form, then pulled the sheet over his lap to save Calla any embarrassment. If it had just been the men, nobody would've cared that he was naked.

Tarron got right to the point. "Teague found

something." He nodded to the hacker, who took up the explanation.

"I've identified two large groups who are communicating via e-mail with the one we believe is their leader—the hunters and rogue vampires. But in the last few weeks another e-mailer has joined the discussion, and you'll never guess where those messages originated."

Nick waited a couple of beats as what they were getting at became clear. "From either my compound, or here at the stronghold?" That anyone among his team or support staff would betray them was inconceivable.

"Here," Tarron said, every line in his body radiating with fury. "Someone among my coven, or your team, is talking with those bastards. Possibly feeding them information."

Nick shook his head and snapped, "Not one of mine. I can personally vouch for every single one of my Pack members. Each one of them would take a bullet for any of us."

"Don't you think I feel the same way about my men?" Tarron shot back. "No one takes on a man thinking the worst of his intentions. But clearly, one of us has misplaced our trust."

"Okay, gentlemen," John interrupted. His voice was quiet and even, injecting calm into the situation to prevent it from escalating into an argument. "We're not going to get anywhere by discussing anything but hard facts. We have a culprit and we need to find out who it is so we can follow him to the source. He has fucked up and we're going to take advantage of the fact that he probably doesn't realize it yet."

The other men blinked at him, obviously not used to the man previously known only as "Hammer" being more vocal and taking charge. When he chose to, John was and always had been a man to make other people sit up and take notice. Nick was glad to see him growing within the team.

"You're right," Tarron agreed, backing down some. "The facts will bear out the truth, and we'll know what direction to take. Teague, where in the stronghold did the suspect use the computer? Or is it possible to tell?"

"That we *do* know. I've traced those e-mails to a computer in the main library. The problem is, those computers are used by dozens of coven members and their children every day and they aren't that closely monitored. There are also no surveillance cameras in the library, because quite frankly we've never had cause to install any."

Tarron nodded. "That will be remedied with a few hidden cameras that are trained on the bank of computers, at least until he's caught."

"I'll take care of it," Teague said.

"Good. In the meantime, Nick, tell your most trusted Pack members to keep a sharp eye on any strange comings and goings among anyone in the stronghold, man or woman. Or any behavior that seems suspicious. I'll do the same."

Nick didn't bother to reiterate that he trusted all of his team implicitly. He was also ninety-nine percent sure he would know, via his gift, whether one of his men had turned. He didn't have the ability to see *everything*, but this much he felt confident about.

"I'll tell them," he said. Then he waved a hand at the door. "As soon as I get some clothes I'll meet with my team."

The men left the room, John volunteering to send someone with fresh clothes for Nick, then get the team together in the prince's conference room. Calla studied him with worry, and he knew it wouldn't be long before she voiced it. He was right.

"I think it's too soon for you to jump right back in to work."

"Honey, I'm healed. That being the case, there isn't any way I'm going to sit on my ass while everyone else takes care of our current problem."

"I know, but that doesn't make me feel any better."

His lips turned up at her adorable pout, and he smiled. "That pretty face could get me into a lot of trouble if I let it. But I'm not going to give in," he teased, trying to lighten the mood. It worked, better than he expected.

Winding her arms around his neck, she took his

mouth softly at first, moving against him. She smelled so good, felt so fantastic, his body responded with fervor, tenting the sheets over his lap. The kiss deepened and they explored, dueling tongues, and his blood fired up.

She pulled back with a sensual, satisfied smile. "What was it you weren't going to do?"

"I forgot."

"Jesus," Micah said as he came into the room, holding a bundle of clothes. "Man, you need the doc to come back and take a look at that?"

Calla giggled at Nick's annoyance. Then Nick really looked at Micah—the younger man's hands were shaking as he handed Nick the clothing, and his eyes were bloodshot, the pupils blown. A familiar buzz settled over Nick's brain, and the vision caught him swiftly.

Micah and an attractive dark-haired woman faced off in an unfamiliar bedroom. "What the fuck is this, Micah?" she shouted, shaking a small bottle in her fist. The contents rattled ominously between the couple. "You told me you'd stopped using! You lied to me, to your team!"

"Jacee, please—"

"Please, what? Give you another chance, and another, while I wait for the day one of your brothers comes to tell me you're dead of an overdose? Or were gutted by the enemy because you were stoned during a fight?"

"No," he denied, voice tight. "That won't happen."

"You need to go." Looking defeated, she turned her back on him. "Now."

"Baby, please. Don't throw me away. I'll get help. I'll quit. Anything—"

"Now, Micah."

She meant it. Micah had no right to stay, no grounds to defend himself. Taking a breath, he said, "I love you. That won't change, ever. I'm always here if you need me, or change your mind."

Numbly, he walked past her and out the bedroom door. Kept going, all the way outside to his motorcycle, where he sat and stared at her house for long moments. A tear trailed down his face and he wiped it away with his sleeve. Trying to keep it together.

Failing.

Cranking the bike, Micah sped away from the house. From the loss tearing out his insides. He ran from his ruined life, the destruction of his hopes and dreams. With the Pack, with his mate.

And so he didn't see the shifter with the huge wings swoop down from the sky, talons extended, intent clear. Nick couldn't scream. Couldn't warn Micah of the danger.

The creature hit Micah from the side, hard, knocking him from the speeding motorcycle. Micah went airborne, flying through the air for awful seconds—until he slammed headfirst into a tree. Falling to the ground in a crumpled heap, head at an unnatural angle, he stared into the sky. Struggled to breathe.

And then stopped, brown eyes fixing on a point he could no longer see.

Nick propelled himself from the horrid vision, fighting to regain the here and now. Calla's and Micah's concerned voices coaxed him back to reality, and slowly the room came into focus. His lungs were burning and he heaved a great breath, focusing on the worried wolf in front of him.

"Nick? Boss, you with us?"

Can't interfere with free will. But I can suggest, and that doesn't mean they'll listen.

He wanted to tell Micah to sell his bike. Not to get involved with Jacee, the bartender from the Cross-eyed Grizzly. To quit using. Any number of things to avert the terrible future he'd just witnessed. In the end, he went straight to the heart of the matter.

Leaning toward Micah, he said, "Take a serious look at your life and where it's going, because I just did."

The man paled, the scarred side of his face standing out in stark relief. "You had a vision? About me?"

"Yeah. And your story doesn't end well, if you keep on your current path," he told the man grimly. "Kick your addiction, now—and keep your eyes on the skies."

"Shit." Micah swallowed hard. "The skies? I don't get that part."

"Me, either. But apparently you're going to make some nasty enemies in the near future, and you're going to need to be alert to fight them. With our help, of course. You can always count on your team, Micah. Don't forget you're never alone in your struggles, okay?"

Wide-eyed, the man nodded. "I won't. But I'm not an addict, okay? Mac *prescribed* this stuff I'm on. I know it's an experimental drug, but it really helps me cope, you know?"

"Maybe it did at first, but now it's killing you, kid. We're going to talk to Mac and see about alternatives."

"All right," he agreed, clearly shaken. As he should be.

"I'm going to get dressed, and I'll meet you and the others in the conference room in a few."

"Got it." After hesitating, Micah walked out.

First the disturbing vision about Phoenix and Noah, and now this. Every one of the guys had endured his share of heartache, and it seemed there was more on the horizon.

"Nick?" Calla said softly. "Is Micah going to die?"

"We'll all die sooner or later." He regretted his flip response the instant it left his mouth. "I'm sorry. Believe me, baby, you don't want to know what I saw. But what I said to him was the absolute truth—if he doesn't get his act together, he's headed for a brutal and abrupt end."

"Gods!" Taking his hand, she brought it to her face. "I don't know how you cope with being able to see the future. That's one so-called gift I'd never wish for, ever. I'm here for you, though, however I can be. I'll help keep an eye on him when I can."

He kissed her forehead. "Thanks, baby. What I see isn't written in stone, thank God. Events can change, because the choices people make constantly change."

"Well, I hope his choices change, and soon."

"Me, too." He sighed. "I've got to get to this meeting. Can I come to your quarters afterward so we can talk?"

"Of course." She wrapped him in a hug, holding tight for a minute before letting go. "My door is always open to you. You're my mate."

That went a long way toward warming the place that had gone cold in his heart after the vision. After giving her another lingering kiss, he slid from the bed and put on the jeans and black T-shirt John had sent with Micah, then pulled on his boots. Feeling more human, he walked out, holding Calla's hand.

"You were supposed to wait for my clearance," Viktor admonished as Nick approached.

"Sorry. Things to do, people to see."

Whatever else the doctor might have said was lost as Nick hurried out of the infirmary. In the corridor, he turned and gave his mate another quick kiss. "See you soon."

"Not if I see you first."

With a short laugh, he left her, reluctantly. He'd rather be anywhere in the world with his mate than working, but he figured most newly mated guys felt that way. It might sound cliché, but she really was the bright spot in his darkness and he didn't want to be away from her long enough even to hold a simple meeting.

Forcing his mind to the task at hand, he made his way to the meeting. The guys were restless when he walked in, and met him with a chorus of greetings. He caught some good-natured shit about his run-in with the basilisk, which he knew by now meant they counted him one of them. After almost a year and a half leading the team, their complete acceptance meant more than they knew.

Unbidden, thoughts of Damien and his incessant phone calls infiltrated his brain. His brother hadn't given up trying to reestablish a relationship with him, and it was wearing Nick the fuck out. He didn't know what to say to the asshole past hello, and didn't care to try.

Selene would be disappointed in him. God, that hurt. His daughter held out such hope that her father and uncle would reunite. *When hell freezes over.*

"John," he said, getting started. The team looked to the big man, some of them wearing curious expressions that indicated they were still getting used to his real name. "Were you able to speak with the basilisk?"

John stood and came forward to lean against the wall near the front of the room. "Yeah. Her name is Sasha. Her story is she was abducted from her nest a few days ago and held captive in a dark cell underground. She was tortured and starved, bound by a tight collar around her neck to keep her from shifting. Her bruises and physical condition support that claim."

"Christ," someone muttered.

"Can she identify who took her?" Nick asked.

"Humans in cammo pants and carrying assault weapons."

"Hunters," Jax said, hate filling his eyes.

"They weren't the ones calling the shots, though, according to Sasha," John continued. "That would be the mysterious vampire everyone was bowing and scraping to, trying to please."

Nick leaned against the edge of the table with one hip. "Did she get a description?"

"Pale complexion, longish dark hair. No name."

"Wow, that really narrows it down," Aric drawled sarcastically, rolling his eyes. "I don't know a single fuckin' vampire who fits *that* description."

Nick shot the redhead a glare, and the wolf shut up. Miraculously.

"Did she catch any talk among them about their agenda?"

"Now, that she *did* manage," John confirmed. "Seeing as how they all thought we'd kill her when we got to the scene, their lips were pretty loose. It's pretty much what we thought—letting loose a basilisk in the city, one who had been tortured and starved, was a lure for us. Only it *was* supposed to be an ambush, so something obviously went wrong."

"Could've changed their minds at the last minute," Micah suggested.

"After going to all that trouble to set it up?" Ryon, healed and out of the infirmary as well, shook his head. "Don't think so."

"Dissension among the ranks, maybe," Jax speculated. "Someone didn't follow orders."

"Or just fucked up. It happens." This from Kalen.

"Whatever the case, we'll be ready if they pull that shit again," Nick told them. "But I'm inclined to think they'll have something different planned."

"Like?" John asked.

"A full-scale attack. They may have decided to test and observe us, note our individual strengths and fighting skills so they'd be better prepared when they hit us," Nick said. That was a chilling thought, and the men stilled as this possibility sank in.

Zander blew out a breath. "That would mean we're really in the shit. You guys have to be careful out there, especially with my healing abilities not up to par."

Jax clamped a hand on his best friend's shoulder. "You just look out for yourself. We'll be fine."

"I'll tell Tarron what we've talked about," Nick said. "We've posted more guards around the stronghold and he's got drills planned to practice sneaking the females and offspring out and off the mountain in case of emergency. I'm not sure what else we can do but be ready."

"Find out who their leader is, where they are, and wipe them off the planet first?" Kalen suggested.

Nick's lips turned up. "That would be the best scenario, and we're working on it. The minute we have any information, we'll smoke their asses. Believe me." He paused. "Unless anyone has something to add, I have an announcement. This is why I wanted to meet just with you guys today and not with Tarron and his men."

Most of them knew, or had a clue. They were just waiting for him to say it.

"Calla Shaw and I are Bondmates."

A cheer went up, and a round of congrats, followed by more ribbing. Nick took it all in stride, not mentioning the issues he and his mate were still working out. But they had deserved the words from his lips before they found out elsewhere.

"Where are you two going to live, Nick?" Jax asked, a slight frown on his face as he pulled at his goatee.

"We haven't gotten that far yet, but I'll let you all know. One thing I can say for sure is I'm not leaving the team or stepping down."

"Damned straight!" Aric exclaimed. Laughing, the others agreed and Nick was promised bodily injury if he tried to so much as type a resignation letter to Grant.

That made him feel pretty damned good.

Dismissing his team, he endured the backslaps as he left the room. How different this life was from when he was under Damien's rule. His brother was so unbending. Practical. Ruthless. Damien's men were definitely not his brothers; they'd feared him. And fear bred hatred.

Nick almost felt sorry that the bastard would never know this camaraderie. Almost.

Hurrying his steps, he started for his mate's chambers. He got as far as the corridor he should turn down to get to her room when his cell rang. He half expected the caller to be his brother, but he was surprised to see it was Tarron.

"Westfall," he said, answering.

"Nick, we have a problem."

"Not on the phone. I'll come to your office." Hanging up, he walked briskly, not wasting time but not wanting to alarm anyone. When he reached the large door, he knocked.

"Come in."

The prince was pacing the carpet, and looked up in relief when Nick came in. "One of my guards has left the stronghold without my permission. I put him on the last shift, and found out he begged off, claiming to have fallen sick from a bad batch of blood. After his shift was covered, one of the perimeter cameras captured him leaving, acting very furtive."

"Who was it?"

"Graham."

"Damn," Nick said angrily. "He's the only one who was with Calla when she was taken. I should've taken a closer look at him before now. Is someone following him?"

"As we speak. Care to join me in catching up?"

"Are you kidding? Let's go catch ourselves a traitor."

Briefly returning to his own bunk, Nick changed into cammos and loaded up with his weapons. His wolf prowled restlessly inside, wanting in on the action.

"Soon," he promised.

With one last check of his ammo, he went to meet Tarron out front.

Time to find out just what the fuck was going on, and destroy the asshole who was behind it all.

Ten

O ut front, Nick and Tarron jumped into a Land
Rover driven by Ian.

Micah accompanied Nick, appearing surprised
and pleased to have been chosen for this mission,
when the simple truth was Nick wanted to boost
the young wolf's confidence—while keeping an
eye on him.

"Why are we not tracking Graham on the
ground, in wolf form?" Nick asked as the vehicle
peeled from the driveway. He still had the guard's
scent programmed into his wolf's brain, so following him wouldn't be a problem.

Tarron answered from his spot in the front passenger's seat next to Ian. "Teague is tracking the
SUV Graham took, using the tracking device in-
stalled in the vehicle." The prince pointed to the ear-
piece and wire Ian wore. "He's giving Ian directions."

"That's certainly easier."

Micah spoke up from beside Nick. "Good old shifter methods fall to technology. It's sad, really."

He sounded so sincere, Nick and the others chuckled. Nick said, "Don't worry, kid. You'll have plenty of opportunity to use your talents."

Micah, being the easygoing type normally, didn't take exception to their amusement or being called "kid." Nick was good at reading people, and Micah had a big heart. He just needed to believe in himself, and to do that he had to get past the horror that had put those scars on his face. The best way Nick could help him do that was to keep him on the front line.

Anything to keep his vision from coming to pass.

Ian drove on, getting directions now and then from their tech god, winding them through the mountains for a good hour. At last, Ian pulled over to the side of the road and addressed the group.

"We need to stop here and walk the rest of the way so we don't alert Graham and whoever he's meeting."

The vampires had brought a camera and a recording device, which struck Nick as so practical he knew Micah had a point. Sometimes having special abilities couldn't take care of everything.

They set out across the green terrain, picking their way around rocks and brush. The sky was a clear blue, a few clouds drifting past. A good day for surveillance, but also to be seen. They'd have to be careful.

A single voice reached them, and Tarron waved them to a halt. "Graham," he whispered. The conversation was one-sided, and the guard sounded uneasy. Annoyed. "Sounds like he's on the phone."

As they approached, they took cover in the brush, in a spot that overlooked the relatively flat area where Graham had parked the borrowed SUV. He was alone, pacing, running a hand through his dark hair. The vampire was obviously nervous, and Nick thought he should be, getting into bed with the enemy. Though they still had to see for themselves. Innocent until proven guilty.

Ian snapped pictures and Tarron gave Micah the job of recording with the small handheld device he'd brought. The foursome watched and listened as Graham quietly unraveled while waiting for a meeting to take place. The poor bastard made a terrible villain, Nick thought. He was so outwardly nervous, he was going to get eaten alive.

Finally, a beat-up pickup truck rounded the bend, and three men hopped out. Two were wearing cammos and carrying their beloved assault rifles. The third was . . .

"Motherfucking hell," Nick hissed. "That's Scott Morgan."

"Who?" Tarron peered at the innocuous-looking man with a frown.

Nick took a fresh look at Scott, knew they saw a slight man of average height and a friendly face, with shaggy brown hair and dark eyes. "The Pack's new mechanic," he supplied, seething. "The little bastard is a plant, to spy on us, obviously."

"But by whom?" Micah questioned. "Who has the power to replace Tom so suddenly?"

Only Grant should, but Nick refused to believe the general would betray them. "I don't know."

The unlikely trio approached Graham, but the two hardened hunters stayed a step or two behind, allowing Scott to take the lead. One even threw the "mechanic" a wary—no, fearful—glance and put even more space between them. What the fuck?

Graham must've had the same thought. "Your tough leader sent a boy to do his job?" he sneered. "I thought he possessed an ounce of cunning."

So Graham and Scott hadn't met before today. Apparently, Scott had been recruited by either the hunters or the rogues for their vampire boss.

Scott's face darkened and he held himself dangerously still. "Vampire, you're the only boy present, and a stupid one at that. Never presume until you know exactly who you're dealing with."

The vampire's confidence waned some and he shifted his stance. "Don't suppose you'd care to clue me in, finally?"

Scott smiled, and right before their eyes began to transform. His incisors lengthened by inches, wicked sharp and deadly. His height grew to top seven feet, and his build went from slim and average to lean but muscular. Shaggy brown hair became wavy and dark, reaching his shoulders. The rest of the glamour lifted, and the stranger stood before them wearing leather pants and a sleeveless black shirt that showed off the dragon tattoos and other scrollwork adorning both arms.

Nick stared, pulse kicking as he recalled where he'd seen this man before.

"Haven't seen you around," a voice said idly.

Nick eyed the dark stranger standing in the shadows. Reaching out with his PreCog senses, he found the walls surrounding this man to be nearly impenetrable. That bothered him more than he cared to admit. "Can't say I've seen you, either. You know Calla or her brother personally?"

"Not really. You could say I'm gate-crashing." His smile was feral. *"Friend of a friend. You know how it is."*

Something about the man put him on edge. "I'm Nick Westfall, com—"

"Commander of the Alpha Pack. Yeah, word gets around. Nice gig if you can get it."

Rage fired Nick's blood. He'd been played by this creature all along. They all had. The vile monster had been observing, feeding information to his master. And enjoying the game in the bargain. Toying with his prey.

Another snippet of their conversation replayed in his head.

"I didn't catch your name," Nick said.

"I didn't say." He polished off the cheese, eyeing Nick. *"But it's Jinn."*

"Jinn . . . ?" he prompted.

"Just Jinn. No last name."

Inside him, Nick's wolf shifted and rumbled in warning. Nick had recognized the name from his vision about Nix learning of Noah's abduction. *"And how is that?"*

Moving closer, he got a whiff of Jinn's scent and found he wasn't a shifter, or a vampire. He wasn't Fae, human, or anything from this world at all, it seemed.

The man—creature—laughed, showing off straight white teeth with very large incisors. "Did you know that in Arabian mythology, the Jinn are the third creation of God, after angels and humans? It's said that we're made of smoke and fire, can take human form, and travel between dimensions. And we can be either good or evil, as the mood strikes us."

Shaking his head, Nick brought himself back to the present and watched the train wreck unfold. Graham had stumbled backward and was staring at the creature who definitely wasn't a human named Scott Morgan.

"Wh-who are you?" Graham stammered.

"Don't you mean *what*?" Jinn's smile was terrifying, his eyes cold.

The vampire shook his head. "Never mind. I

don't care as long as I get my cut for doing my part."

"Prince Tarron and Princess Calla dead, and control of his coven, correct?" His tone was cool.

"Yes, that was the deal." Graham gained back a bit of nerve, standing straighter. "And I *have* done my part. I let you know that Calla was going for a walk to the waterfall so your men could move in and take her as bait. I let myself get *stabbed*, for fuck's sake. All your hunters had to do was wait for Tarron and Westfall to come, and wipe them out, and your leader and his morons managed to fuck it up."

That fucking traitor. Nick shot Tarron a glance, and the prince appeared ready to rip out Graham's throat.

"You worthless piece of bloodsucking shit," one of the hunters yelled, surging for him. He was stopped by a flick of Jinn's wrist, frozen in place, blinking angrily.

"So far, your contribution has been abysmally small compared to your demand," the creature observed. "What you do not understand is that Prince Ivan's power and motivation is much greater than yours. What do you have that he can actually use?"

Ivan . . . Cardenas? Nick looked to Tarron again, who mouthed, "Cardenas is their mysterious leader?"

The light dawned. Cardenas had attended the

planning meeting for the alliance of covens. "Maybe," Nick whispered back. But what the hell was Cardenas's motive for vengeance that Jinn referred to?

Graham tried to humble himself, backing off a bit. He seemed to be reminded of the slippery slope he was treading as he removed a small device from his jacket pocket. A mini tablet, it appeared. "I have something he'll want. I assure you it will help achieve his aims."

Tapping quickly on a couple of apps, Graham brought up something for his cohorts to see. Some sort of document, perhaps. Whatever it was couldn't be seen from a distance, but the hunters began to chortle with glee.

"Fuckin' A," one hooted.

"No shit."

"You've come through," Jinn purred. "Send that to Prince Ivan's e-mail right now, and copy me."

Oh, Graham can't be that stupid. But he was, and he completely missed the sly smirk Jinn exchanged with the hunters while his head was down, doing as Jinn ordered. When the e-mail was sent, the vampire raised his head.

"There. I've done as you asked. When will Ivan get this done so I can gain control of the coven? I have plans for the world alliance, as well." Graham's eyes gleamed at the prospect.

Jinn smiled. "Do you? That's too bad, because unfortunately, your plans and my master's are at complete odds."

"What do you mean? We had a deal!"

"That's what *you* believed." Jinn laughed. "He was never going to give you control of the coven. He's going to take it and destroy every man, woman, and child as revenge for the murder of his mate. You are no longer of use to him at all."

Beside Nick, Tarron's expression was thunderous.

"What?" Graham moved back, eyes widening. "I am of use! Haven't I proven that?"

Without answering, Jinn held out a hand. A wisp of smoke floated from his upturned palm, thickening as it floated toward Graham.

"What are you doing?" the vampire choked out.

Those were his last words. The smoke coiled like rope around his throat and tightened. He clawed without effect as he fell to the ground, his fingers merely slipping through the horrible mist that was strangling the life out of him. His face turned red, then purple. His arms went limp at his sides and his eyes stared heavenward as his body shook violently. Then the shakes subsided to an occasional twitch.

And then nothing.

Jinn sauntered over and knelt by the body. Nick wondered what the bastard was doing as he grasped Graham's shirt and ripped it open down the front. When Jinn held up a hand, claws lengthening to lethal razors, he was afraid he knew.

The creature plunged his talons into Graham's chest, splitting his breastbone in two as though slicing butter. He then dug downward, and even from his position Nick could hear the awful slurping sounds the dead vampire's flesh made as Jinn ripped Graham's heart from his chest.

Eagerly, Jinn tore into the organ with his fangs and closed his eyes in ecstasy. The hunters had backed away all the way to their vehicle, revulsion on their faces, and as much as Nick hated them, he couldn't blame them. Jinn ate every last bite of his snack, then wiped his mouth and hands on the tattered remains of the dead vampire's shirt.

"Heart of the fallen," he said in bliss. "Nothing on this plane or the next tastes better."

Beside him, Micah made a soft gagging noise. His hand was over his mouth and he looked about two seconds from hurling all over the grass. Nick placed a hand on his shoulder to steady the wolf. The last thing they needed was to be discovered by a creature whose power quite possibly equaled Kalen's.

Jinn scooped up Graham's mini tablet and walked back to the vehicle. In seconds, they were driving away and had disappeared.

"What the fuck *is* that thing?" Tarron asked, his voice colored with horror.

"His name is Jinn," Nick told the group, a cold chill of fear joining the anger. "At least, that's what he told me when I met him at your party. He's a demonic paranormal creature, not a Sorcerer. There's not a drop of human blood in his body. He's the equivalent of a trickster who wields powerful black magic, and for some reason he's attached himself to Ivan."

"Love is blind," Micah muttered sarcastically. Under any other circumstances, that would've been funny.

"I don't know another Ivan besides Ivan Cardenas, but I can't understand why he'd be after me with such vengeance." Tarron looked lost. "Revenge for the murder of his mate? In the entirety of my long existence, I've never to my knowledge killed a female."

They all digested that for a few moments.

Then Micah said, "His mate could've been a man."

And there it was. The flip of the light switch they needed. The missing motive. Tarron turned and locked eyes with Micah. "Mother of the gods. Carter Darrow."

Ian cursed. "Maybe. It's just a guess at this point."

"How could I have missed the fact that Carter was mated?" Tarron wondered aloud. "Why did this not come to light before?"

Nick tried to soothe him because the guilt was already there, in his brother-in-law's voice. "Listen, if that's true, nobody knew it. Carter obviously kept Ivan in the background, maybe to protect him. Even as evil as he was, the need to protect one's mate transcends everything else."

"If Ivan *was* his mate," Ian interjected. "I'll get on that with Teague as soon as we get back to the stronghold, see what we can dig up."

Tarron nodded, clearly shaken. "All right. If Carter was Ivan's mate, Ivan will stop at nothing to bury me. We need to find out what Graham passed along to him just now."

"We'll get into Graham's account and find that out, too," Ian promised.

"Should we take back his body?" Micah asked, still visibly disturbed by the grisly sight before them.

Tarron thought about that. "No. Should they come back, they'll be suspicious if he's gone too quickly. Let the traitor stay for now, and I'll send some men out on a mission to 'find' my missing guard tomorrow. We'll give him a proper burial, and keep this between those who need to know."

Everyone in agreement, they loaded into the Rover again and headed for the stronghold. The mood was somber because Tarron was right. Revenge on behalf of a murdered mate was a fury nobody in his right mind wanted to face. It wouldn't have changed Carter's demise, but if they'd known Ivan existed, they would have taken him into custody right then to determine his threat to them.

Too late now. All they could do was gain more information.

Back in the conference room, they spread out as Teague tried to work his hacking magic. He found several accounts belonging to Ivan Cardenas of Barcelona, including two e-mail accounts and multiple bank accounts.

He also found a couple of bank accounts that had once been jointly owned by the couple before Darrow's death. The joint accounts were linked to an address outside Chattanooga.

"Answers that question," Teague said with a sigh. "Christ on a stick, we're fucked."

"Your confidence is overwhelming." Tarron glared at the tech.

"Sorry." Throwing his prince an apologetic glance, he went to work on getting into Graham's e-mail. But as time ticked by, he sat back and stretched. "Damn. If Graham sent something important that Ivan wanted, he didn't send it from his regular e-mail account. There are no attachments here at all. I'll keep searching, but this could take a while. He must have another account under an assumed name."

"Let's get out of here and let Teague work," Tarron said. "I'll let you all know if he finds something."

Teague grinned. "*When* I find it, you mean."

Nick bid them good-bye and headed down the corridor. It took him a few seconds to realize he was instinctively heading toward Calla's chambers. He wasn't sure she would be there, but it seemed a good place to start. He had missed his mate.

He hoped she let him show her just how much.

Calla roamed the hallways, trying not to let herself worry. She'd learned secondhand that Nick had left the building with her brother, and the guard she asked didn't know why. Nick hadn't bothered to communicate with her to tell her that he was leaving, and that bothered her the most.

He was the commander, and a busy man. He was also used to being alone. She understood that, or her head did. Her heart ached a little.

As if to punctuate her melancholy, a cramp seized her stomach. She got up and made her way to the bathroom, planning to splash some water on her face, but a wave of dizziness nearly sent her to the floor.

"Damn my stupid pride," she muttered. "Should've just *told* him I needed his blood instead of expecting him to figure it out."

And there was no doubt he hadn't learned yet that his was the only blood she could take. This wasn't something he would let go unattended.

Bracing herself against the bathroom wall, she wobbled to the sink and turned on the warm water. Splashing it on her face felt good, but the reprieve was temporary. The room tilted at a crazy angle and she gripped the counter as she started to fall sideways.

Her strength deserted her and she fell. The counter slipped from her grasp and she hit the floor with a weak cry, bumping her head on the tile. Lying there, she tried to clear the fuzzy webs from her brain. Nothing doing. She couldn't focus, or think.

Well, she couldn't think of anything except the burning in her stomach that demanded sustenance. She needed her mate's blood, fast.

Nick, she thought. Even though he couldn't hear her, she called out.

And kept calling until the darkness took her.

Calla. Calla, wake up! Baby, come back to me!

Her head was grasped in strong hands. A pleasing male scent teased her nose, and she tried to open her eyes.

"That's it, baby! Wake up. You can do it."

Her body was lifted and she felt herself being carried in those wonderful arms and then placed on something soft. Her bed? Hands caressed her face, then checked her scalp and limbs for injuries as Nick continued to speak softly.

"You have a bump," he said. "Here. Doesn't seem too bad. Can you hear me?"

"Mmm."

"Look at me, honey. Please."

With a great effort, she opened her eyes and found herself staring into his beautiful blue ones. "Hungry," she whispered.

Confusion and concern mingled with the panic on his handsome face. "Why haven't you eaten, baby? I'll get you something."

"Need blood."

"Okay. Do you use a donor?" His expression said he didn't much like that idea. "Or bagged blood?"

"You."

"I'm sorry?"

"You," she said quietly. "Need yours."

"Me?" A hint of fear darkened his face. "But you vampires can take any blood. Why haven't you fed?"

"Not *any* blood. Not after we've mated," she told him. "Can only have yours now."

The truth settled over his features and she regretted the outright horror there. But if she'd thought the horror was for himself, she was wrong.

"You mean to tell me that you've been suffering since I claimed you?" he whispered, shame coloring his voice. "That you've been starving yourself? Why, for God's sake?"

"I know you're not comfortable with me biting you, Nick," she whispered. "After what happened to you."

"That doesn't matter—not when it comes to this! Not when it endangers your health!" Sitting on the edge of the bed, he took her hand and swallowed hard. "What do you need? My neck? Jugular?"

He would do this for her. Push aside his fear, for her. She squeezed his hand.

"No, your wrist will be fine. It won't be a claiming, but I can feed."

"Here, let me help you."

Sitting her up, he plumped the pillows behind her head. Then he helped her recline on them so she could get to him easily. Holding out his arm, he said, "Do it, baby. Take as much as you need."

Taking his wrist, she spoke lovingly. "When I do, it will probably arouse you. Thought you'd want to know because of what Carter did to you. But it should be a very good experience, not a bad one."

He nodded. "The arousal is normal. I know that."

"Yes, between mates especially. There will be a tiny sting, but that won't last. You'll feel pleasure, and there's nothing wrong with that. Nothing wrong with riding it to its natural conclusion."

He laughed, looking suddenly shy for a big, tough wolf commander. "Okay. I'm ready as I'll ever be."

No sense in drawing out his nervousness. Time to show him that allowing his mate to feed from him was the most natural and sensual experience in the world.

Gently, she slid her fangs into the tender part of his wrist. Droplets of blood welled on his flesh and she began to suck. Instantly, a shock of sheer lust went through her body. As she revived from the much-needed blood, she also thrived on the very sexual connection of taking a part of her mate into herself.

He was aroused as well, judging from his shortened breath. Her mate gazed down at her and shifted his position on the bed, sitting so he had access to the zipper of his jeans. As she'd guessed he might, he unfastened his jeans and lowered the zipper. In short order, his cock popped free, red and leaking.

"Yes, my love," she murmured around his wrist. "Like that. Stroke yourself for me."

"God."

Any trepidation he had before went out the window when she started sucking his wrist again. With a groan, he fisted his erection with his free hand and began to pump the rigid flesh. She enjoyed watching her mate pleasuring himself. There was no shame in any sensual act between a vampire and her mate. He was learning this and it was mind-blowing to see.

She took all she needed as he stroked himself faster and faster. Careful not to take too much, she removed her fangs as soon as she was sated and gave him a knowing smile. "I'm going to scoot down to lie on my back. Straddle my face."

"Are you sure?" he croaked. His cock twitched in anticipation.

"Very. I'm more than fine now." She winked. "And I'm hungry in an entirely different way."

"Shit, baby."

Scooting down, she waited as he placed both knees on either side of her head. She loved this position, her big strong mate crouched over her face. Reaching around him, she cupped and kneaded his ass, and began to mouth his balls. The tortured groan that escaped his lips made her smile before she went back to tonguing every part of him she could reach. Every single crease and bit of sweet flesh.

Arms and thighs trembling, he braced himself over her and let her eat and lave him. Finger and suck him. His balls, cock, and taint. Getting him nice and wet, riling him past endurance, right where she wanted him. Taking his cock deep into her throat, she sucked him without mercy, until he was trying desperately to pull back.

"I'm gonna come, honey! Let me fuck you."

Tightening her grip on his fine ass, she released him just long enough to order, "Come all over my face. Mark me, wolf."

His eyes flashed with sheer lust and possessiveness. She'd appealed to the basest part of a shifter and they both knew it. When she took him into her mouth again, he pumped with long strokes, sliding his flesh between her lips. She loved every second, making sure he knew that with the pleased sounds coming from her throat. That drove him higher, higher—

Then he stiffened, yanking himself out. And he came all over her face and throat, pearly streams bathing her with warmth. Marking her, just the way they both wanted.

After squeezing out the last bit of come, he climbed off her and laid his body over hers. Kissed her deeply, come and all, even tasting himself with a growl of pleasure.

"That's a good look on you," he said, obviously proud of himself.

"You put it there." She smiled up at him, and he grunted in male satisfaction.

"You were the instigator."

"Verdict?"

He took her mouth in a sweet kiss. "Everything I could've hoped for, and more."

"No fear?" She waited anxiously for his answer.

"None. Not with you," he said in a low, husky voice. "You were right—being bitten by your mate is nothing like I endured before. It's not even in the same realm."

"I'm so glad." Tears pricked her eyes as she wound her arms around his neck. She toyed with his hair, fingering the luxurious strands threaded with silver.

"No sadness, baby. We're figuring things out, you and me. We've got this."

He kissed her again, then went to work removing her clothes. She offered no protest when he finally had her sprawled naked underneath him and spread her thighs to crouch between them.

"How often do you need to feed?" he asked. "Don't fudge the truth."

"Every day, at least once."

"I'll make sure I'm available to you." Then he frowned. "What if I'm on a mission? Sometimes I might be gone for days."

"We can keep several bags of your blood in storage for me. Fresh from the source is obviously more pleasurable for all parties, of course." He returned her grin and kissed her nose.

"Of course. Problem solved, then."

Done talking for the moment, he bent and placed light kisses on the insides of her thighs and worked his way north. All the way to her slit, where he made her squirm by employing his talented tongue to make her a very happy vampire.

He licked and sucked, showing her exactly the same mercy she'd shown him moments before— none. Before long, she was writhing under his ministrations, every part of her on fire. Impending release coiled in her sex, and when it hit, she couldn't hold back the tidal wave.

"Oh! Gods, yes!"

She bucked into his face, riding the storm. He wrung every last drop, lapping until she stilled, panting, under his hands.

At last, he gathered her into his arms and cuddled her on top of the covers. She snuggled into his chest, listening to his heartbeat and counting herself lucky. After all these lonely decades, since Stefano's murder, she'd found joy again.

"Are you happy?" she asked.

"Yes," he said softly. The truth was in his voice, his touch. "More so than I ever thought I deserved to be again."

"You deserve everything. I'm going to make sure you get it."

"Same here, baby." He paused. "I want you to claim me."

Rising up, she looked down into his earnest face, heart pounding in excitement. "Really? You mean that?"

"I do." He smiled. "I want to plan something special for the two of us, to get away from the madness for a while. Then I want you to claim me as yours, forever."

"Nick." A tear escaped, and she smiled. "I'd love that."

"Then it's done. I don't care what else is going on; tomorrow night, you and I will have some alone time to cement our bond."

"Oh, Nick, that would be amazing."

Snuggling into her mate's side, Calla drifted off. This was how it was supposed to be. Two mates looking forward to their future, not living in fear.

Tomorrow night, for just a while, they would forget their troubles.

And they would be Bondmates, for good.

Eleven

A strangled shout jolted Calla from a sound sleep.

"No! I won't!" Nick thrashed beside her in bed.

"Nick!" She shook him, hoping to wake him without alarming him more. "Honey, it's me."

His reaction was swift, and violent. Moving like a ninja, he pinned her to the bed and hovered over her, teeth bared. He was glaring down at her in the darkness, but his eyes weren't seeing her.

"I'm going to fucking kill you," he growled. "Why won't you fucking stay dead?"

Oh, gods! "Nick! It's me!"

He reached for her throat, and she reacted instinctively—she brought her knee upward and slammed him in the balls. Howling, he fell to his side on the bed and clutched his abused package. Her pulse thudded with fear as she scooted away, watching to see whether he'd go on the attack again.

He didn't. Instead, the rage slowly left his eyes. He stared, waking by degrees until he rose up on one arm, gazing into her face as though he'd never seen her before.

"Calla?"

"Yes. Are you all right?"

"What did I do?" Shame filled his face. "Did I— Oh, God. Did I just *attack* you?"

"It's okay," she said, reaching for him. She wasn't expecting the reaction she got.

Flinging her hand away, he snarled, "It's not okay! I tried to attack my own mate! Christ, maybe this was a mistake."

"What?" No. Not after last night.

"What I said. Maybe we should just stop before I end up hurting you for real."

She couldn't help the bitter laugh that escaped. "You think it takes a physical blow to hurt someone? I can't believe you'd ruin something as special as what happened between us last night by saying these things to me."

"Fuck!"

Propelling himself from the bed, he punched the wall so hard, the stone actually cracked under his fist. She flinched and shrank away from him, starting to become truly frightened. This wasn't the loving, passionate man who'd given himself to her last night.

"You're scaring me," she whispered. Tensing, she prepared to run.

He turned, and in that moment, she saw rationality return. Shame and guilt were close behind as he seemed to shake off the last effects of his nightmare.

"Calla, I'm so sorry," he said hoarsely. "Forgive me."

He moved to the bed and sat next to her, not making any sudden movements as she watched him warily. "I'm sorry," he repeated.

"You can't say our mating was a mistake and expect to brush it away." Her throat burned with unshed tears.

"I didn't mean it. I swear to you." Anguish filled his face. "I was in the grip of the nightmare when I first woke up. Then I lashed out because it drives me crazy that it still affects me like that."

"I understand that, but I can't unhear what you said. I can't forget how you looked when you wanted to strangle me." The tears fell, and she couldn't stop them.

Reaching out, he gathered her into his arms. "I'm sorry. I'm trying. I fight this battle every day and I'm scared I'm going to lose."

"I'll fight it with you! And you *won't* lose, as long as you don't quit on me." She sniffed. "But maybe you do need some space. Maybe I've pushed you too hard."

"Never," he denied.

Then he kissed her. Despite herself, she leaned into him, seeking more. She wanted him, and nothing would change that.

Nick brought one hand around and gently placed a finger under Calla's chin, tilting her face upward. Their eyes locked and, despite her hurt, she returned his desire in equal measure. Vaguely, she remembered her suggestion to give him some space. To hell with that. She fervently hoped he would kiss her again. She wasn't disappointed. He cradled her close and took her mouth, savoring her. At last he drew back and regarded her silently for so long she started to worry.

"What are you thinking?"

"That we need some time alone," he said, touching her face. "Just you and me. Some hours away to take things slow and enjoy each other, see where things go."

She liked that idea, a lot. "What do you have in mind?"

"Have dinner with me tonight."

"Where would we go?" she asked. Her pulse quickened in excitement at the thought of a real date with her Bondmate.

"I'm not sure, but I'll work out all the details by tonight," he said with a half smile. "Do you trust me?"

"You know I do."

"We need this. I need *you*, all to myself for a while. What do you say?"

Finally, she gave him a tentative smile. The hope on his face, and another, stronger emotion, was a balm for her soul. He was such a beautiful man, inside and out. "I think you're right," she said softly. "We do need this."

His smile was brilliant. "I'll pick you up at eight."

"Pick me up? But you're staying here with me," she said in confusion. "Where will you be until then?"

"Yes, I'm staying here. But I have an idea for our getaway, so I can't tell you where I'll be."

She paused, looking up at him as if considering. In truth, she'd forgiven him. Nothing short of nuclear war could have kept her from accepting.

"All right." Intrigued, she nodded. "Eight o'clock it is. How should I dress?"

"Whatever you want. All I'm going to say is, no fast food tonight. I'm pulling out all the stops. Does that suit you?"

"It sounds perfect. I'll be ready," she said, hoping her voice came off confident.

Through her renewed optimism, a dose of doubt crept in. Would tonight be the night? She'd tried to claim him before, with near-disastrous results. There was no guarantee it would be different now, even after their wonderful evening last night.

But the need for her mate was all she had to hold on to.

*   *   *

Late-afternoon shadows slanted across the porch of the cabin Nick had rented.

There had been no time to hire someone to clean, so he'd spent the last few hours scrubbing. Shirtless and dripping with sweat, he stood in the living room and surveyed his efforts with satisfaction.

Every piece of furniture shone and the fresh scent of lemon oil permeated the air. The carpets were vacuumed and everything dusted. There were fresh sheets on the bed, too. At the thought of Calla claiming him, he felt a twinge of unease, but he pushed it down, replacing his fear with thoughts of how sweet and sensual his mate was. He could do this. It was going to be fine.

A throb of pain shot through his almost-healed leg, reminding him of the basilisk, and the rogues and hunters doing their best to get rid of him and his allies. As he rubbed his thigh, his thoughts naturally drifted to their enemy—Ivan Cardenas.

"Very soon, you sick fucker, I'll find out where you're hiding. Then we'll have a whole new ball game, asshole."

Glancing around, he decided the place was ready. All that was left was to fetch his mate.

Jumping in the shower, he got cleaned up quickly. After drying off and getting dressed in a pair of black pants and a blue dress shirt, he took one last look around. Satisfied, he headed out the door.

Smiling to himself, he got into the low-slung

Ford GT and fired it up. The engine started with a throaty purr, and he silently thanked Tarron again for loaning him the car for tonight. He wanted everything to be perfect. A hot car, a rented cabin, and a man determined to fully give himself to his mate—an unbeatable recipe for romance.

The drive didn't take long, and less than half an hour later he pulled up to the entrance of the coven's grounds. Recognizing him and Tarron's car, the sentry there waved him through the gate. Reaching the end of the road at the main entrance, Nick swung the vehicle around in the driveway and saw Calla already waiting. Her expression lit up and she seemed glad to see him.

Hurrying over, she climbed into the car and leaned over, giving him a sweet, slow kiss. "I've missed you, even if it was only for the day."

"It's not like you haven't seen me," he pointed out.

"I know. But I felt like we were miles apart and I hated that."

Taking her hand, he kissed the soft skin on the back of it. "Me, too. I hated feeling like I'd let you down. That's why I pulled away."

"Oh, Nick. You didn't let me down. I don't believe you ever could, unless you gave up on us without a fight."

"Told you, not going to happen—in spite of my big mouth."

"Good."

"You look beautiful, by the way," he said, eyeing her in appreciation.

"Thanks. So do you."

She had on a classic little black dress, sleeveless, that fell just above her pretty knees. The material hugged her curves without being too tight. Her hair was loose around her face and shoulders, and her eyes sparkled. His heart did a weird lurch. His wolf may have claimed her, but it was the man who was falling in love.

Had *fallen*.

The cabin was far enough away from the stronghold to feel like an escape, but close enough that she could teleport them in seconds, if necessary. As far as their safety, he wasn't taking any chances. She'd never see the team of wolves he'd placed in the forest to stand guard for the night.

When he rounded a bend in the road and the structure came into view, Calla gasped in surprise. It was impressive, built of logs and stone, with a wall of glass facing the forest. Chuckling to himself, he made a note not to get dirty in front of the windows, or the guys would get a show.

"What?"

"Nothing. Do you like it?"

"It's beautiful," she breathed as he parked. Getting out of the car, she gazed at their place for the night. "Let's go in."

He unlocked the door and let them in, leading

Calla by the hand. Once inside, she twirled around, wide-eyed, clearly delighted with the fat leather sofas, oak furniture, and soaring ceilings. A dining room had its own space next to the kitchen, and was open to the living room as well.

"Are you cooking?" she asked, looking toward the kitchen. "You did promise dinner."

"Hungry?"

"Starved."

"Then I suggest you open the door."

Looking puzzled, Calla crossed the foyer, peered out the peephole, then opened the front door, where a tall, thin man dressed in a tuxedo stood regarding her down the considerable length of his hawklike nose.

"Good evening, madam," he said, bowing gallantly. He introduced himself as the maître d' of the Duck, the fanciest restaurant in the county. "I'm here with your dinner, and I hope you're famished." He gestured to a rolling cart behind him, laden with covered silver dishes.

Calla's eyes rounded. "All that? I'm glad I'll have help eating it. You can bring it right through here."

"Certainly, madam." He turned abruptly and snapped his fingers toward the open doorway. A younger waiter leapt forward from the shadows to maneuver the cart inside. They followed her to the formal dining room, where they made a great show of setting the dishes just precisely so.

As she watched in astonishment, they spread out two place settings, complete with china, crystal, and flatware. Nick grinned and took in her reaction with immense satisfaction. Calla clearly wasn't used to being pampered, which surprised and pleased him, given her status. He was going to get used to spoiling her. The thought sent a small shiver of happiness through him.

"Will this do, madam?" the tall man asked.

"It looks terrific," Nick broke in. "Thank you for coming all the way out here. We appreciate it."

"Our pleasure, sir."

Nick handed him a large wad of bills and saw them out. When the door was shut and locked firmly behind them, he turned back to her. "Shall we eat?"

"Definitely. It smells wonderful." She sniffed appreciatively.

"I'll get the wine."

Nick reappeared in moments, filling Calla's glass and holding out a chair for her to sit down in. He uncovered the dishes one by one as Calla's jaw dropped in amazement. The table abounded with Caesar salad, seafood linguini marinara, delicate asparagus, fresh bread, strawberries and cream, and two huge slices of cheesecake.

"There's enough here to feed every neighbor within ten miles! I would feel guilty if I weren't so busy salivating," she said, shaking her head in wonder. "You really didn't have to go to all this trouble."

"Oh, sure. Picking up the telephone was a lot of trouble," Nick teased. He loved watching the childlike joy on her face and sensed it had little to do with the food.

Nick filled their plates and they talked quietly, basking in each other's company. The shadow of this morning seemed to fade into the past, for which he was profoundly grateful.

Finally, they turned to the subject of Graham's surprising betrayal. "And Ivan Cardenas?" Calla pondered. "I barely remember him. I certainly didn't know Carter was his mate."

"Neither did anyone else," Nick said. "We're going to find him, though. When we do, he'll have to face justice for trying to overthrow a prince."

"It's really sad," Calla said, her brow knitting. "Grief can do terrible things to a person."

"True. But he was mated to Carter, and since Fate chooses those who are supposed to be perfect for us as our Bondmates, I'm not sure how innocent Ivan ever was to begin with."

"There is that. But he's going to be extremely dangerous, with grief driving him. I know something about that, after Stefano. . . ." She trailed off in apology, but Nick shook his head.

"You can always talk about him. You can say *anything* to me, and I'll always be behind you."

"In some ways, I understand where Ivan is coming from. Carter was evil and he hurt many. He *deserved* what he got. But as a mate, I *get* Ivan's grief.

I didn't go after Stefano's killers—Tarron did—but sometimes I think if I had it to do over again, I would make a different choice." She let out a sigh.

"What would you do, sweetheart?" he questioned softly, taking her hand.

After a pause, Calla took a deep breath, looked him in the eye, and said, "I wouldn't rest until I found the hunters who kidnapped and starved my mate to death. I would follow every lead to the ends of the earth until I skewered the bastards and roasted them on a spit." She looked down at their joined hands.

"Why didn't you?" Nick searched her face and hated the pain he saw reflected there.

"Because I was numb. I couldn't even breathe, much less mount a manhunt. I relied on my brother to exact justice, and he did."

"There's no shame in that, baby."

"I know. But you asked." Her lips curved into a smile and the shadows left. "You know what I would *never* change? Meeting you."

They finished their meal, chatting companionably. When they were done, he wiped his lips with a napkin and said, "We'll leave the dishes. I've got someone coming to clean up and return the dishes to the restaurant tomorrow."

"Thank you," she said. "This was wonderful."

"Oh, the evening isn't over yet." Her smile was worth all the effort of preparation. "Want me to start a fire? It'll get a bit cool tonight."

"Sounds lovely."

Pushing from the table, he took care of that without any trouble. In minutes, a fire was blazing cheerfully in the hearth. Calla had taken a place on the sofa, and kicked off her high-heeled shoes. Settling next to her, Nick took off his jacket and ditched his shoes as well. Then he tucked her into his side and they simply sat for a while, holding each other and enjoying the closeness.

Reaching up, he stroked her dark tresses, running his hand down the length of it. She felt so warm against him, so right. His blood quickened. She shifted a bit so she could look at him, and started to say something. He beat her to it.

"I need you so much," he rasped.

"You have me."

The desire on her beautiful face matched the fire inside him. He brought his mouth down on hers and kissed her slowly at first. Then more hungrily, sending the flames between them leaping. He kissed her deeply, savoring her, as she entwined her fingers in his hair.

Calla sucked in a sharp breath as his attentions traveled downward to the curve of her neck. He liked her reaction. All afternoon he'd been waiting for this. Any lingering fear about allowing her to sink those sharp little fangs into his throat was gone. This was Calla, and she'd never hurt him.

There was no point in denying it any longer— he belonged to her, body and soul. He was ready to be claimed. Her hand snaked upward. Before he realized what she'd done, his shirt was halfway unbuttoned and she was gently caressing his chest. It wasn't enough.

"Take my shirt off."

She didn't need any further encouragement. She helped him tug off the offending garment and sent it flying across the coffee table with a smug smile. His heart hammered as she leaned forward and pressed her lips to his neck, downward to the hollow of his throat, then lower still, across his chest. When her tongue flicked seductively across his nipple, he groaned and felt himself harden.

"Calla, yes."

Emboldened, she explored the scars from various battles that decorated his torso and stomach. There weren't many, due to his shifter healing, but she spread butterfly kisses across each one, as if by doing so she could erase the pain they'd caused him.

"Hang on a second." Spying drapes that would cover the large glass windows, he got up and closed them gladly. He didn't really want to move from their spot, and now they could have privacy.

When he rejoined her, his hand came around to the back of her dress and deftly unzipped it. He watched, spellbound, as she stood and let it fall in a heap at her feet. The undergarments she wore were nothing more than tiny, filmy black scraps. The curve of her breasts swelled generously over the top of her bra. His eyes traveled the length of her, taking in her trim waist. Her long legs, which were well toned and shapely.

Calla knelt before him. He cupped her breasts, brushing his thumbs across the silky material until the hardened peaks tightened. Then his fingers found the clasp nestled in the center, and he freed her. She looked at him with naked desire, so powerful it nearly made him lose control right then.

"Tell me you'll claim me," he said hoarsely. "Because I want this, baby. For real."

She looked deep into his eyes. "Only if you mean it. If you're really ready."

"I am."

Reverently, he caressed her face. The dancing firelight illuminated her skin and caught her hair in a cascade of fiery highlights. She must've been part Sorcerer, because she'd cast a spell on him.

"God, you're beautiful."

She took his hand and drew him down to the rug in front of the fire. He straddled her with his knees on either side of her hips, looking down at her. Chestnut hair fanned out from her sides, around her shoulders. Her skin was the color of cream. As she captured him with her entrancing green eyes, he knew he wouldn't rush this. Calla deserved so much more than him, but he was hers and he wouldn't let her down again.

Nick bent over her and took a rosy-tipped breast in his mouth. She gasped in pleasure as his tongue swirled lazy circles around it and his teeth grazed it gently. He splayed a hand across her stomach, then continued downward to the silky material of her panties. He sat up, sliding them slowly over her legs. For a moment, he could only stare. She was every inch his princess.

His mate gave him a wicked grin, pulling at his belt. "It's your turn. It's only fair, you know."

He laughed and stood, shedding the rest of his clothes, then hesitated. This was it. He would be fully, completely bonded to a woman he loved for the first time since that hot summer night that nearly destroyed him. Awful memories crowded in, threatening to overtake him. But he wouldn't let them. Not tonight.

"What's wrong?" Her voice sounded from behind him, tinged with concern.

"Nothing, baby. For the first time in years, everything is right."

"Then stop torturing me with your gorgeous naked self and come here," she teased.

Nick turned to face her then, his smile gone and his entire being humming with raw, sexual energy, and another emotion begging to be voiced. He moved to her side and knelt, taking her face in his hands, his expression sober.

"I'm a mess and I don't have a clue why you want the trouble that comes with me and my life with the Pack. But I'm yours, if you'll have me. Yours completely." He held his breath as if his life depended upon her answer.

"From the second we met, I knew you were perfect for me in every way," she whispered, reaching up to slide her palm down his chest. "Nothing else matters but us, my mate."

Nick crushed his lips to hers, plundering her sweetness, tasting. He rolled her taut nipples between his fingers, marveling at how they seemed to be made for his touch. She arched her back in delight as his hands and mouth explored her everywhere, scorching a hot path to her breasts and down the plane of her soft belly. When he slowly, deliberately parted her knees and found the warm center of sex, he relished driving her crazy. He brought her to the edge of the precipice with his mouth, again and again, nearly sending them both over.

Finally, she could stand it no longer and pulled frantically at his hair. "Make love to me. Now."

"That's what I'm doing, baby."

He moved over her, covering her body with his own. Grasping her wrists, he placed her hands on either side of her head, palms up, then linked his fingers with hers. As he looked down, the complete trust and utter sensuality on her face was his undoing. Something fierce and primal rose up inside him, a feeling he'd never known before. His. Calla was his, and he'd never let anyone hurt her again.

He thrust inside her, burying himself deep, his eyes never leaving hers. She moaned as he moved with agonizingly languid strokes. Writhing beneath him with wild abandon, she set his body on fire. Gradually increasing the speed of his thrusts, he brought them to a perfect rhythm, her hips rising to meet his. When she wrapped her legs around him, he let go of her hands and cradled her, crushing her against his chest, driving deeper still. He was certain he would never feel closer to anyone than he felt right now.

"Do it," he groaned, cupping the back of her head. "Claim me."

He tilted his head to the side, heart about to pound out of his chest. She struck quickly—and his world detonated.

The pleasure was like nothing he'd ever known, but it was more than a physical sensation. With her fangs buried deep in his throat, marking him as hers for all time, the ecstasy was almost too great to be endured. It was as though every cell in his body had been blasted like a supernova, turned inside out and made joyful and whole again.

They rode the pulsating, crashing waves together to a feverish pitch, until neither could stop the tide. They tumbled over the precipice of their release together, clinging tight to each other. With one last thrust, his passion exploded into a million tiny shards. Holding her close, he shuddered as he spilled his seed deep within her.

He was alive. At last.

His Bondmate clung to him, riding the last wave before floating softly to earth.

"Oh, my gods," she moaned, burying her face in his neck.

"Are you okay?" he asked in alarm.

"What?" she said, blinking at him owlishly.

"Did I hurt you?" Anxiety flipped his guts into a pretzel.

"No! Not a chance." She gave him the sweetest smile. "That was simply wonderful."

Not realizing he was holding his breath, he let it out in a rush. "For me, too, baby. That was incredible."

"How do you feel?" she asked, smoothing back his hair to peer into his face.

"I'm good. No, fantastic." Rolling onto his back, he pulled Calla with him, his arms steel bands around her. *Can you still hear me?* he pushed into her head.

Yes, she thought back, then giggled.

"I heard you," he said.

"It works!"

"That it does." He couldn't be happier, or prouder, of his mate.

She sighed in contentment, settling her head onto his shoulder.

They stayed entwined for a long while, basking in the glow of their lovemaking, reveling in their mating. They touched constantly, spoke in low tones, reliving the moment she'd claimed him.

It was beautiful to him, and he made sure she knew it.

"Calla?"

"Hmm?" She lifted her head to peer into his face. Maybe she sensed what he was going to say before the words left his mouth.

"I love you."

Her eyes misted with tears as she smiled and stroked his hair. "I love you, too. So much."

The entire night was more than he'd ever dared to dream. He'd hold on to this feeling with both hands, as long as he could.

Until the day he stopped breathing.

Holding Nick's hand, Calla walked with him toward the dining room. She couldn't be prouder to be at her mate's side.

Word had spread like wildfire this morning that their bonding was complete, and official. All it took was for one vampire to spot the mark she'd left on his neck, and the news spread almost as fast as if she'd posted it on the Internet. Gossipy vampires. For once, she didn't mind.

Now it was lunchtime, and as they walked in, conversation ground to a halt. Then the clapping started and her wolf commander grinned sheepishly at his new extended family before following her to Tarron's table. Her brother was sitting with Ian and Teague, and the two were in deep discussion as she and Nick sat down.

"I'm searching as fast as I can," Teague was saying to Tarron. "I'll find that account and what Graham sent. I just need a little more time."

"That's a luxury we don't have at the moment," Tarron snapped. "Don't give me excuses. Just do your fucking job."

Teague flinched, mouth pressing tightly closed in anger and embarrassment. Calla's brows rose. She wouldn't dare correct her brother in front of their coven, but she could make her irritation patently clear without words. When he met her gaze, she made sure her expression was as glacial as possible. He blinked at her, and then looked down at his plate of fish and chips as though it held the answers.

When he raised his head, he met Teague's gaze straight on and apologized. "I'm sorry. The tension is getting to all of us, trying to figure out what they have planned, and I took it out on you. Forgive me."

The tech's expression eased. "No problem, man. It's all good."

Calla couldn't help but grin. Only Tarron's inner circle of good and trusted friends could get away with addressing him so informally, or not even think of refusing his apology. Lunch proceeded without further unpleasantness.

Until Nick's cell phone rang. "Sorry about that," he said, pulling it out. "I know it's not polite to answer your phone at the table, but with everything that's been going on . . ."

Tarron was in the same boat, so everyone understood. Calla heard Nick greet Selene, clearly happy to hear from his daughter, and she relaxed. The feeling vanished, however, when he paled and pushed back from the table.

"What?" he barked, his fork clattering to his plate. "How bad is he?"

She and Tarron exchanged a look of alarm as Nick paused. Leaning in, she touched her mate's arm, lending silent support as they listened.

Nick stood, expression filled with rage. "I'll be there as quickly as I can. Hang on, honey. I'm coming."

As soon as he ended the call, she stood as well and took his hand. "Who's hurt, my love? Is it Zander?"

"No, it's my brother." His jaw worked as the tortured emotions flooded his face. "Damien's car was ambushed by more than a dozen hunters and rogue vampires, and three of his men were killed."

"Is he . . . ?"

"No. But Selene doesn't know if he's going to make it." Suddenly he looked stunned, as though that reality was just sinking in. "I've been so fucking angry, so intent on making him pay again and again for our past. And now I might lose the chance to reconcile with him before I even get my head on straight about him and me."

"You need to go to him."

"Yeah." Looking lost, he ran a hand down his face.

"I'm going with you."

He didn't argue with her as they left the dining room in a hurry. Silently, she sent up a prayer to whatever powers were listening for Nick's brother to survive.

For both of their sakes.

Twelve

Nick was losing his mind.

None of the vampires could teleport him to his brother's Pack in the Smoky Mountains of Tennessee, because none had ever been there before. Nick himself was sketchy on the exact roads, since it had been more than twenty years since he'd last set eyes on what was little more than a camp.

So Tarron had his private jet carry him, Calla, and Zander, plus a few Alpha Pack members, as far as Gatlinburg, and had a car waiting to take them the remaining thirty miles to Damien's clan. With every mile, Nick berated himself for holding on to his anger for so long. Yes, he had reason to be furious with Damien. The man had thrown him out of the clan and taken Nick's child to raise.

But Damien had been following Pack law to the

letter. Their father had raised them to adhere to the strict rules, and everyone knew there was no excuse not to obey them. Nick deserved to pay a steep price for using his gift to the detriment of another, even if his heart had been in the right place.

That didn't make Damien's actions hurt any less. Didn't make the ache in his soul go away. Losing the brother he had idolized. His mate. His daughter.

Even with Calla at his side lending her quiet support, the thoughts chased around and around in his brain. The guilt.

He'd promised he would try to meet Damien halfway, to repair their relationship. So far he'd done nothing to make good on that promise. Dozens of deleted messages weighed like an anvil on his chest.

When the car turned down the road to the clan's spread, Nick found it hard to breathe. The last time he had been there had ended so horribly, with such finality, he knew he'd never be back. And yet here he was.

His first impression was one of near shock. Instead of the ramshackle sprawl of wooden cabins he'd left behind, a well-ordered village of brick buildings had taken its place. The family homes were small, but they were attractive and well maintained, set back from paved streets and sidewalks. There was even a store or two nestled among them.

Damien had provided well for their clan. Better than Nick could ever have done.

Memories flooded his mind, and along with them a sense of melancholy. Time hadn't stood still, and when Nick found himself searching for the modest house he'd shared with Jennifer and Selene, he was a little saddened to realize it no longer stood. That caused an ache in his heart he figured might never totally go away.

"Honey? We're here."

A gentle touch on his arm brought him from his musings. Calla was looking at him with compassion, and his throat tightened. "I don't know if I can do this."

"You can. He wants you here, so focus on that and nothing else, okay?"

Nodding, he took her hand and they got out of the car. After giving her a quick kiss on the lips, he turned at a woman's voice calling to him. He saw Selene jogging toward them from a two-story building across the street. For a second, he saw her as a smiling little girl with platinum blond hair running toward him with open arms.

The image faded and the girl was grown. But she was no less happy to see him as she threw her arms around him.

"Dad," she said with a sob, burying her face in his chest.

"Sweet girl. How is your uncle?"

Pulling back, she wiped her face with her hand.

"I'm sorry. Actually he's better. It's just that when I heard what those bastards had done to him, and then I saw the shape he was in when I got here . . . I kind of lost it."

"That's understandable," he said quietly. "What about Tag? Is he all right?"

Taggart was Selene's lifelong friend, and a wolf determined to mate with her before she'd met and mated with Zander. Tag hadn't taken the news well at first, but after leveling a warning at Zan to treat her right, he'd backed off.

"Tag wasn't in the car, thank God." She sniffed. "I don't know what I would've done if I had lost him."

"Well, there is me," Zan said, stepping from behind Nick. Immediately he had his arms full of his mate.

"You know what I meant." She gripped Zan tight. "Tag is one of my best friends."

"I'm glad he's okay, sweetheart. Why don't we go see Damien?"

Nick led his family inside the building, which turned out to be the clan's hospital. It was a nice facility, almost as well-appointed as the Pack's new hospital. He couldn't help but be even more impressed. It didn't escape his notice that Damien's care and attention to his clan's needs might ultimately save his life.

A clan doctor met them on the second floor, and Nick made introductions. The doctor introduced himself.

"I'm Dr. Simon York," he said politely, shaking Nick's hand. "Why don't we talk in the family room for a moment?"

Once they were settled, with the doctor seated in front of them, Nick asked, "How's Damien?"

Dr. York nodded. "Weak, but hanging in there. He suffered multiple lacerations, sustained both from the wreck caused by the attack, and the fight itself. He's had internal bleeding, which we've managed to stop, and a few broken bones, which will mend when he shifts."

"When will that be?"

"Depends on Damien. The Alpha is healing quicker than we thought he would, which is a terrific thing. Could be tonight, but more likely tomorrow."

"So, in your opinion, he'll survive?"

"Yes. He passed the critical point while you were en route, took a turn for the better. I'm confident he'll be good as new in no time."

Nick pushed aside the relief he felt. "May I see him?"

"Sure. Room two twelve. He's been asking for you."

He had? That choked Nick up all over again, and Selene, too. Now that the crisis was past, he was tempted to run again. Far and fast. But he couldn't do it. Not this time. Not when he'd almost lost his brother.

He did let Selene and Zan go in first, though.

Selene had been in already, but Zander wanted to pay his respects to her uncle. Then a couple of Damien's clan, but they didn't stay long. Too soon, it was Nick's turn.

Walking to the room on wooden legs, he had no idea what to say. Then he was out of time to think, because he was through the door and Damien was lying there, face cut and bruised, lip busted. His arm was in a cast and there was an oxygen cannula in his nose. Dark hair was swept back from his face and he stared at Nick hard for a few seconds before his expression crumpled.

"I thought I was being a good Alpha. I followed the letter of the law instead of my heart," he whispered. He didn't bother to hide the sheen of moisture in his eyes. The devastation. "Forgive me, brother, please. I can't stand to face one more day knowing I drove you away when you needed me most."

Nick's legs started moving, and before he knew it, he was crouched at Damien's bedside. Pulling his brother into his arms, he choked, "I forgive you. I've got a long way to go to forget, but I do know I don't want to be without my brother in my life."

"That's a good start."

"Yes."

After a few moments, Nick forced himself to let go and took a seat in a nearby chair. He wasn't sure what to say, so he settled on his first impression. "You've done so much for the clan. You've turned it into a community to be proud of."

Damien's smile was pleased, but not for himself. "The clan pulled together to do all the work. I just made the money available from the clan account to make improvements and boost our businesses and jobs."

"You know, you sound nothing like Dad in your vision of what community looks like," Nick observed. "He didn't believe in spending clan money. We never could convince him that funneling the yearly dues back to the community would help everyone in the long run."

"Thanks." Damien flushed at the compliment. "He was a good man, but stuck in the seventeenth century."

"Literally."

"Yeah."

They were sharing a smile, and it was weird. But good, too. His brother's exhaustion took over, and slowly his eyes drifted shut. Nick sat by his side for the longest time, studying his face and thinking about how lucky he was to have the chance to rediscover their bond as brothers.

This time, Nick meant it.

More people came in to visit, and left. Nick began to doze, and at some point he realized that the sun had vanished and he was covered with a blanket. His chair had been reclined and his head was resting on a pillow. *Calla.* She always knew what he needed, and right now that was to be here.

Before he knew it, early sunlight was filtering through the drapes. Yawning, he stretched and looked at his brother—to find him curled up in wolf form. He couldn't help but laugh softly at the sight of the big brown wolf taking up the bed, snoring. At least he was healed.

Rising from the chair, Nick slipped from the room and went in search of his mate. He didn't like that he'd been away from her, but surely she'd understood. Spying the nurses' station, he walked over.

"Excuse me. I was hoping to find—"

"Ooh, you must be the Alpha's brother," one young nurse enthused. "You look so alike!"

"Yes, I'm Nick Westfall," he said politely. "I'm looking for my mate but I'm not sure where she went."

"I think Taggart put her in cottage number eight. It's just across the street."

"Thank you."

The nurses were giggling as he walked off, though he couldn't fathom what was so amusing. He quickly crossed the street and knocked on the cottage door. Before he could open his mouth or knock again, the door was yanked open and Nick was pulled inside.

Calla hugged and kissed him soundly before

ushering him to the sofa. He sat with a groan. "Feels good. That chair about did me in."

"Sorry. I should've got you up to come to bed."

"No, I was glad to be with him." He squeezed her hand. "I think we've finally made a start on repairing things. It'll take a while, but it can be done."

"That's so great," she said, smiling.

"Yeah."

When his cell phone rang, he groaned again. "I'm seriously going to run over that thing with my SUV if it rings one more time."

He looked at the screen. "It's your brother," he told her. "Crap, it's early." He had barely greeted the prince when Tarron broke in. "Nick, I need you back at the stronghold! You and your men. Leave Calla there, but come back as soon as you can!"

He frowned. "Why? What's going on?"

"Teague found the file that Graham sent Ivan before he died. It was a detailed blueprint of the fucking stronghold!"

"Shit!" He met Calla's eyes. So *that* was how Ivan planned to destroy the coven—a direct attack. God.

"Every single fucking room, corridor, doorway, every detail! We're already evacuating the women and children—"

Tarron's words were cut off by a loud noise coming from the other end. A boom that echoed through Nick's brain and made his blood turn to ice. "Tarron? Tarron!"

There was no answer. The line went dead.

"What is it?" Calla asked, voice rising. "What's happening?"

"The file Graham sent to Ivan contained detailed blueprints of the stronghold. Tarron was telling me about evacuating the women and children, and the line went dead."

Her face paled. "Oh, my God!"

"I'm going and I need you to stay here—"

"No! I can help! You'll need me to teleport you there and bring men back here to get the rest of your team, now that I know where it is. It'll be much faster than hours traveling by plane and car. If they're under attack, they need us now!"

One look at his mate's determined expression and he knew there was no point wasting time on an argument he wouldn't win.

"Fine. But when you get my men back to the stronghold, you get the hell out and go to the Pack compound. You'll be safe there until your brother and I hand those guys their asses."

He didn't wait for an answer but rounded up the rest of his team and explained the situation.

"This isn't going to be easy," he finished up. "They've been ambushed, and it's up to us to turn the tide in our favor. Questions?"

"How soon can we kick some sorry ass?" John growled.

"That's the spirit."

They were going to need more of it to beat some really bad odds.

Calla never thought she'd experience the terror of actually watching her beloved mate rush headlong into battle. Especially to save her coven.

The grand foyer was smoking rubble, the scene chaos. Blood ran thick on the stone floors, and everywhere the screams of the injured and dying rang out in the morning air. Horrible. Incongruous with the start of a new day that had been filled with such hope.

Losing sight of Nick, Calla forced herself to focus on her task. She summoned three guards who were running past.

"Princess, we have to fight!" one cried.

"First you have to come with me to get the rest of the commander's wolves! We need all the help we can get!"

The number of rogues and hunters was almost overwhelming, perhaps two to one in the enemy's favor. She couldn't believe what she was seeing.

Just then, a pair of hunters appeared, carrying rifles. Quickly, Calla grabbed the guards and vanished, teleporting back to Damien's compound. Nick's men were waiting on the lawn in front of the hospital building, along with every able-bodied man, it seemed.

And Damien himself. The man looked exhausted, but fiercely determined. "My men are at your disposal, Princess."

Tears stung her eyes. "I'm grateful, but do you understand the risk? Chances are you'll suffer losses."

"There's no greater loss I could suffer than to lose Nick now," he said. "Our clan is behind you."

"All right. You have my thanks, and my friendship. Whatever you need after this day, I'll see that you have it. But we have to go. I'll send more guards after you and your wolves."

"We'll be waiting."

She and the guards teleported Nick's men, who instantly shifted and joined the fight. She lost track of them in the mass of bodies clashing. Swords flashed; gunshots popped. In front of her, two wolves attacked and dodged by turns, slashing at the rogues, muzzles bright red.

Neither of them was a white wolf, and her heart cried out for her mate.

Nick?

Calla, hide! Stay safe!

She wasn't a fighter. But today, she had to be. If she hid like a coward, there was no way she would ever be able to face her people again. Moving swiftly, she ran, dodging combatants and searching the fallen for weapons. There! A hunter was facedown, a pistol in hand. Crouching briefly, she pried the gun from his dead hand and sprinted for a pillar some thirty yards away.

It wouldn't afford much cover, but she could get off a few good shots before—no. Best not to think of that.

A sting pierced her side, but she kept going, ignoring it. Once she had achieved cover, she observed the fight and chose her marks carefully. Tarron had taught her to shoot, and she wasn't bad at it. A short distance away, a brown wolf was fighting a rogue. A hunter was sneaking up behind the wolf, taking aim with his rifle. Calla brought up the gun and fired a round into his skull, and he dropped like a stone.

The wolf shot her a look of gratitude before finishing the rogue. She made several more kills before the hair stirred at the back of her neck. Whirling, she found herself face-to-face with a rogue, teeth yellow, fetid breath making her gag. His eyes, however, were wide and the tip of a sword was protruding from his chest. He fell, and Tarron pulled the sword from the rogue, then decapitated it for good measure.

"Thanks," she shouted.

His face was a mask of anger. "What the fuck are you doing out here? Get to safety!"

"No! I can fight! I've killed several of the enemy already!"

Her eyes widened as she spotted a hunter rushing at Tarron from behind. Gritting her teeth, she shot the bastard between the eyes, and he fell at her brother's heels. "See?"

"Thanks," he rasped, shaking his head. "But I don't want you here. Please, sis, go."

"I can't. You need me."

There wasn't time to keep arguing about it. A new surge of the enemy came at them like a solid wall, and bitter fear clogged her throat. There were more of them than before. Where were Damien and his wolves?

A hoarse shout sounded at her back, and her blood froze. She spun in time to see Tarron fall, crimson spreading across his chest.

"No!"

She tried to run to her brother, but a hand fisted in her hair from behind and slammed her face into the pillar. The world spun on its axis.

Nick! Tarron's down! Help me!

Then all went dark as she was lifted and carried away.

God help them all. This wasn't a fight—it was a slaughter.

Nick had shifted to his wolf form as soon as they dove into the battle. If he hadn't, he'd already be dead. His wolf was faster, more agile. Able to take more physical abuse before he went down for good.

His focus was narrowed to a razor-sharp point. Seek. Attack. Kill. Move on.

There was nothing but blood and death. The only question was who would be the next to fall.

All around him, Tarron's men lay broken on the stone floor. Many beheaded. No coming back from that.

Nick tried to keep tabs on his own team, but it was impossible to spot them all.

Aric was the first of them to fall.

Nick almost got himself beheaded as he whirled to see the red wolf lying in a dark pool of blood. His eyes were closed, and it was impossible to tell whether he was alive. Forcing himself back to the fight, he shut out the grief. The fear. Nothing could keep him breathing but rage.

And love. This was his family. The enemy was trying to take that away, but he wasn't going to let that happen. No matter how badly they were out-numbered.

Across the foyer, he saw Kalen grow still, Sorcerer's staff in one hand. Kalen's eyes closed as he concentrated on whatever spell he was going to unleash on the enemy. Nick silently urged him to hurry.

But a cruel laugh rose above the mayhem. Nick's guts twisted as he saw Jinn appear a few feet from his Sorcerer, eyes gleaming with malice and antic-ipation. Quickly, Nick shifted to human form.

"Kalen, look out!" he shouted. Just in time.

Kalen's eyes flew open and he assessed the new threat briefly before they engaged in a magical battle the likes of which Nick had never seen. Lightning shot through the rooms and bounced off the rocky walls. Sparks rained down as black and white magic clashed, battled for dominance.

The two magicians were snarling at each other, teeth bared, muscles straining as they faced off. Threw spell after spell in an attempt to overthrow the other. Nick shifted back to his wolf and started toward Jinn, hoping to distract him long enough for Kalen to win the fight.

Then a pair of hunters came at Nick and he was forced to face them.

Redoubling his efforts, he fought on.

Calla came awake gradually, her head pounding. When she finally became aware of her surroundings, a number of things seeped into her brain.

First, she had no idea where she was, but wherever that might be, it was uncomfortably chilly. Second, she wasn't alone. Stretching, she found herself lying on her right side on the hard floor, pressed into the curve of someone's body. Wetness invaded that side, and she shivered.

Next she realized that her clothing was disheveled. She was barefoot and her jeans were torn. Since her left wrist was handcuffed to something metallic, she clutched at her shirt with her right hand. Still there, not torn.

Opening her eyes, she tried to focus her vision. Somewhere above, a dim bulb chased away the shadows of the dank room—and far above that, she heard sounds of a distant battle.

"Nick!" It all came rushing back. Tarron had fallen, and someone had hit her, knocked her out. Who was next to her? What was this place? Lifting her head, she saw a steep flight of stairs in a far corner with a metal railing running down the side. Finally, she recognized the space as an old storage area below the stronghold's living quarters.

A low, anguished moan broke the silence behind her. With sudden, startling clarity, she knew exactly who was there and braced herself. He'd been bleeding, badly injured, and was bound to be in bad shape. She maneuvered onto her stomach, then her left side. Shock and outrage left her gasping.

"Oh, Tarron, no."

Although grateful to find him alive, how this was possible she couldn't imagine. A savage beating had left his body broken and bloodied, the purple bruising forming a multitude of fist-sized patterns all over his torso. Straining against the shackles around his wrists and ankles had cut deep gouges, exposing the bone. The wound in his chest might be from a gun or blade. She couldn't tell. But it was oozing red, his vampire healing not quite sealing off the gash. Hopefully it would close soon. While she'd been out, someone had been methodically torturing him.

Reaching out, she placed her palm on his cheek. Cold. Too icy, his skin dry rather than hot and sweaty. He struggled with each breath, the sound like the rustle of crackling leaves deep in his chest.

If someone didn't find them tonight, or she couldn't orchestrate their escape, he would surely die.

They would die anyway, if their side lost the battle.

"Tarron, can you hear me?" Carefully, she tilted his head slightly toward hers.

He stirred and opened his lids with a great deal of effort. His eyes, normally so warm and full of love and humor, were like spun glass. Drugged as well? What the hell could those bastards have in their possession that would drug a vampire? Anger fired her blood. Tarron gazed at her with the barest spark of recognition. Indeed, she wondered whether he was aware of what was happening.

"Do you know who I am?" she tried again.

His face clouded in confusion. For several seconds he stared as if trying to make sense of what she was saying. Then something flickered in his expression.

"Sis?" he rasped. Hope.

Her heart cracked. "Yes, brother. It's me, Calla," she said softly.

His brow furrowed, then cleared again. "Calla," he pleaded, straining. "Got to get free. Get back. . . . Help them."

Her throat threatened to close up.

"Neither of us is going anywhere for now. Stay with me, Tarron. Do you hear? Just hang on. They're gonna find us real soon." That, she feared, was an outright lie. Nick, his team, and Tarron's men would be frantically scouring the stronghold looking for them soon—but only if they won the fight. If they didn't . . . Well, she tried not to think of what Ivan would do to them when he came.

And he would come; she was sure of that.

Tarron's lids fluttered closed again and his body shuddered as he let out a long sigh. He'd gone completely still, and for one panic-stricken moment, she thought he'd stopped breathing. Then there it was, the shallow rise and fall of his chest. He hadn't given up.

"That's it. Keep fighting," she encouraged.

Gently, she caressed his cheek, stroked the sable hair falling to his shoulders. Perhaps her touch could keep him connected to this world long enough to make it out of here.

Her thoughts turned to Nick. She was numb with terror for him. Ivan could use her and Tarron to lure him into some sort of trap, even if the battle went in Nick's favor. What, if anything, could she do to thwart Ivan's plans?

"Calla."

Tarron's soft murmur jarred her. His eyes were open again, looking at her with such intensity, she shivered.

"In my pocket," Tarron gasped. "Take it."

Falling silent, he let his eyes close again. She studied his jeans, but there didn't appear to be anything in his pockets. Still, she reached with her free hand into his right front pocket. Nothing, save a ball of lint. Next, she wormed her hand down into the one on the left. The tip of her index finger bumped something and she dug deeper.

Calla's fingers closed around something oblong and smooth. Immediately, she knew what he'd wanted her to find. Drawing it out, hope flared as she perused the object. It was a small pocketknife, about three inches in length. A dot of hope began to grow inside her as she held the tool.

Securing the knife, she wedged her thumb and index finger in the groove of the main blade and pulled. The first time, the knife slipped from her grasp. The second time, the blade popped open. Now she had to decide how to position it. She settled on making a fist with the blade protruding between the two middle fingers of her right hand. It wasn't ideal, but it was the best she could do, and she silently thanked her brother.

Ivan or one of his underlings would be here before long. The small knife was her only protection and she would save it until absolutely necessary. Then what? The small blade was a one-shot proposition. Calla tucked her right hand under her body, hidden from view.

And she waited for the devil's return.

Thirteen

Nick wasn't sure how long he'd fought before he realized that Calla and Tarron had disappeared.

Quickly, he dispatched the closest rogue and curled his lip in disgust. They weren't difficult to tell from the good vampires. The dirty teeth and sour breath gave them away, if the madness in their eyes didn't.

Leaping over the body, he frantically searched the living area. He fought his way into the ballroom, sad to find the once-glorious room in shambles, along with the rest of the place. Strangely, broken furniture was heaped in piles everywhere. Then the distinct stench of kerosene reached his nostrils and he knew what the bastards had planned.

They were going to set the stronghold on fire.

The flames wouldn't destroy the mountain itself, but everything and everyone trapped inside would die. He couldn't let that happen, and he still had to find his mate and brother-in-law.

"Nick!" Micah yelled, avoiding a blow that would have taken his head. "They're going to light this place up!"

Nick shifted back to his human skin as well, so he could yell back.

"I know! Get as many people as you can to find fire extinguishers, and to douse the interior with water, anything that will stop the flames!"

"On it!" Micah spun away and started shouting orders to that effect.

Maybe there was hope for the kid yet.

Not bothering to shift again, Nick worked his way through the living and dining areas. Then he began to search the corridors, and off the main living area, he found a stone staircase that descended below the earth. There was no doorway, just a wide opening and the steps. He peered around the corner, listened. There didn't seem to be any movement from below, so he took a step.

The blow from behind caught him off guard.

Propelled forward, he fell. Tumbled down the stairs until his skull slammed into the sharp edge of a step and the world went dark.

The pounding wouldn't stop. The relentless thrumming, the roaring in his ears. Eerie laughter meshed painfully with the noise in his head. God, his head. He tried to reach up, only to find that his hands were tied behind his back. Tugging on the bindings didn't help.

Nick opened his eyes and attempted to focus, but it was like trying to see through crimson wax paper. Blinking helped a little, but his vision was still blurry. Was that Ivan's voice? Nick squinted and could just make him out.

The vampire was standing over Calla, laughing. The glint off the massive blade in his hand made Nick's blood run cold. Nearby was a gun Ivan had obviously laid on the floor where he thought it would be out of reach. *Think again, asshole.*

Nick put all of his concentration into sitting up. Pain lanced through the back of his skull as he pushed himself up on his knees. Sickness rose and he fought it down.

"Calla, my dear, your quick tongue is one of the things I've always admired about you," he was saying in amusement. "I'm going to enjoy that tongue, too."

Nick's movements caught the vampire's eye. "Ah, there you are. I suppose it's time now to get on with business. I was going to send your mate's brother on his way first, but there hardly seems to be any point now, does there? He'll die soon enough, and he's not the one who wronged me anyway."

"You sonofabitch," Nick breathed, shaking with fury. Indeed, Tarron hadn't stirred. If not for his labored breathing, Nick would have thought he was dead. "If you've wanted to kill me for so long, why don't you just do it? Here's your opportunity, you bastard. There's no need to hurt anyone else."

"Nick." Calla's broken voice tore at his heart, but he didn't meet her eyes.

"*Savoring* killing you is nearly as satisfying as acting upon it will be, I think. First you will watch me kill your mate, as you did mine."

Above them, the battle still raged. Nick felt helpless, not knowing which way the tide was turning. Anger swamped him, and he pulled on his bindings, trying to rip them with brute strength. They gave some, but Ivan's reaction was quick.

In an instant, the blade was pressed against Calla's throat. "Move one muscle, and I'll slit her lovely neck. Keep still and she'll live a bit longer."

The vampire leaned over her. His free hand groped under her sweatshirt until he found a breast and squeezed. She gasped in pain, tears filling her eyes.

Nick's wrath bubbled up in his chest, hot and roiling. No matter what, he wouldn't sit by and let Ivan rape her. The sonofabitch would kill them anyway, so he had nothing to lose. But before he could get to his feet, he saw her right hand swing upward. Nick thought she intended to slap him and pushed up quickly. Then her fist, clutching a small pocketknife, connected with Ivan's face and he leapt away, holding his cheek, blood pouring from between his fingers.

"Bitch!" he screamed. "Goddamn bitch!"

Nick was already closing the distance, his heart in his throat. Ivan lunged for her, thrusting his huge blade outward. Nick barreled into him, blocking the assault with his own body and knocking the vampire to the floor. Nick fell across Calla, panting, pain spreading through his side in rolling waves.

"Give me your wrists! Hurry!" she cried.

Nick sat up and held his hands toward her, his eyes never leaving his enemy. Still clutching the knife, Ivan was getting up now, murder etched on his features. A deep, ugly gash ran the length of his cheek. Calla frantically sliced off the thin nylon bindings. Keeping himself in front of her, Nick grabbed the gun from the floor and pointed it at the other man's chest. The wicked blade in Ivan's hand was covered in blood.

The vampire saw the look in Nick's eyes—the look of a man pushed completely over the edge—and seemed to realize he was carrying a knife to a gunfight.

Self-preservation took over. Ivan turned and dove toward the stairwell as Nick opened fire. The killing shot sailed over his head, slamming against the far wall. He scrambled up the stairs, bullets pinging off the railing. None of them connected with their intended target and Nick swore violently.

"This isn't over, Westfall," Ivan shouted. "I'll see you burn in hell!" Then he vanished.

Nick panted, burning with hatred. If he wasn't wounded, dammit, his aim would have been true.

"One of our men will catch him, surely," Calla said in a shaky voice. "Are you okay?"

"I'm fine," he lied, turning to face her. "Are you all right, baby?"

She started to answer. Then she spotted the wet stain spreading on his naked side and sucked in a breath. "He stabbed you," she moaned. "I thought it was *his* blood on the knife."

"It's not bad, I promise. Listen, we have to get out of here. He's gonna set the place on fire. He's got broken furniture stacked up and soaked with kerosene on the main floor."

"But we're chained up! Leave us here and go for help."

"I'm not leaving the two of you here! Especially when he could double back or send reinforcements while I'm gone. Let me try something. I want you to stand up and hold out your wrist."

"You're going to shoot the links?" She shook her head. "That's dangerous. Only works in the movies."

He shook his head as he projected a message to

Ryon, their Telepath. *Ryon, I'm with Calla and Tar-ron and they're shackled in the basement storage area. Tell Kalen to send a spell through the stronghold to release all metal shackles or something. And I need some clothes, too.*

Got it, the wolf sent back.

A tense few moments went by, and then—

All of the shackles snapped in two with a loud *pop*. Calla jumped back involuntarily at the noise, then checked her hand, and her brother's. They were free.

"It worked!" she shouted. "Let's get out of here."

Just then, a bundle with jeans, boots, and a black T-shirt appeared a few feet away. Nick pulled them on as he spoke to Ryon again.

We're headed up. Situation?

Grim, boss. The wolves your brother brought are helping, but we need an atom bomb. Fast. That fucking Jinn is still keeping Kalen neutralized and unable to bring out the big guns to wipe them all out.

Fuck! *Who can we call on? I don't know how to reach the other covens, and Tarron's in no shape to help me. Who's left, Ryon? Think!*

A moment passed. *Kalen says to get Sariel. He's the only one who has the power to put an end to this thing.*

Sariel? The Fae prince was the gentlest creature Nick had ever known. He had serious doubts about Sariel's skill as a warrior. *Blue's not a fighter.*

He doesn't have to be! He just has to drop that A-bomb we need. That's all. Boss, we can't hold out much longer!

All right, send one of the vampires to get him! Do it now!

"Nick?" Calla asked, bringing his focus back to them. "What's going on?"

"We're sending someone after Sariel," he told her. "He'll try to turn the tables in our favor."

"I hope it works."

"Me, too."

Looking down at Tarron, he knew there was no point in trying to rouse him. Even if he awakened, he was too far gone to have any idea what was happening. Nick tucked the gun in his jeans.

"Come on, big guy," he said gruffly. He bent and gathered Tarron into his arms and lifted him with a grunt. "Calla, stay behind me."

"Want me to get his feet?"

"No. That would leave you exposed." He started off, then hesitated. Turning back to Calla, he sent her a look filled with regret. "Baby, I'm so sorry. For everything. I—"

She put her fingers to his lips. "I love you. Nothing will ever change that." She tilted her face to his and he brought his lips to hers.

"I love you, too, baby," he said. "Now let's get the hell out of here." Shifting her brother higher in his arms, he took the metal stairs, Calla on his heels. At the top, they stepped out into the dim hallway.

And smelled the acrid odor of smoke.

As he climbed the stone staircase to the main floor, Nick's chest and arms ached from the strain of her brother's weight. Compounding the problem was the knife wound in his side, which was worse than he'd led Calla to believe. Already, dizziness threatened to overtake him, but adrenaline propelled him on. As they neared the main floor, the smoke grew thicker. Almost there.

"Baby, when we get up there, I want you to stick as close to my back as you can," he said over his shoulder.

"Do you think he's waiting for you?" she asked worriedly.

"My guess is he's still here somewhere, and he's not going to give up so easily. He's got a lot riding on the outcome," Nick pointed out.

They ascended the final distance to the main floor and stepped through the archway. Nick was nearly knocked down by the blast of heat as he continued on into the main living area. Either Ivan or his thugs had set the piles of furniture and other items ablaze, or at least the ones Nick's men hadn't been able to douse with water, and flames were just beginning to lick up the walls and leap toward the ceiling.

He spotted a ragged hole that had been blown through the rock about fifty yards away.

"There! Let's go!" he yelled above the noise. The roaring flames and the fighting around them obstructed any view of the other routes out of the stronghold.

He wanted to get Calla and Tarron out of here. Then he'd return to the battle.

Starting off, he felt a gentle tugging at his waist and realized Calla was hanging on to one of his belt loops. Ten yards gained, then twenty. Freedom was so close at hand he could almost feel the fresh air on his face. Then he heard the popping. At first he thought it was only noise from the fire. Then a splinter of wood exploded in front of his face.

"Get down!" Nick yelled. He dropped to his knees and laid Tarron on the floor, then grabbed Calla by the arm. He pulled her down next to her brother, then crouched over them, shielding them from the gunfire. Bullets whizzed dangerously close, ricocheting everywhere. He raised his voice above the din.

"Calla, listen to me! I'm gonna cover you. When I say go, I want you to make a run for it!"

"No! I want to stay with you and Tarron!"

"When I tell you," Nick repeated, leaving no room for argument. "Go!" He stood, spun around, and opened fire in the direction of the shooting.

Though she was terrified of leaving Nick at Ivan's mercy, Calla was left with no other option but to run.

She sprinted for the ragged hole, not daring to

look back until she reached relative safety. Gaining the outside, she turned to see whether he would follow and saw Ivan on the opposite side of the room. Nick was out in the open, drawing the other man's attention away from her. It was clear from where she stood that he was firing blind through the smoke and Ivan now had him in his sights.

"Noo!" The scream tore from her lips even as the shot spat from the pistol in Ivan's hand.

The world ground to a stop. Nick's body jerked and he sank to the floor beside Tarron, arms flung out to his sides. She ran into the daylight, her only thought now to get help. Where? After gaining a few yards across the rocky ground she halted, her sides heaving.

There was no one. She clasped her arms to the sides of her head, keening her grief, tears flowing down her cheeks. Ivan was going to murder the man she loved, the man who'd risked his life to save her. To save them all.

The inferno leapt from the torn mountainside into the sky.

"Nick?" Someone was speaking anxiously, patting his face. Hard.

"Wake up, man. We've got to get you guys outta here. Help me!"

Nick opened his eyes, dazed. "John."

"Can you get up? This place is about to go up

like a Roman candle and take every fucking one of us with it. Come on. You can do it!"

"The bullet hit my leg." John helped him sit up. "Think I can make it, though."

"What happened to your side?" The big man pointed.

"Ivan stabbed me with that big fucking knife." Nick grabbed his friend's arm. "Wait. Get Tarron the hell out of here. He's worse off than me. I'll cover you."

The boiling heat was now nearly unbearable. The fight had moved to the fringes and people were scattered.

Nick propped himself on his elbows, ready. "Get him out, now!"

"Hang on," John said grimly. "I'll be right back, okay?" He lifted Tarron into his arms with a grunt, whirled, and took off in as close to a dead run as he could manage.

Nick returned the volley of gunfire, buying John precious seconds. Throwing a look over his shoulder, he almost collapsed with relief to see the man disappear through the hole. He raised his head and caught a glimpse of Ivan sliding along the wall, much closer now.

The vampire was circling around, closing in on him. Nick raised his arm, sighted him, and pulled the trigger. The only response was a metallic *clink*. Empty.

"Shit," he gritted through his teeth. He heaved

the useless object away, wiping blood and sweat from his eyes. His brain screamed at him to shift into his wolf. To fight.

It had to be now. Nick pushed up only to find himself shoved roughly to the floor again. Ivan was standing over him, smirking in triumph, one foot braced on his chest. With the ceiling high above his head consumed by writhing flame, he was struck by how very much the vampire resembled Satan.

"This is how it ends, wolf," Ivan said with a sneer. He brandished the big knife. "It's almost a shame to end our dance, but my mate deserves your blood. Are you ready to die?"

"I'm not afraid to die, Ivan. But I think you should go first!" He grabbed his enemy by the ankle and yanked with all his strength. The other man, caught unprepared, lost his balance and fell onto his back.

Agony seared through his side and leg, but Nick ignored it as he rolled and pushed himself up. Bracing his weight on his good knee, he launched himself at Ivan as the knife swung up. Nick landed on top of him, grabbing his wrist and twisting the blade away from his own body. Locked together, they fought for control of the weapon, nose to nose, staring each other down. Malice gleamed in the depths of Ivan's eyes.

Nick strained, his muscles bunching, the cords of his neck standing out. Though fueled by hatred,

Ivan's physical strength was no match for his. Breath coming in short puffs, Nick began to feel the tide turn in his favor. The other man realized it, too, and snarled in rage. With one last, great effort, Nick wrung the dagger from Ivan's grasp and lunged.

The blade sank deep into Ivan's belly and the vampire's eyes flew wide in disbelief. Nick gave the handle another shove inward, then up, sending it all the way to the hilt. Ivan's hands fell at his sides, an odd gurgling sound coming from his lips.

Pushing himself up, Nick stood, keeping most of his weight on his good leg. He stared down at Ivan impassively, and felt nothing but relief.

"End it," the vampire gurgled. "I want to join my mate."

For a second there, Nick almost believed the vampire felt remorse. "My pleasure. Burn in hell together."

Faster than he ever had, Nick dropped to his knees and shifted. He lunged for Ivan's throat—and ripped it out.

Even though the vampire was dead, Nick savaged the body until there was no hope he could revive. The bastard had touched his mate, terrified her. Had almost killed Tarron and had killed many others.

At last he was done, but the devil hadn't yet reaped his due. To Nick, the final scene unfolded in slow motion, as if underwater. No sound, no sense of time.

Calla ran back into the inferno, screaming Nick's name. John was on her heels, reaching for her.

Across the room, Jax fell at last. Then Ryon, and Micah. They didn't move again.

Rogues and hunters started laughing, celebrating. In wolf form, Nick ran for Calla, ignoring his healing injuries. The battle was all but lost, but he would save his mate. Or die trying.

Then a loud clap of thunder shook the mountain. Pebbles were dislodged from the walls, and people lost their footing. Nick reached Calla and pushed her behind him, backing her toward the escape route—and then stopped to stare in awe at the sight before them all.

Sariel.

The Fae prince was hovering above the now-halted battle, looking down upon their enemies, his face etched with a smoldering rage Nick had never seen before. His hair cascading around him like a jeweled blue waterfall. Matching wings were spread to a great width, easily keeping him aloft above the carnage.

A hunter raised his rifle, prepared to take a shot.

And Sariel reduced the unfortunate man to a puff of smoke with the flick of a wrist.

"Hunter and rogue vermin," his steady voice

proclaimed. "For your crimes against my friends and family, who've never done you any harm, I sentence you to death. Go to the devil, if he'll have you. I really don't care."

With that, his arm swept out and blue fire shot like a torch from the palm of his hand. Everyone hit the ground, friend and foe alike, but the fire only incinerated their enemy. Men screamed, their voices cut mercifully short. Probably a kinder end than they'd deserved—except for the fear they'd experienced while staring at Sariel in shocked awe.

That they'd deserved in spades.

When the cries finally died, the blue flames gentled. They danced among the wreckage, and touched the fallen. Caressed them with care, almost lovingly. Nick's throat grew tight, thinking it was a fitting good-bye to those they'd lost.

And then everyone the flame touched began to stir, and come around with a groan.

"Holy fucking shit," John whispered.

"Nick," Calla said, fingers digging into his fur. "He's—he saved them. Gods, he's saved them all!"

It was true. The injured and formerly dead began to rise, looking down at their whole, uninjured bodies. Patting themselves in disbelief, looking around them with wide eyes.

Uncaring of his nakedness, Nick shifted back. A slow smile spread across his face as Aric, Jax,

Ryon, and Micah came into view. Whole and without a scratch, and totally dumbfounded.

"Nick, what the fuck just happened?" said Jax.

"Sariel just saved our collective asses—that's what." He'd never forget the sight as long as he lived.

Or his debt to the Fae prince.

Calla flung her arms around him, squealing as her confused brother stepped through the hole in the rock. "Tarron's okay, too!"

"I think so," her brother said, walking over. "Jesus, this is unbelievable. Your Fae prince wiped them out."

"That I did," Sariel said, landing in the middle of the group with a flutter of wings.

"I don't know how to thank you," Tarron said, getting emotional. "You saved my coven. My family."

"And mine," Sariel pointed out.

"Still, I know what using that kind of power must've cost you. So thank you." It was all Nick could think of to say.

"I'm all right. I'm a lover, not a fighter," the Fae quipped, "but when I'm called, I'll come. Especially for those I love."

Nick clapped a hand on Sariel's shoulder as his friend went on.

"In my own realm, I'd be executed for what I just did," Sariel said with a half smile. "I'm not allowed to interfere with destiny any more than you are, Commander. But I'd do it again in a second. Know that."

"Thank you," Nick said again. "I don't know how we'll ever repay you."

"I'm sure I'll think of something."

With that, the Fae prince spread his wings and took to the sky, bound for home.

Nick couldn't wait to do that as well. Wherever home was going to be for him and Calla, he didn't care.

As long as he was with his mate, nothing else mattered.

But the next words out of John's mouth gave Nick pause.

"Hey, where's Kalen? I see everybody but him."

Nick frowned. "I haven't seen him since he was battling with Jinn."

That caused some mild concern, but the consensus was Kalen was around here somewhere, that Sariel's magic had destroyed Jinn as well. But as they searched the stronghold, calling Kalen's name, Nick started to really get worried.

Kalen was nowhere to be found. At least not inside.

The search moved to the outdoors. Nick pulled on his clothes again and strode into the sunlight. He, Calla, and the others spread out while Aric and Micah changed to wolf form and tried to catch Kalen's scent. There wasn't a sign of him, until a loud barking reached them from about a hundred yards away.

Grabbing Calla's hand, Nick walked with her through the brush. At last they reached the spot where a group was gathering, all of them staring at a wide black swatch that had been cut through the trees and brush, all the way down the mountain.

Nick nodded at the path. "Looks like maybe Kalen and Jinn fought it out all the way down to the bottom."

Aric appeared worried about his friend. "But that means Kalen and that monster weren't inside when Sariel showed up and saved everyone."

That was a horrible and sobering thought. Some of the guys exchanged looks and then Nick shouted, "Follow the trail to the bottom. Leave no stone unturned!"

Next to him, Calla searched. Nick couldn't understand why if the trail was clear, the sun was out and birds were singing, they couldn't find Kalen. He refused to consider that Jinn had taken him hostage. That would be more than anyone could take right now.

Especially Mackenzie, home with their baby son.

The black path stopped at the bottom, right at the waterfall Nick thought of as his and Calla's. The pool glistened as usual, not a thing out of place.

Except for the Sorcerer's staff rising majestically from the water, embedded in the sand below. Oddly, the staff was still glowing with power. Nick called out and moved forward as others joined him. He was aware of Aric jogging past, and the redhead stopped and stared at the staff in bewilderment.

"What's that supposed to mean? Has that ass-hole kidnapped Kalen?" He started forward.

"Aric, don't touch it," Nick ordered.

He moved to the edge of the pool. "I'm not. I'm just going to see—"

The red wolf broke off as something under the water caught his attention. His eyes widened. And then he shouted, long and loud, the sound filled with anger and pain. He vaulted over the rocks and into the water, yanking furiously at the staff.

"What the hell?" Nick and a couple of the others followed Aric, and when Nick saw what had happened, he struggled not to be sick.

Kalen was there. Under the water, impaled through the chest by his own staff, pinned to the bottom of the pool. His eyes were half-open, small bubbles clinging to his mouth.

"Mother of God."

"Shit! Kalen!"

Working together, they loosened the end of the staff from the bottom of the pool and lifted Kalen out, staff and all. They didn't dare remove it yet.

Carefully, they placed him on his back in the grass and Nick knelt, checking his breathing.

"Need to get some air into him." Tilting Kalen's head into the right position, Nick started rescue breathing. It seemed to take forever, but was probably less than a minute before Kalen coughed, water spewing from between his lips.

That the staff hadn't impaled the Sorcerer's heart was a miracle. Or perhaps that was due to the magical staff protecting its master. Nick snapped his gaze to Ryon. "Get Zander down here, fast."

"Boss, he's not supposed to heal—"

"Do it!"

"Yes, sir."

While Ryon concentrated on contacting Zan, Nick did his best to keep his team calm. Especially Aric, who was losing his fucking mind.

"Get that thing out of him! How's he supposed to heal with that in his chest?"

"Aric, look at me," Nick said calmly. "Probably the only thing that has kept him alive is this staff. And until Zan gets here to tell us what to do, it stays or we could hurt him worse. I know he's your best friend, but you're not helping him if you can't keep it together."

Aric swallowed hard. "Yeah. Okay."

After that, Zan appeared and fell to his knees at Kalen's side with a curse. He took a few moments to examine the wound, then appeared to come to a decision. "Here's what we're going to do. Remove the staff, slowly. As you do, I'm going to heal the wound from the inside out."

"Can you withstand a healing of this type now?" Nick asked. "I won't endanger two of my team."

"I can. I'm much better and I'm immortal now, remember?"

He was. Mating with Selene, a born wolf like Nick, had seen to that.

"You can still die," he said. "Be certain."

"I am. Let's start. He doesn't have much time."

They got to work, carefully inching out the staff as Zan worked his healing talent. The squelching sounds the rod made as it was withdrawn were horrible, making him ill. It was necessary, however, and they kept to the grisly task until at last it was done.

The hole in Kalen's chest was gone, but the danger to him wasn't over.

"I need a couple of vampires to teleport him home, to the compound."

Immediately two volunteers ran forward, and Aric informed him they'd need three. He wasn't leaving his bud until he had to. Another vampire escorted Aric, and the whole group vanished.

"Zan, are you all right?" Nick asked.

"Yes, I'm fine." The Healer stood; he was a bit pale, but otherwise he seemed to be telling the truth.

Selene was still going to chew his ass out. He wasn't looking forward to the confrontation. Nick wiped the blood from his hands on the grass and stood with a tired sigh. Calla wrapped her arms around him and held on, her love the only thing that made sense in this moment.

"Kalen was the last one," Calla said. "He'll be fine and everyone's okay now."

"I hope you're right."

"I am."

Over Calla's shoulder, Nick saw Tarron making his way down the slope. When the prince reached them, he gave them both a collective hug and stepped back.

"Will your Sorcerer recover?"

"We think so, but we'll know more soon. It seems as though Jinn pinned him to the bottom of the pool, thinking he'd drown. But the staff must have saved his life somehow."

"I don't know how magical things work, but that's possible. Perhaps it knows its master somehow and kept him alive."

Nick gave Tarron an apologetic look. "I need to get to the compound and see about Kalen, and check on some things I've been neglecting. I'll leave some men here to help with cleanup, but—"

"Go, Nick." Tarron smiled. "You've spent so much time taking care of us, it's time you took care of your own for a while."

"Thanks."

"You going with your mate, sis?"

"Was that even a question?" She smiled at her brother and Nick.

Nick's heart lightened. Especially when he spotted Damien walking down the slope. Moving toward him, Nick enveloped him in a bear hug and lifted him off the ground.

"Whoa! No PDAs, man!"

He was kidding, though, and everyone laughed, including Nick, who set him back on solid ground and clapped him on the shoulder. "I appreciate you and your clan coming to the rescue."

"It's your clan, too, if you'll accept us back."

The enormity of that statement almost bowled him over. He cleared his throat. "I'd be glad to be a part of the clan again, even though my duties lie at the compound. Whatever I can do to help, I want to take part."

"Music to my ears, brother."

"I really do need to get back."

"I understand," Damien said. "My men and I will stay here for now and assist Tarron. I'll catch up with you later."

"Sounds good." It did indeed sound fine.

Nick hooked his arm through Calla's and they were home in seconds.

Or at least where he hoped would be the permanent home for them both.

Fourteen

Calla's mate's first task on their arrival at the compound was breaking up a catfight. Or was that a she-wolf fight?

Selene had started by tearing into her father for using Zan's healing, even though Zan strenuously protested that he had been careful not to overdo it. When Mac stepped in, the game was on.

"Of course you're going to defend Zan's actions! He risked his health to save your mate!"

"Selene," Mac began. "Zan has been cleared to heal within certain limits. And of course I'm grateful. How could I not be? I love Kalen, and our baby needs his father."

"Oh, pull out the baby card, yeah? You know—"

"Enough!" Nick's voice boomed down the hospital corridor, making everyone jump. "Selene, that's enough!"

Turning, she blinked at him. "Dad."

"I know you love your mate, and so does Mac. Everyone works together here. We're family, all of us, and it serves no purpose for us to be at each other's throats."

Selene hesitated, then looked at Mac, eyes shining with tears. "I'm sorry. I just can't stand the thought of losing Zan the way I did not so long ago. Or almost did."

"I understand," Mac said softly, taking her hands. "I almost lost Kalen like that, too, more than once now. Peace?"

"Yeah."

Dr. Mallory interrupted. "Nick, Kalen would like to see you now. He's still on the mend, so make it short."

"I will." He turned to Calla. "Come with me?"

"Sure."

Kalen was propped up in the bed when they walked in, looking awfully pale with his black hair falling around him. "Nick! How do I keep getting myself into these messes, eh?"

Her mate chuckled. "You're a troublemaker—that's how. Didn't I tell you that the day we met?"

"Not in so many words, but you were right." His grin banished some of the shadows. "So, did you and the guys catch that Jinn creep yet?"

Nick shook his head. "Not yet. We've got feelers out for him in the paranormal community. Now that Ivan's dead and Jinn's got no mission to perform, I'm not sure if that'll make him easier or harder to track."

Some of Kalen's good mood faded. "Yeah. Sorry I couldn't kill his ass. That fucker's a lot more powerful than I gave him credit for at first. He's got more black magic in his little finger than I have in my whole body."

"But your white magic saved you. Don't forget that. Good always wins in the end."

"Does it?" the Sorcerer asked.

"I hope so. That's my story, anyway, and I'm sticking to it."

Kalen gave a quiet laugh. "Sounds like one I can get behind. When I'm out of here, I'll help you guys look for that bastard. I owe him, big-time."

Nick leaned forward. "Did he say why he was pinning you under the water like that? Did he know you'd survive?"

"He said he was doing it because he could," Kalen said thoughtfully. "As for whether he knew my staff would protect me, I can't say. But I would think a powerful creature like him would know that."

"Which means he could've been toying with you."

An idea struck Calla. "I think he left Kalen like that as a message to all of us. He could've killed him and chose not to, this time. But he can get to us anytime he wants."

Those words brought the memory rushing back

again—Nick's vision of Noah being kidnapped by Jinn. Why would the creature want Noah? How would Nix's mate fall into that horrible creature's clutches? His gut churned at this possible future threat, but he put that aside to deal with later. Somehow, he managed to keep the vision to himself.

Kalen nodded. "Makes sense. But does he have the motivation now? Was he that attached to Ivan that he'd seek revenge for his death?"

"I don't know," Nick said. "But I do know he's angry. And that makes him dangerous."

"True." Kalen sat back into the pillows, visibly worn-out. Just then, there was a knock at the door, and Sariel strolled in. Kalen smiled at his half brother, obviously pleased to see him. "Well, if it isn't the hero of the month."

"I do try." The Fae fluffed his feathers and grinned.

"On that note, we'll let you visit with Blue and get some rest." Nick stood. "I'll check on you later."

In the hallway, Calla stood on tiptoe and kissed her mate on the lips. "I think lying down is a great idea. But how about the rest comes . . . *after*?"

"God, baby," he groaned, his cock hardening between them. "I like the way you think. Just as soon as I take care of some business, like finding out what happened to Tom, our mechanic."

Calla sobered and regarded Nick thoughtfully. "He could be anywhere."

"Anywhere Ivan was," Nick corrected.

Just then, a thread of an idea came to him. Something about Ivan and Carter's joint bank accounts—

"They had an address," he said, straightening.

"What?"

"Carter and Ivan had an address in Chattanooga listed on their joint bank accounts. What if Ivan held Tom there?"

"It's a long shot, honey," she cautioned him. "Isn't it more likely he killed the poor man and dumped him in the woods somewhere?"

"Maybe. But even though Ivan was consumed by anger and revenge, he still needed to feed." He shuddered at the thought of the friendly mechanic enduring with Ivan what Nick had at Carter's hands. "I've got to check it out."

She nodded, taking him into her arms. "I understand. Go. I'll be waiting when you get back."

"Thanks, baby. I need to know one way or another what happened to him."

After giving her a lingering kiss, he left. Quickly, he rounded up a few of the team and explained where they were going and why. The guys were in full agreement—Tom hadn't vanished into thin air, and if he was out there, they were going to do their damnedest to find him.

Nick considered taking the Huey, but that area of Tennessee was very hilly and forested. It meant hours of travel, and they'd have to set the craft down miles from their destination. Too much wasted time.

In the end, he was forced to call on Tarron for help one more time, but his new brother-in-law was happy to assist. He'd been to Chattanooga before, and a few of his guard accompanied the team and provided transport. Then they made their way across town to the correct address after they'd searched for the location on the Internet.

Once they appeared on the porch of the house, Nick quickly double-checked the address, then gestured for them to move around back where they'd be out of sight. The house was in a rural area rather than a busy neighborhood, which made sense for a couple of vampires who'd wanted to retain privacy. But they couldn't be too careful.

The lower level of the house was built into the side of the hill, as so many were in the region. At the rear entrance, Nick stood to one side of the door and held up a hand for silence as the rest of the men gathered on either side of him. Once he was satisfied he heard no movement inside, he moved quickly.

Stepping in front of the door, he raised his foot and kicked with all his strength. The wood splintered near the doorknob, and another kick sent the door crashing inward. The lower floor had the look and feel of a basement, he noted as he stepped inside. It wasn't finished. No carpet on the concrete floor, no paint on the walls. Just a serviceable area with a wood stove, a pile of logs beside it. A pool table.

To the right of the pool table was a long hallway. Nick nodded toward it, leading the way. Soft footsteps sounded behind him, the men at his back ready. Tense. The narrow corridor wasn't the ideal spot for a fight, should there be one.

"Hey," a voice called out. It was quiet, muffled. But there.

"Did you hear that?" John whispered.

"Yeah." Nick listened, and the faint cry came again. "Careful. It could be a trap."

Cautiously, he moved forward. He crept down the corridor until he came to the last room on the left. Taking a steadying breath, he kicked in the door. Rushed in, ready to do battle.

And stopped short at the sight of Tom, chained to a bolt in the cold concrete floor. His clothes were filthy, his face gaunt. But the younger man gave them a weak smile as he raised his head.

"What the fuck took you guys so goddamn long?"

Nick hurried over, and without Kalen there to spell the shackles, getting the man free took some doing. Finally, someone found a key on the upper floor and the mechanic was unchained. Zander checked the man from head to toe, scanning for injuries.

"You're anemic and we need to get some food and water into you, but you're going to be fine," he told Tom.

The man looked relieved, though his hands shook with nerves. "I'm glad. After what that crazy fucking vampire did to me, I wasn't so sure."

"His name was Ivan Cardenas," Nick told him. "How did he get you?"

"*Was* Ivan?" The man zeroed in on that word like a hawk.

"I killed him."

"Good," Tom spat. "Was on my way to work one day. My car was run off the road, and the vampire snatched me before I even knew what was going on. He brought me here and has been feeding off me ever since. Only, he hasn't come back since last night, and now I know why."

"Tom, this is important. Did the vampire mention how he was able to pull off putting another mechanic in his place?"

"Yeah. Asshole bragged about it. Said that Sorcerer of his spelled Grant to think I'd quit and sign off on hiring the Sorcerer in disguise as some guy named Morgan. Grant never knew, according to the vampire."

Damn. Jarrod was going to feel terrible about this, even though it wasn't his fault. But they'd deal with that later.

"The important thing is, you're going to be all right," Nick told him, giving him a reassuring smile. "We're going to take you back to the compound where you're going to be on strict rest for a few days, and that's an order."

"My job?" he asked anxiously.

"Is still yours. That wasn't even a question."

"Thanks, Nick."

Tom was fading fast, and needed medical attention. They whisked him back to the compound, and Nick left him in the capable hands of his medical team. Once Tom had been taken away, Tarron turned to Nick.

"I'm going to go. Give my sister my love, and I'll see you both soon."

"I will. And thank you, for everything."

The vampire smiled, showing off a hint of his fangs. "I'd say we helped each other. Besides, there's no thank-you necessary among family."

Family. Nick had one now. A real family. His life truly had turned into a walking miracle.

He couldn't ask for more.

When Calla awoke, the first gray streaks of dawn were just beginning to spread across the sky, chasing the darkness back to the other side of the world. She knew exactly what had awakened her.

Nick was wrapped around her, but he wasn't asleep. Not even close. He was nuzzling her neck, one arm draped across her, his fingers tracing the swell of her breasts.

"Baby, are you awake?" he whispered playfully.

"No, I'm not. Go back to sleep." Of course, he'd do no such thing and she'd have been disappointed if he had.

"You feel so good. Come here," he growled, rolling her onto her back.

"You're insatiable." She smiled up at him.

"Only when it comes to you."

Nick captured her face with both hands and lowered his lips to hers. God, she couldn't get enough of him. He was becoming an addiction. The more she tasted him, the more she wanted. He'd loved her for hours the night before, in every conceivable way, but it still wasn't enough. Moving over her, he covered her body with his, enfolding her in his embrace.

He claimed her once more, this time loving her with great tenderness, as if she were a priceless treasure. In her entire life, she'd never imagined sharing this sort of intimacy in lovemaking. Nick wasn't like anyone else, ever.

He was the man—wolf—for her.

Moving within her, he stoked the fires until the blaze consumed them both. Their passion erupted with force as they melted together, riding the pulsating waves. At last, he collapsed with a shudder, holding her tightly.

Calla ran her hands over his back, wondering how she'd ever lived without this, without him.

"Where are we going to live?" he asked. "I've been meaning to broach the subject, but there hasn't been time. I'd be glad to travel back and forth between here and the stronghold."

"But that would make your work harder for you," she said.

"Some. But what you do with teaching the children is important, too."

"I love you for that," she said, stroking him. "But it's easier for me to travel than you. I say we live here and travel to my brother's as needed."

"Are you sure?"

"Positive."

He kissed her soundly. "It's settled, then."

He became quiet, and she asked, "Is there something else on your mind?"

"There is." After a pause, he said, "You know how you said it's rare for vampire females to give birth?"

"I remember." She pulled back and looked into his earnest face, already smiling inside and out.

"Well, do you think we could try? If you want to, I mean. I know I already have a daughter, but I missed out on so much of her growing-up years, it aches," he whispered.

"Oh, honey."

"Please, consider it? He could be a little vampire, or a wolf. Could he be both? I wonder."

"Well, I can't consider it."

His face fell. "Why not?"

"Because it's already a done deal, my commander."

"You mean—?" His face lit with untold joy.

"Yes. We'll just have to find out what special gifts our baby has when he arrives."

Laughing, her mate pulled her into his arms and made love to her again. And again.

Life was full, and happy. With Nick.

Her wolf that chased the shadows from them both, for good.

Turn the page for an exciting excerpt from
J. D. Tyler's Alpha Pack novel

COLE'S REDEMPTION

Available now from Signet Eclipse.

The white wolf scented the air, searching for her prey.

The commander hadn't ventured into the forest lately, but that would change. Sooner or later, the traitorous bastard would come out of his stronghold, venture beyond the protection of brick and mortar, past the magical boundary erected by the Sorcerer.

He'd put aside the shadows on his soul, even if temporarily. He'd forget that his ability as a Seer was severely hampered when it came to his own impending death. Longing for solitude, to feel the wind in his face, his toes digging into the soft earth, he'd let his wolf loose. Go for a run.

And if all went as planned, he would never return.

Settling in, she watched. Waited. She burned to

see the expression on his face when he realized his past had finally come to call. That, in a great twist of irony, he had sired his own executioner, and his sins would be paid for with his blood. It was all that mattered, all she lived for.

Soon, her father would die.

"The vampire problem is becoming increasingly unstable," Nick Westfall said, face grim as he studied each member of his Alpha Pack team of shifters. "If we don't get a handle on the rogues, they're going to end up exposing the entire paranormal world to the human race."

Resting his elbows on the conference room's table, Zander Cole struggled to understand his commander's briefing. It wasn't as if he was *completely* deaf anymore. When he was a kid, he and his friends would while away the summer at the local swimming pool. Sometimes they'd entertain themselves by yelling to one another underwater and trying to decipher the messages, to little success and a great deal of laughter. His current predicament was like that—without the amusement.

But over the past few months, he'd gotten better at reading lips. As long as he was looking directly at the speaker and concentrating hard, he could catch most of what was said.

It was a vast improvement over the total deafness he'd been left with after the Pack's Sorcerer had created an explosion of lightning that had literally rocked the earth. Progress, yes—but a long way from being healed.

Because his brain injury had left him to contend with so much more than just his hearing being shot to hell.

Despair swelled in his chest, and he fought it down yet again. The blinding headaches were as bad as they'd been in the beginning. Maybe worse. Every day, the feelings of helplessness, uselessness, got harder to take. He feared he was no longer an asset to his team, but a burden. A waste of space.

Sort of hard to swallow, considering Zan was the Pack's Healer. His Psy gift allowed him to heal everyone except himself, and even that was in jeopardy of failing him altogether.

For years, his Pack brothers and their mission of battling the world's most dangerous paranormal predators had been his whole life, and now his future wasn't looking too bright. His days on the team appeared to be numbered, and rejoining the "normal" human world wasn't an option.

Where that left him was a very, very frightening place in his head.

Shaking himself from his misery, he forced himself to focus again on what Nick was telling them.

". . . capture one of them alive if we can. Find out why there's so goddamned many of them lately." Pausing, he consulted some notes in his hand. "Our latest report cites a rogue problem on a ranch in Texas."

"Texas?" Zan mused out loud. He glanced around and saw the same curiosity reflected in his brothers' faces before returning his attention to Nick.

"Not their usual stomping ground, for sure. They normally keep to big cities, where it's easier to blend in and feed and where one more dead homeless person will hardly be noted. But for whatever reason, it seems we have a group targeting a ranch in East Texas. The owners were shocked last week when a couple of hands found two cows with their throats slashed and only a minimal amount of blood around their bodies when the ground should've been soaked."

There was a murmur around the room as Nick went on. "We know vampires will drink from large animals if they're desperate for food. What's unusual is that the animals were killed during the daytime."

A loud exclamation came from Zan's right, and he needed no clarification to interpret it as a curse. Glancing over, he saw Aric Savage lean forward in his chair and rest his elbows on the conference table. The redhead looked pissed as he pushed his long hair from his face.

"The bastards are walking during the day now? How the hell are they managing that?"

Nick shook his head. "No idea, which is another reason we need one of them alive."

"I doubt this reached your desk because of a couple of dead cows," Zan said, working to enunciate clearly. He hated how his voice must sound to everyone, strange and flat, and tried hard to ignore the gazes that swung in his direction. "There must be more."

"You're right. It wasn't the cows that got our friends in Washington moving—it was the dead cowboy who was found this morning, throat slashed and body drained. He went out early to check the cattle, and his horse came back alone. Our contacts were already aware of the slaughtered cattle, so when this news came over the wire, Grant called me while the government sent in a couple of suits to keep local law enforcement at bay."

General Jarrod Grant was an old friend of Nick's and one of the only allies in Washington whom the Pack trusted. If Grant was involved, the rogue situation was serious.

Zan snorted. "I bet that went over well. When do we leave?"

Nick paused, giving Zan a searching look, and a lead ball formed in his gut. For one excruciating moment, he feared the commander would order him to remain behind at the compound, despite their previous talks. Even Packmate Micah Chase, with his nightmares and heavy meds, was now allowed to join their missions. If Zan had to stay behind, confirming his status as useless to everyone, he'd crawl under a rock and die.

Then the man nodded at him slightly and said, "Thirty minutes. We'll take a couple of the Hueys."

Zan fought to hide his relief. Nick had placed his trust in him, and Zan couldn't let him or the team down. As the team stood and began to file from the room to make ready for the flight, he felt a hand on his shoulder and turned to see his best friend, Jaxon Law, gazing at him with a slight smile on his face, not an ounce of sympathy evident. Thank God. Jax of all people knew that pity was the one thing Zan wouldn't be able to handle.

"You ready?" Jax asked.

"Yeah. As I'll ever be."

"You'll do fine."

"I'm not worried about doing my job," he snapped, then immediately felt bad about it. Especially since that statement was a big lie. And because Jax was simply standing there wearing an expression of patient understanding instead of giving in to the fight Zan suddenly craved.

As though reading his mind, Jax smiled and said, "Good. Save that aggression for the enemy and we'll both be proven right. Come on."

He felt like an ass. His team had been nothing but supportive in the aftermath of his injury and throughout his recovery. They knew how tough these past few weeks had been for him, and nobody gave him a hard time. They didn't dare, considering that if they were truly doing their jobs, every single one of them would end up out of commission sooner or later. The difference was that being shifters, their injuries typically healed within days.

Zan's wounds were severe, possibly permanent.

Giving Jax a grin he didn't feel, he nodded. "Sorry. Lead the way."

They hurried out, taking only seconds to dash to their living quarters and retrieve the new laser guns they'd been issued, along with the big bowie knife Zan liked to strap to his thigh. Unlike Aric, he wasn't a Telekinetic/Firestarter and didn't have the power to hurl objects or set the enemy on fire in a fight—though that would be awesome. Being a Healer was rewarding, but it certainly didn't give him an edge in battle, so he preferred human weapons. Teeth and claws and superior speed were cool when he was in wolf form, but the knife was just as effective in close combat.

Meeting in the hallway, he and Jax made their way through the compound and down a corridor leading to the huge hangar that housed all of the Pack's vehicles. In addition to the helicopters, there were several SUVs, cars, and a jet, along with their personal modes of transportation. Zan's baby, a big, macho Ford Raptor, sat on the far side of the building, and he spared it a longing glance before climbing into one of the Hueys with Jax, Nick, Ryon, Micah, and Phoenix. In the other copter rode Aric, his mate, Rowan, Kalen, Hammer,

A.J., and finally, Noah, a nurse who worked in the compound's infirmary. It was quite common for one of them to need patching up in the field, and Noah's presence was a great help to Zan these days.

Zan tried not to think about why. It wasn't like Noah's being around was a vote of no confidence, since one of the doctors or nurses usually accompanied the Pack on a mission. But an insidious voice inside him whispered, *Yeah, but for how long? What happens when you've got nothing left to give?*

Inside him, his wolf growled at the thought.

Once they were in the air, he lost himself to the dull roar of the aircraft and paid no particular attention to the shouted conversations going on around him. That was one dangerous thing about being practically deaf—it was all too easy for him to retreat from the world. If he didn't look, he couldn't participate. Both a blessing and a curse.

Eventually, however, his gaze was drawn to his Pack brothers. Especially Micah and Phoenix. It was strange, getting used to having the two of them with the team again, especially after they'd been believed dead. Zan was glad they'd been rescued from the horrible labs after being tortured for months, and wondered how they were really coping.

One side of Micah's face was ruined, like melted wax, the result of molten silver being poured on him. God knows he had to still be in pain, but Micah claimed that his medications were helping. He'd come out of his shell in recent weeks, had stopped hiding his face. He smiled more, though the expression was still reserved. The man was a walking miracle; so what if his eyes were a bit too bright, almost feverish?

Nobody questioned it, at least not to Micah. No one wanted to risk setting back his progress.

Phoenix was a completely different story. Rescued separately from Micah, the man had come away malnourished but with no physical scars and seemed to be handling the horrors he'd been through with relative ease. Too much so, which had Zan concerned. But if he was hurting inside, he was hiding it well. Nix appeared to be quite happy lately—and even a blind man could see that it was due to his attraction to Noah.

Were those two Bondmates? A betting pool had been started, and Zan hadn't bothered to chip in on what he figured was a *yes*. The great thing was, not one of the guys had expressed a negative attitude about it. In the shifter world, a man's Bondmate just *was*, like the leaves on the trees or the air they breathed. If fate blessed a man with the other half of his soul, he didn't question his good fortune. He simply seized his destiny with both hands and thanked God he didn't have to walk through life alone.

Zan knew he sure as hell would, if he were so lucky.

Dammit. Not going to think about one more impossible dream heaped on the bonfire. The rest will be a pile of smoldering ashes soon enough.

As if to punctuate that miserable thought, Zan glanced over just in time to catch a snippet of conversation between Micah and Nix.

"Don't know, man," Micah was saying. "I'm not one to talk about whether *he's* ready to be on duty. I mean, look at me." He gestured to his own face, but Nix shook his head.

"Your scars don't affect your ability to do your job, buddy. His situation is totally different. Just sayin'."

Unable to bear witnessing another word, Zan averted his gaze and stared at the ugly gray wall of the Huey. Hurt speared him like a lance to the gut, and he rested his elbows on his knees. Was that what all of them were saying? Speculating out loud on whether he was fit to be in the field?

Doubting himself in private was one thing.

But seeing his brothers do the same—in front of him, as if he were stupid as well as deaf—was a whole different level of pain.

Lost in his head, he let the hours roll by, scarcely making an attempt to join in what little talk the guys managed. By the time they landed in a wide, grassy plain in Texas, Jax was gazing at him with worry etched on his brow as he stroked his goatee. The second he saw Zan noticing, however, he put on his poker face. Already on edge, Zan wasn't about to let him get away with pretending nothing was wrong.

As soon as they were clear of the transport, Zan grabbed his friend's arm and held him back as the others walked across the pasture to meet a trio of men in suits.

"Don't do that," he hissed. "Don't pretend to my face that you're okay with me being here when you think the same as everyone else."

Anger flashed in Jax's eyes. "You telling me what I think now? News flash—you're a Healer, not a Seer, so you have no clue what's going on in my head."

"I have eyes. I can tell you're second-guessing whether I can do the job."

"Am I?" He took a step forward, got in Zan's face. "I doubt any one of us could possibly second-guess you more than you're doing all on your own. You saw concern, yes. But that's because I'm your *friend*, jackass. I give a damn about you, that's all."

Put like that, the perspective made Zan feel about an inch tall. Blowing out a breath, he looked away for a moment, scanning the horizon without really noticing much. One of Jax's hands clasped his shoulder, and he returned his attention to his friend.

"The thing is, *your* doubt is the only thing that matters. Don't you see? When you have your confidence back, when you've lost the anger and fear and you can join the mission knowing you're back to one hundred percent, then what anyone else believes won't amount to shit."

He swallowed hard. "But what if I'm never the same? What if I don't heal?"

"Then you learn to compensate, like I did after my leg was mangled."

"That's different—" he began.

"No, it's not. My leg physically healed, yes, but the strength and agility I used to have in that limb are not equal to the good leg. And it won't ever be the same. But I've learned techniques to help me make up for it in a fight—techniques you and the others helped me perfect, I'll remind you."

"I get it," he muttered.

"Do you? Nobody wants anything but the best for you, Zan," he said, warm sincerity evident in his expression. "The guys are worried, and they may run off at the mouth too much, but every one of them is in your corner. Believe that."

Hey, guys? Ryon pushed into their minds telepathically. *Nick's giving you both the stink eye, so you might want to cut the lovefest short, get your butts over here, and join the party.*

Jax made a face and turned, starting off toward the group of Feds, who appeared decidedly unhappy. With a sigh, Zan followed him, sort of glad for Ryon's interruption. Save for a mated couple, who could speak telepathically to each other, the Channeler/Telepath was the only one who could push his thoughts directly into others' heads. Zan relished being able to hear someone's voice clearly, even if just temporarily.

Those brief periods of contact might be all he had to look forward to.

As they reached the spot where Nick stood in front of his Pack, Zan noted that the meeting between his commander and the Feds looked more like a standoff.

"So, are you guys military or not?" one of the agents asked with a frown, arms crossed over his chest.

Nick had his back to Zan, but whatever the commander said did not go over well with the suits. A second agent, short and stocky, pushed the issue.

"Your outfit doesn't look like any Special Ops team I ever saw. More like mercenaries, if you ask me." This was said with a slight curl to his lips, as though he'd tasted something bad.

Zan got close enough to maneuver around and catch Nick's response.

"Nobody *did* ask you." The commander's stare was hard and flat. "And now that we're here, you all can pull back and let us do what the White House sent us here to do. Unless, of course, you'd like for me to get the president on the phone so he can tell you personally."

The agents froze, and several of the Pack members blinked at Nick in surprise.

"You've got President Warren on speed dial? You're full of shit," the stocky agent sneered, recovering some.

"Try me. But fair warning—you'll be out of a job before I end the call. Up to you if losing your career is worth the attitude."

Way to pull rank, Zan thought with a smirk. *Nothing like the mention of the Oval Office to chap their asses.*

Holy crap. Did Nick really have that kind of clout? The Feds eyed Nick's stony expression for a few tense moments, seemed to buy it, and reluctantly backed off. Once they'd moved off to stand elsewhere and act official—*translation, be completely useless*—the commander turned to a tall, beefy rancher who'd been hovering on the perimeter of the gathering, weathered face grim under the brim of his hat, broad shoulders drooping with the weight of what had occurred on his property. Zan pegged him as either the owner or the foreman.

Taking off his hat to scratch his head, the rancher also looked plenty baffled. "I don't understand why the government sent damned near two dozen people to investigate poor Saul's murder, unless you're looking for a serial killer or something. Whatever the reason, I'm glad you're here."

"We're looking for a specific type of killer," Nick informed him, before fudging the truth. A lot. "There have been a rash of cult killings, and this murder fits the pattern. We came as soon as we heard."

"That was damned fast, but I'm grateful. Sure might take a military group to stop a bunch of cult crazies." The rancher eyed Nick, then the team in general. "I'm Tim Edwards, by the way. What do you need me to do?"

"I need use of a couple of trucks, if you have any to spare. We want to look around the area where the cattle and your hand were found."

"Sure. I'll send a couple of my men out to show you—"

Nick shook his head. "Just to tell us. We can find it. I'd rather not put more of your men in unnecessary danger when the culprits are still at large."

Zan tried to imagine what the rancher would do if he knew that the team could simply sniff out the murder scenes with their canine noses when they got close enough. That would probably finish off the poor guy.

Thankfully, the rancher seemed to agree with Nick's plan. "That's fine. I've got three trucks that belong to the Bar K ya'll can use if you promise to bring 'em back in one piece."

"Thank you. We'll do our best."

Zan fell into step with his Pack as they walked the rest of the way to the main house. The mood was somber, rugged-looking men milling around not knowing what to do and clearly uneasy with the recent events. He spotted more than one cowboy with reddened eyes and knew their fellow hand's murder must've hit them hard. Zan could empathize with the horror of losing a close friend to violence.

None too soon, they'd gotten directions, borrowed the trucks, and were on their way to investigate the sites where the bodies were found. He felt a little guilty for his relief at leaving the heavy cloud of grief behind him and getting on with doing what they did best.

The lead truck followed a well-worn dirt road for a mile or so before veering into the pasture. After it had traveled about forty yards, it came to a halt and the vehicles behind it did the same. Everyone got out and trailed Nick to a pair of bloated carcasses on the ground a few feet away. Zan wrinkled his nose at the stench.

"Jesus."

The bodies of the cattle were stiff, getting ripe. Each one's throat was laid wide open, the wound sort of messy, the meat chewed.

Micah pointed. "Not what I'd expect from a vampire bite. They don't typically ravage their victims like that when they feed."

"But I can scent them all over the place," Zan put in. His lupine sense of smell was one of the traits that hadn't deserted him yet. "Definitely a vampire kill."

There were nods of agreement. Nick squatted,

his blue eyes narrowed. "These rogues are out of control. Not that we didn't realize that—they've killed a human out in the open—but this is beyond the ordinary. Even for rogues, this shows a lack of control I haven't seen before. A certain amount of . . ."

"Recklessness?" Zan supplied. "Balls?"

"Yes." The commander stood. "There's no thoughtful cunning here. No discretion."

Jax shook his head. "There's almost a sickness permeating the area."

"We have to find out why," Nick agreed. "Nothing else to see here, though. Let's move on to the ranch hand's body."

Just then, Zan noticed Micah wandering away from the group, sniffing the air. He walked toward the back of the property, in the direction they'd been heading before they stopped. Then he crouched and palmed a handful of dirt, inhaled, then dropped it and brushed his hand on his jeans.

"There was a human here," he told them. "This scent stands out because it was joined by at least one vampire, and then both scents head that way." He pointed toward a copse of trees a ways off.

Zan peered into the distance and remarked, "That's where they told us we can find the body. Maybe he came out here alone to take another look at the dead cattle and they snatched him. A kill of opportunity."

At that grim prospect, they loaded into the vehicles and drove the rest of the way to the murder scene. As they approached, Zan noted that there was a vehicle there and two men in suits standing near what he assumed to be the body, which was covered with a tarp. Made sense that they couldn't leave the body unguarded, though Nick wouldn't like them hanging around.

They must've been informed in advance about visitors, because they stepped aside and moved a fair distance away with a minimum of protest. Still watchful, they leaned against a couple of trees while Zan and the others surrounded the tarp.

Nick pulled it back and Zan grimaced. *God, that poor bastard.*

The victim's head was turned to the side, eyes wide and staring across the field. Like the cattle, the man's neck was savaged, to the point Zan was surprised it was still attached to his prone body. The Pack had seen some pretty disturbing things in their line of work, but this? This guy had suffered before he died. He had blood and tissue under his fingernails, scratches on his arms. He'd fought. Had been desperate as he'd been dragged across the field to the tree line. He must've known he'd end up like those cows.

What a fucking shitty way to die.

Nick motioned Jax close to the man's body, and Zan knew what his best friend would be asked to do. As the Pack's RetroCog, Jax could touch a person or hold an object in his hand and get a reading on past events. Sometimes that event was a movie clip of the last moments of the person's life, or some other significant happening tied to the mystery they were trying to solve. Other times he got only snapshots of the past that didn't make sense until much later.

As Jax laid a hand on top of the man's head, Zan stepped up close to his friend, ready to catch him if necessary. These sessions usually left Jax drained.

Exhaling a long breath, Jax closed his eyes and grew still. Zan pictured how his friend always described the process of reading a body—there were threads attached to every person and object, and those threads led to the memories. Jax gathered those threads and pulled them close to see where they led.

For several long moments Jax was still. Then his body began to shake, and a soft moan of distress passed through his lips. Suddenly he fell backward with a cry, and Zan caught him from behind, steadying him.

"I've got you."

Before Jax could protest, Zan sent gentle waves of healing energy into his friend's system, cleansing the bad remnants of the memories and chasing away the exhaustion. As he finished, a dull throbbing began at his temples and crept to encompass his skull, and he knew it would get worse before it went away. But he'd do it again and again, to take care of his brothers.

Jax pulled away and turned to glare at him. "You shouldn't do that when you don't have to. Save your energy."

"Save your breath," he countered. "The day I can't heal, you can put me in the ground."

"That's not funny."

"Wasn't meant to be."

Looking frustrated, Jax let the subject go for the moment. He hadn't heard the last of it, however. His friend was like a dog with a bone when it came to making sure the people he cared for stayed safe.

"What did you learn?" Zan asked, changing the subject.

"I saw how he died. Lived it." He shuddered. "It was horrendous, what he suffered. They played with him, enjoyed causing him pain and . . . fuck, you don't want to know the details."

"What about the vamps themselves? Did you see any of them?"

"Yeah. There were two who killed the victim, but there were more hiding deep in the woods. Of the two, one was younger, blond, maybe early twenties when he was turned. The other was a few years older, brown hair, tall and slim, sort of dirty. I didn't get names."

Zan helped his friend to his feet. "You did good."

"It's not enough. I don't have a sense of whether they're still around."

Nick made sure Zan was looking at him before he interjected. "They are. I don't know how many, but they're here. Waiting."

"For what?" Zan asked.

"Us, maybe? I don't know. But I do know we have to go after them."

That was creepy as hell. Especially since Nick frequently *knew* things about the future that he either couldn't—or wouldn't—tell them. He didn't believe in interfering with free will or tampering with the future. Rumor had it he'd once tried to change a terrible outcome, with disastrous results.

None of that mattered at the moment. Any of them would follow Nick into hell on his word alone. The Pack waited as he told the disgruntled Feds that he was taking charge of the body and removing it. Unbeknownst to the suits, the dead man would wind up at the Pack's top-secret compound being studied from head to toe for any clues they could glean about the rogues. Eventually, the body would be released to the man's relatives, if there were any.

They split up into twos and threes to search the woods, spreading out. Zan found himself walking with Nix and Micah, which was fine by him. It was good to work alongside his old buddies again. He'd missed them even more than he'd realized.

Keeping a sharp eye out, he studied his surroundings despite his growing headache. It was strange not to hear the birds in the trees, the crunch of leaves underfoot. No wind, no voices. Just the steady presence of his companions. He had his knife and laser gun, not to mention his wolf's teeth and claws. He could do this after all. Be a contributing team member still.

It was that exact moment when things went to hell.

A rush of air and a scrape on his neck was his only warning as a body barreled into him, knocking him to the ground. He had a split second to realize Nix was the one who'd shoved him—saving him just in time from having his throat ripped out by the razor-sharp claws of a rogue vampire.

And now Nix was fighting for his life.

Zander unsheathed his knife and threw himself at the rogue, just as more of them emerged from the trees and flew at them like the hollow-faced horrors they were.

Also available from

J.D. Tyler

Cole's Redemption
An Alpha Pack Novel

Wolf shifters Zander Cole and Selene Westfall are damaged souls—Selene lives only to avenge her mother's death and a battle has left Zander deaf and his powers dimmed.

When Zander and Selene are forced together, they come to terms with their unlikely, turbulent bond. A love neither expected may be all that stands between them and a killer trying desperately to keep the past dead and buried....

__Also in the series__
Cole's Redemption
Hunter's Heart
Black Moon
Savage Awakening
Primal Law

Available wherever books are sold or at
penguin.com